FAKING IT

KATE ASTER

PROLOGUE

~ CASS ~

I remember the first time I saw him. I was channel surfing, sitting in front of the TV on my parents' brown shag rug because the remote's batteries were dead.

I flipped past the summer Olympics and was already two channels away when his image seeped into my brain, unleashing a maelstrom of teenage hormones.

My fingers punched the remote fiercely till I found him again—short blonde hair and glacier-blue eyes. He shot the camera a smile before wrapping those sumptuous lips around a water bottle and chugging it, readying himself for the next match.

I had never been into men's freestyle wrestling. But for that half-hour of the broadcast I was addicted, watching his muscles flex and tighten as he struggled on the mats with another competitor. I'm not even sure what country the other guy was from. Did it matter?

Dylan Sheridan took home a silver that day, something I never thought twice about until six months later when I saw his first shaving ad from America's *second* largest razor manufacturer with the tagline: "Never overlook the guy in second place."

I secretly cut those ads out of magazines when I found them, and they fueled my fantasies for longer than I care to admit.

All the way up until about thirty seconds ago.

"I'm the irresponsible one," he says, reaching out his hand to me. He's in a tux that fits his broad frame meticulously, and I'm sure it's not a rental. Not in *his* family, it isn't.

"Dylan," I reply, taking his hand.

He laughs and I can smell the top shelf whiskey on his breath. "You're named Dylan, too?"

He is drunk off his ass (his remarkably fit ass, I might add).

"No. I'm Cass. I'm a friend of Allie's."

"Well, I guessed that from the bridesmaid dress you're *almost* wearing."

My brow furrows, glancing down at the strapless gown that I had to use a full paycheck to purchase. It's pretty conservative, barely showing any cleavage and extending all the way down to my ankles for Allie's formal wedding. But seeing as this guy is clearly three sheets to the wind as we approach the final hour of the reception, I'm pretty sure he is seeing something completely different from what my eyes are seeing.

"Um, okay. Well, it was nice to meet you, Dylan."

He sits down next to me just as I start to stand. "So what do you do, Cath?"

"Cass," I correct him, raising my voice over the live band playing their own renditions of Etta James' classics. "It's short for Cassidy. And I'm a model."

He laughs—actually laughs. "So you want to be a model?"

I narrow my eyes. "I *am* a model." I've paid my bills, or at least a good chunk of them, for the past six years doing catalog modeling and a commercial or two. It isn't the fame and fortune I had planned when I left my hometown to move to New York City, but I'll be damned if I'll let him minimize what I've accomplished.

He laughs again, and even drunk, the sound of it is low and sexy. If I can just block out the words he's saying, I might still find him as attractive as I once did.

But then he opens his mouth...

"Models will do anything to get ahead. I know," he says with some authority, even though he's slurring his speech. "They're always trying to sleep with me to get their faces in the press or their hands on my money. So damn tiring."

"But I'm sure you sleep with them anyway."

He shrugs. "I'm the irresponsible one, remember? Logan is the patriot, you know—the freaking Navy SEAL—"

"Former SEAL," I correct. "I know. I'm at his wedding, remember?"

"Yeah, that's right," he responds too thoughtfully, as though I had just said something shocking. "But once a SEAL, always a SEAL, you know? There's no competing with that. Then there's Ryan..."

My eyes follow his to the tall, handsome man at another table, having a conversation that looks more like a board meeting than anything else. He's hotter than hell, but I swear he barely smiles. Even though my friend Kim is happily engaged to him and is utterly in love with the guy, he still kind of scares the crap out of me when he gets that all-business, *I'm gonna buy you, chop you up, and sell your parts for profit* look on his face.

"Ryan's the dependable one. Took over our family business. Head of my family's multi-billion dollar housing development company, JLS Heartland. Never makes a mistake. Never fails."

He leans back, his eyes almost meeting mine. I think he sees two of me right now and is looking somewhere in the middle.

"And then there's me. The loose cannon. I'm just riding their coattails, so if I can get a piece of ass from a few dumb models who want to use me, who am I to complain?"

My eyes widen and my mouth drops about an inch. I almost feel sorry for the guy. If it weren't for the *dumb model* proclamation that hangs between us, I'd be tempted to remind him that he's an Olympic medalist and owns a successful chain of gyms he started with the money he made off of his endorsements. I read that in a *People* magazine article. That's pretty accomplished in my book.

But of course, I'm just a dumb model.

I stand, extending my hand and giving his a firm shake. "Well, Dylan, I better be going or I'll be the next dumb model to fall for your abundant charisma." I walk away, flagging down a waiter and asking him to deliver some strong coffee and a glass of water to the hot Olympian who is going to have a major headache tomorrow.

My blood is boiling, and not even because my career choice has been attacked, and my intelligence questioned.

It's because the reality of Dylan Sheridan just ruined my favorite fantasy.

CHAPTER 1

SEVERAL MONTHS LATER

~ CASS ~

Just shoot me now. Please.

I stand adorned in my forty-pound gown of satin, taffeta, and crinoline, hoping the Earth might take pity on me and swallow me whole. I would feign illness—I'm feeling pretty sick now, anyway—but there's a mile-long line of whining kids waiting to meet me and I need this job.

Brenna Tucker is standing ten feet away from me, her grinning, capped teeth smiling behind her iPhone as she snaps a photo of me with her adorable and perfectly dressed daughter. The same Brenna Tucker who was senior class homecoming queen, class gossip, and reigning bitch extraordinaire.

Please don't recognize me, I silently will her.

How could she? I'm dressed as a freaking princess with my sparkly, thick makeup and false eyelashes, and standing in Buckeye Land, Ohio's second rate Disneyworld knock-off.

It's not like Brenna Tucker was even part of my crowd in high school (not that I even *had* a crowd). So luck should be on my side. And if I'm *very* lucky, she might not remember how I announced to every living person who would listen in that school that I was going to ditch my backward hometown and become the next supermodel in New York City.

Looking back, I shouldn't have been so vocal about it. But I thought success was a sure thing.

I flash another saccharine smile at our amusement park photographer so that Brenna and her mini-me, who together look like a Hanna Andersson ad with their matching flower-print outfits, can buy the photo on T-shirts and other official Buckeye Land merchandise.

As I send her kiddo on her way toward her mother, I feel a flood of relief when Brenna turns her back on me to exit my palace stronghold.

But then she stops cold and looks over her shoulder toward me.

No, no, no.

"Cassidy?" she asks. "Cassidy Parker?"

I glance from her little girl up to Brenna, weighing my options. I could pretend it isn't me. In my costume, I probably don't look much like the unassuming 18-year-old she sat next to in physics class and barely acknowledged.

But I'm caught. "Brenna Tucker." I smile. "I was wondering if that was you."

"What are you doing here in Ohio? I thought you were going to New York City to model."

Clearly she's not impressed by my job as Princess Buckeye, and I'm tempted to point out that for two summers in a row now, I beat out two hundred applicants for this job. But that would look desperate. "Oh, I do live in New York. My agent got me this job for the summer, though. I just needed a break from the city. You know how it is." I bat my hand through the air.

Her face is blank, telling me she has no idea how it is.

"What are *you* doing in Ohio?" I ask, hoping she's about to tell me that she's unemployed, divorced, or in some kind of drug rehab—anything that would make my job in Buckeye Land look a little less pathetic.

"My husband was transferred to Cincinnati last year. He's CEO of an aerospace engineering company. I had to give up my career in the hotel industry to follow him, but it's really been wonderful to have more time with my daughter. Do you have children?"

I spot our photographer darting a look at me, and he's right. I'm not supposed to break character. Ever.

I force a laugh. "Well, I actually have about 270 right now, standing in line waiting to see me." I open my arms to her. "It was so great to see you, Brenna." We hug in that superficial way that people do when they aren't really happy to see each other.

"Good to see you, too."

My face droops as they leave, noting the look of glee in Brenna's eyes as she walks toward the exit with her perfect child. I'm sure her photos of her kid and me will be on the class Facebook page within five minutes.

My life is crap right now.

I'm six hundred miles from my hometown. What are the chances of her running into me here?

But that's just the reality of being a princess in the not-so-enchanted world.

7

Cinching on my dress every morning as I start my work day, I find myself thinking a lot about those stories I was fed as a kid—the ones where the princess has a chance meeting in a forest while she sings to animals (which, by the way, I never do, even when I'm in costume) and the prince sees her and immediately falls in love. When in reality, a girl is much more likely to run into an evil witch in that forest than a handsome prince.

A witch like Brenna Tucker.

I swear I'm going to write a book one day called *The Princess's Guide to Life in the Not-So-Enchanted World*, and set the record straight for these sweet girls so they don't end up like me.

No handsome prince has come to my rescue, as I've sweltered in the heat in my castle-like structure for the second summer of my life, even though I swore when I left at the end of last season, I'd never be back.

Don't get me wrong. I wasn't always this way. I was once as starry-eyed and optimistic as the next girl as I charged out of my small, Kansas City suburb to live in my flophouse in Queens, New York, with another wanna-be model, a wanna-be actress, and a girl in nursing school.

You can imagine who among the four of us is actually making a living wage right now.

What I did was so stereotypical, reeking of at least a dozen old movies I've been addicted to since I was five years old, back when my grandma used to babysit and we'd wile away our days watching the Turner Classic Network and eating dry cereal out of the box.

I'm not unlike Ginger Rogers in the opening scene of *The Major and a Minor*—a grossly overlooked classic, in my humble opinion. Small town girl escapes to the big city to make a name for herself. But instead of meeting Ray Milland and falling in love on a train, I got my dreams knocked out of me when I realized there are literally thousands of blue-eyed blondes in New York City who look just like me. And most of us end up regretting skipping college to follow our dream.

Lord knows I do.

Especially today, as I smile again at the camera even though the kid standing next to me smacks of body sweat and sunscreen. But I slap on a smile because that's what princesses do.

"Can I have your autograph?" She thrusts a Princess Buckyeye coloring book in front of me.

"Why yes! I'd be delighted!" I reply with a wide grin, using a voice remarkably similar to Glinda the Good Witch. I don't worry about kids recognizing the voice from the classic of Hollywood's Golden Age. This generation of kids skipped *The Wizard of Oz* and went straight to *The Hunger Games* for entertainment.

"You have a sparkling day," I say just as I've been directed to, as the little darling departs, leaving a peculiar cloud of fumes in her wake.

Glancing over to the line again, I recognize the next girl approaching me.

Eight-year-old Hannah Sheridan is a breath of fresh air to me, quite literally because she always smells like McIntosh apples and looks at me like I have the power to make the sun rise every morning.

My friend Kim is engaged to her billionaire dad, Ryan Sheridan. And my friend Allie just married her Uncle Logan a few months ago. So with my two closest friends in Hannah's life, I tend to see this kid around a lot.

Besides that, it's the fourth time she's been to Buckeye Land this summer. Yet she still stands in the long line to have her picture with me, even though she knows me in real life.

She's at that stage when she actually thinks my job is the coolest thing on the planet.

I guess Brenna Tucker outgrew that stage.

"Hannah!" I greet her, opening my arms for a hug.

"Princess!" she says, her exuberant embrace sinking her into my layers of crinoline.

I glance upward, expecting to see her dad with her or maybe her uncle, Logan. But the sight of the man approaching me has me reeling.

Dylan Sheridan.

When Allie told me she was dating his brother Logan last year, I'd often envisioned how I'd meet the mouthwatering Olympian-turned-MMA-fighter—always at Allie's town-home, maybe while I'm over for a drink and he'd saunter in looking for Logan who lived next door to her last year.

I'd be wearing something casual, but flirty—maybe the short-shorts that show off my legs and a baby doll t-shirt that miraculously makes my 34B-cups look like DDs.

Our eyes would meet, and time would stand still.

I certainly hadn't planned on meeting him at Allie and Logan's wedding last spring, ogling him during the rehearsal dinner and the ceremony only to finally get my formal introduction to him when he was seconds away from passing out drunk on the white-clothed table.

"I'm Dylan. Hannah's other uncle," he states, extending his hand. He says "other" uncle with some import.

"I know. I'm Cass—" Mortified, I remember I can't even say my real name without getting in trouble. Our photographer is giving me the evil eye again. He's worked here six summer seasons and I'd probably be as mean as he is if I worked here that long. "I'm Princess Buckeye. Welcome to my kingdom."

God, I hate my job.

He smiles at me and I want to wither in my gown. It's bad enough running into Brenna Tucker today, but now I have to face this guy so that he can see where "dumb models" end up if they haven't made it big by the time they're twenty-four years old.

"The line was sooo long," Hannah says. "You're famous."

Even a complaint doesn't stay a complaint on this kid's lips. I just adore her.

I lower my head to hers. "Next time, don't stand in line. I'll give you my cell phone number and when you come visit, I'll text you when my break is and we can have a soda together in the break room trailer."

Her eyes light up like I've just handed her the world. "Really?" she asks.

"Really. No one ever goes in there except me." I skip telling her that the reason I'm the only one who goes in the character break room trailer is because Buckeye Land had to lay off the prince, the dragon, and the evil witch at the end of last summer due to cut-backs. I'm the only character left at this amusement park as it teeters on the edge of bankruptcy.

"Cool," she says, her eyes lit with wonder.

"I'll even let you try on my crown," I add under my breath before turning toward the camera and flashing a smile.

Dylan's blue eyes are locked on mine.

"I think she'll take you up on that offer." He pulls out his phone. "What's your number and I'll hand it over to Ryan?"

He punches my number into his phone, even though I'm sure Ryan could get it through Kim anytime he wanted it.

Hannah claps her hands in delight. "Thanks! I'm coming back next week with Grandma. We bought season passes this year." She bubbles over with joy and gives me a hug before they leave.

I can't resist watching him as he exits, those corded muscles in his back betraying him through the thin cotton of his shirt. I wonder if he even has any idea we've met before.

Probably not. All us dumb models look alike.

CHAPTER 2

- DYLAN -

I toss my key card onto the desk, plug in my phone, and turn on the TV. The hotel where I'm staying is the best in the area. But that's not saying much for the general vicinity of Newton's Creek.

Bergin's Hotel and Conference Center isn't really comparable to the kind of places I'm used to when I travel, and I've certainly put on some miles. But the suite is kept spotlessly clean and the people here bend over backwards for me, so I'm perfectly fine spending some time here. Growing up in my family, my mother made sure we never lost our heads to the influx of money in our household as my dad grew my grandfather's construction business into one of the largest housing development companies in America.

So Bergin's version of a Presidential Suite suits me just fine, even though there's nothing presidential about the tired sofa or the slightly frayed bedspread. All I need is a mattress and a shower, and maybe a bit of floor space so that I can do some push-ups in the morning since the workout room they have here is pretty scant.

I pick up the phone to make my usual room service order of steak and potatoes. I've been staying here often enough that I know the menu by heart. When my dad got diagnosed with vascular dementia a while back, I decided to explore the option of opening a gym in the area, eventually settling on a lot just outside of Cincinnati. It seemed a reasonable enough excuse to check in on my family more regularly than I have in the past.

It's been high drama for my clan since Dad's diagnosis, with him stepping down as CEO of JLS Heartland, and my brother Ryan taking over. Then my other brother, Logan, quit the SEALs and left the Navy, and now is working at JLS with Ryan.

To add to the mix, Ryan was handed full custody of his daughter last summer and ended up falling for the love of his life who comes with a son of her own. In two weeks, they'll be getting married.

With all the turmoil, I thought my family would need me around for a while. Or maybe one of my brothers might ask me to pick up some of the load at JLS.

Of course they didn't. They're all thriving, as is JLS Heartland.

I hang up after ordering, trying to look forward to the same cut of steak I've had three times this week. If I stayed at my parents' house like my mom wants me to, I'd be eating a home-cooked meal right now. But I need a little privacy. Unlike my brothers, I'm a consummate bachelor. And there may not be many unmarried women in the vicinity of Newton's Creek, but I'm certain there are at least a few left who aren't wearing a ring on their left hand.

And one of them wears a princess dress.

Cass. At least I think that's what she said her name was before she introduced herself as Princess Buckeye. I crack a smile, remembering how nicely she filled out the bodice of her dress.

A woman who looks like that—with some small town sensibilities—would be the makings of my fantasy woman.

I stare at the cell phone that's charging on my desk, thinking about the newly entered phone number I now have in my contacts. She could be married for all I know. It's not like she'd wear her wedding ring with that costume.

Stepping into the bathroom, I see fresh towels neatly hanging on the towel bars, and the sink completely free of even the tiniest speck of facial hair from my morning shave. Unconsciously, I nod in appreciation for Greta's work, noticing the ample tip I leave housekeeping every day is definitely paying off. I've never seen her, and only know her name from the tiny card she left on the nightstand introducing herself as my housekeeper. She might be built like a linebacker or older than my mom, but I'm in love with Greta.

Shutting my eyes, I step under the rainshower-style stream of water and let the sweat and dirt from five hours in Buckeye Land disappear down the drain. The way the water pours over me reminds me of my shower back in my condo in Chicago, and if I keep my eyes shut a while, I might be able to imagine I'm back there.

Wrapping a towel around my waist, I step out of the bathroom.

"Holy shit." I jump when I see someone sitting on my couch, slicing into my steak. I narrow my eyes on my brother. "How the hell did you get in here?"

Logan holds up a single finger as he chews for a moment. "Room service let me in," he finally says, his mouth half full.

I narrow my eyes. Great security here at Bergin's Hotel

and Conference Center, I see. "Step away from the prime rib and nobody gets hurt," I threaten.

"Hey, I'm hungry. And you didn't order me anything."

"I didn't exactly know you were coming."

"Well, I'm here now, and this is delicious."

I step toward him, and pull the plate out from underneath his gaze, letting it rest on the desk. Glancing at the overdone steak, I frown. Bergin's is definitely not known for their fine cuts of beef, so Logan probably is starved if he's raving about that hunk of meat.

Shrugging, I hand it back to him. "Okay, so I've already spent five hours in Buckeye Land. How are you planning on prolonging my torture today?"

Logan laughs. "Hannah cornered you, did she?"

I nod. "Better watch out or you'll be next. Ryan never should have bought her those season passes." I sit in the chair opposite him. "So, what brings you here on a Friday night?"

"This." He reaches to the side of him where the plans for my latest gym are rolled up and leaning against the wall.

I had dropped them off for him this morning, but didn't exactly expect he'd have a chance to look at them—not with his wife Allie's animal shelter opening up this weekend.

I catch myself biting my lip as I try to get a read on his face. I don't ordinarily involve either of my brothers in my business, because God knows they steer clear of me when it comes to JLS Heartland. But the plans for this gym are special. And I need my brother's input—his approval—even though I'll never admit it out loud.

"You looked at them?" I ask tentatively.

"I did." He pulls them out of the tube.

"And?" I feel myself holding my breath for his reply, and it annoys me. It shouldn't matter what he thinks of the idea.

"It's brilliant, Dylan."

My eyes widen. "You're not just saying that?"

"Hell no. Do you have any idea how well this'll be received by the military community?"

"I've got some idea."

I got the idea from one of the SEALs I met at Logan's wedding, Mick Riley. He'd been treated recently for Traumatic Brain Injury at Walter Reed National Military Medical Center and told me about some of the guys who'd come through there in even worse shape than he'd been in.

Mick told me how hard it is for service members who've faced catastrophic injuries to find a good gym. Even though health clubs are supposed to be ADA-compliant, that doesn't actually mean that they'll have the kind of equipment, trainers, and services that people facing life-changing injuries need and deserve.

Sheridan Gyms have always had a pretty heavy military following, just because we offer them a hell of a discount, and free membership to anyone who is medically retired. So I got the idea of building a new gym—something bigger than I've done before—right outside of Washington, DC, near Walter Reed. This one would serve as Sheridan Gyms' flagship, a state-of-the-art fitness center that's able to rise up to the challenge of serving anyone who comes through our doors.

If it goes well, I plan on modifying my other gyms to follow suit.

"Did Mick help you with this?" He flattens the plans out on the desk.

"Yeah. He hooked me up with some therapists at Walter Reed. I couldn't have done it without him. He hasn't seen the final plans yet, though. I'm flying out there this week for a final meeting with a few people at Walter Reed and to sign some paperwork. I'll tell him then. I kind of owe him a favor, anyway."

"What favor?"

I shrug. "I told him I'd grapple with his guys on the mats for a while. Show them a few moves. You know how he likes mixed martial arts."

"Is he still at the Pentagon?"

I shake my head. "He just started some kind of job at the Asymmetric Warfare Group at Fort Meade."

"AWG? That's Army. Not Navy. Last I heard, anyway."

"It's some liaison job between them and the Pentagon."

"Huh." He's got that faraway look now, the one he always gets when he is forced to acknowledge that the military has marched on without him. It's been hard on him since he left. "That'll be a good morale boost for his Group," he finally adds. "Not often they get to take down an Olympian."

"What do you mean, take down?" I say, giving him a brotherly shove. But inwardly, I shrug. If it weren't for social media and a few tabloids that seem to think I sell magazines, I really think the world would have forgotten that I ever took a lousy silver at the Olympics, or fought in a handful of MMA cages afterward just to keep my face in the press.

I can't complain. Any publicity keeps my business thriving.

I snatch a spoonful of mashed potatoes off my plate. "He got another Navy Cross, you know. For whatever he was doing when he got banged up so bad last time he was in the fight," I add with a shrug.

Logan leans back. "You're kidding me. Why didn't I know that? I would have gone for the ceremony."

I shrug. Mick and my brother's time on the Teams didn't actually overlap, Mick once told me. They had only recently become friends after attending the wedding of a shared acquaintance. "You know Mick. He probably kept it pretty low-key. I only found out because it came up in conversation." Since Logan seems to have lost interest in my dinner, I grab the fork and knife and slice into the tough steak.

"Another Navy Cross. He deserves it," Logan says quietly with a hint of longing. I know my brother, and right now, he's wondering where he'd be if he hadn't left the Navy. I know he doesn't regret his choice, but I think not wearing the Trident every day still makes him feel like there's a piece of him missing.

His eyes look distant right now, but I know the way to bring him back to the present.

"Is Allie excited about tomorrow?" I ask.

Just like that, his expression changes, placing him back in a very civilian here-and-now. A smile touches his eyes. "She hasn't slept for the past two days, I think. Today they're transporting the animals from the county pound to the new shelter."

Allie founded a dog rescue organization and my family's company decided to open up a shelter for her so that she could save more dogs. It's kind of JLS Heartland's way of giving back to our community, I guess.

Tomorrow night is Allie's big night—the grand opening gala and ribbon-cutting ceremony with entertainment, a silent auction, and the whole enchilada right at the new shelter. With JLS's public relations department working on the event, there will be more press there than this town has seen in its 120-year history.

"She's so torqued up," he continues, stealing a swig of soda. "Cass is stopping in early tomorrow to take some pictures of the dogs for the new website."

"Cass." The name rings a bell from earlier today. "The Buckeye Princess, right?"

He gives a quick nod. "She's got a knack with the camera. She's a model, you know. When she's not playing princess, that is."

A model. I frown inwardly. I don't have a good track record with models.

"Must have picked up some tricks from those New York photographers because she can make the most unapproachable-looking dog look adorable."

My eyes widen. "Adorable, huh?" I repeat, wondering when the hell my testosterone-laden brother started talking like a chick. I think he needs a little time on the mats to counteract all the girl talk with Allie.

"Yeah. Damn cute," he finishes with a grunt, as though he just realized he was starting to sound like his wife.

"Is she single?"

"Who?"

"The princess girl."

"Cass." Logan laughs again. "She was in my wedding, you know. Didn't you meet her then?"

"I think I would have remembered meeting a woman who looks like *that*."

A smug smile stretching across his face, Logan leans back in his chair. "Never took you for a guy who goes for royalty."

"Shut up, man. Is she single or not?"

"Single. Definitely single. Don't get attached, though. She's not sticking around Newton's Creek."

"I'm not exactly sticking around either, bro."

"And don't break her heart. Allie will have your head on a platter if you do. So will Kim, for that matter. They're pretty tight, those three."

"I don't break hearts, Logan."

"Not according to what I read in the checkout line at Carter's last week," he says with a mocking smile.

"You know all that's B.S.," I comment, watching my brother's attention move back to my gym plans.

His finger traces along the wide halls leading to spacious workout areas. "This is about fifty percent bigger than your other gyms. Did you buy the space for this yet?"

"I'm in negotiations. Hopefully I'll be signing the papers this week when I'm in DC."

"If you need more money, JLS will chip in whatever you need through the Foundation."

I bristle. I can't help it. I've made it a point to not turn to my family for money while I built these gyms, and I've succeeded. Every one of them is turning a substantial profit.

"I don't need money," I assure him. If either of my brothers ever bothered to look at Sheridan Gyms' financials, they'd know that. "That's not why I showed you the plans."

He holds his hands up. "I know, I know. I'm just saying that this would be something we'd love to back up. Hell, it would make JLS look good."

"I'm not doing it for publicity." I get so tired of organizations scaring up publicity for themselves by playing the pro-military card.

He cocks his head. "Since when are *you* doing something without publicity?"

I give a half shrug. "This is an exception. The people who go to this gym will be there for a good workout. They don't want a bunch of cameras in their faces."

"So, do some interviews *before* it opens. Drum up your opening a bit. Come on—you're the PR monger in the family." He snaps his fingers. "Hey, you should talk to Mick's sister-in-law while you're out there. She does on-air work sometimes at CNN out of their DC Bureau, last I heard."

"I don't need some reporter turning my gym into a circus act."

"She won't do that. She's a straight shooter, Dylan—married to a SEAL like her sister. She'll do right by you." He rolls up my plans and carefully puts them back in the cardboard tube. "And I meant what I said about JLS. We'd give you the money quietly. No PR. Hell, the PR team is going to need a month's vacation, anyway, after Allie's shelter opens tomorrow. They've been working 'round the clock."

"Thanks. But I definitely don't need the money. In fact, the way things are going, JLS Heartland might be coming to *me* for a loan down the road."

He grins. "How's the Cincy gym coming along?"

"Great. You should stop by sometime. Love your input."

"I will. As soon as you get the mats down, we'll do a little sparring. 'Bout time someone schooled you on the mats."

"Ha. You can try." I'm a damn good fighter, but if anyone could beat me, it would be Logan. But only if he's having a good day.

CHAPTER 3

~ CASS ~

The hot August air feels decadent on my legs, now that I'm in my shorts and free of that hefty dress. I've washed myself clean from my cake makeup and watched the sparkles from it disappear down my drain.

Now, feeling fresh-faced and slightly more courageous, I sit in front of my laptop. My heart races as I click the keyboard, bringing it to life.

I know I shouldn't do this. I know what I'll see. But I do it anyway.

"Cassidy Parker," I type into the search line.

And there it is, my photograph with Brenna's little kid on Facebook, on Twitter, and even making today's post on one of my former classmate's blog.

It doesn't take long for news to spread in this day and age.

Biting my lip, I click on the Facebook link first. My photo isn't tagged because I don't have an account. Yes, I realize I'm only one of about twenty-five people on the planet who isn't updating my life on Facebook. Really, why would I? I had enjoyed the idea of people thinking I might be doing something a bit better than playing princess as a seasonal worker at Buckeye Land when I'd had such vocal expectations of fame and fortune when I left my hometown.

But my name is plastered all over the comments section on Brenna's Facebook page today.

- *Isn't that Cassidy Parker? I thought she was living in New York!*

- *Yep, that's her. She's the Buckeye Princess. ;)*

- *Love the gown. LOL*

- *She fills it out well, which is surprising since I doubt she makes more than minimum wage.*

I narrow my eyes. I make a lot more than minimum wage, which is the only reason I'd agreed to come back for a second summer. My fingers itch to respond, but I know it would make me look even more pathetic.

- *I thought Cassidy wanted to be a model.*

- *What's she doing there? She said she hated small town life! Poor Cassidy.*

- *I'll rescue you, Princess! But first let me check out what's under those skirts.*

Very mature group, our high school class.

And then, the *pièce de résistance*, from Brenna herself, just to make her look like a nice person:

- *Now guys, I didn't put this up here for you to insult Cassidy. I just wanted you to see the picture of my beautiful daughter. Isn't she precious?*

Bitch.

I switch to Twitter, and the dialogue is pretty much the same.

My shoulders sag as I push myself back from the desk,

patting my lap. My foster dog, Rascal, pounces up onto me, and I don't even mind that his paws scratch my legs.

"Humans suck, Rascal," I tell him, stroking his fur. His sympathetic eyes meet mine, and I'm betting he agrees, seeing as he's pretty much been failed by humans till Allie's rescue organization saved him from the "kill list" at our county pound.

He lifts himself up, resting his two front paws on my shoulders, and licks my face. I can't help smiling.

God, I love this dog. I love them all, though. And I'll miss not being needed as a foster now that Allie's shelter is officially opening tomorrow.

Sighing, I pull him off my shoulders and wipe my face on my sleeve. Picking up the phone, my fingers hover to call one of my friends and pour my heart out. My friend Allie is probably enjoying a Friday night barbeque with her husband in their new home about five miles from here. No need to drag down her day.

I consider calling Kim instead. Kim may be engaged to the hottest billionaire on the planet right now, and her wedding in two weeks has somehow morphed into a celebration for the entire town, complete with pony rides for the kids and fireworks after the reception. But as a single mom, she's known her share of hardship.

She's also my housemate this summer, renting me one of the spare rooms in her and her five-year-old son Connor's townhome. They'll be moving out in two weeks after Kim gets married to Ryan, and into his 6,000-square-foot home in an elegant part of town. So, for my final month here in Newton's Creek before I head back to New York, I'll have the whole townhome to myself while Kim lists it for sale.

Narrowing my eyes thoughtfully, I picture her schedule in my head. I think she's at a peewee soccer match today, and I'm not sure if I should bug her. But I bring up her name in my contacts and hit the talk button anyway, consoling myself that she can ignore the call if they're in the middle of a heated match.

"Hi, Cass," she answers. "Thought you'd still be at work."

"Got off at four. How's the soccer game?"

"We're losing. But Connor's made the only two goals, so he's on happy. What's going on there?"

I preface my reply with an annoyed grunt. "Oh, just bumped into someone from high school at Buckeye Land, and within minutes she posted pictures of me in my princess get-up online. So humiliating."

"Well, don't they say any publicity is good publicity?"

"I think that only works when you're famous. Not a nobody like me."

"Quit talking like that. You're a successful New York model."

"Kim, I did catalogs."

"And TV commercials."

"Just a couple local ones."

"Sure, local. But the New York metropolitan area is huge."

I frown, remembering the moment when I stood in front of a green screen knowing that a giant deer with antlers would be standing beside me. "Come to Halton's to buy your next used car. We'll save you BIG BUCKS," I had to say, thrusting a handful of fake bills in front of me.

No, that's not really something to brag about. And it certainly pales in comparison to the grandiose plan I once had in my life.

A tone beeps in my ear and I glance at the number on the phone. I don't recognize it. "Hold on, Kim. I have another call." I switch over. "Hello?"

"Cass?"

My heart rate kicks up a notch at the sound of the voice on the other end. "Yes?"

"Hey, it's Dylan Sheridan. I met you today with my niece."

And at the wedding, I'm tempted to remind him. But I'm starting to think he doesn't remember our conversation that night.

I'm almost annoyed at the way my face automatically flushes pink at the sensual timbre of his voice. Even though the guy has the personality of a paving brick, he still sends my hormones into overdrive.

"Logan and Ryan's brother. Yes, hi," I say, trying not to sound like a girl who, during my late teen years, taped photos of him to my bedroom walls like a shrine.

"Yeah. Logan and Ryan's brother," he repeats, sounding a little deflated. "I wanted to see if you were free for dinner sometime while I'm in town."

My eyebrows rise. I should absolutely tell this guy to go to hell, seeing as I know I'm just another "dumb model" to him. Yet there's this part of me that wants to say yes—to take a couple hours to show him I'm more than what he thinks I am—and then wipe the floor with his oversized ego as I march into the sunset.

That would be bitchy, though, and totally out of character for me.

I open my mouth to turn him down, but then remember Allie's gala tomorrow night. My smile hitches upward on one side, my scheme evolving quickly in my supposedly microscopic model-brain. "Actually, I was going to Allie's shelter opening tomorrow."

"Really? I'll be going too."

My eyes flash with delight, picturing all the press that will be there, hopefully taking my picture with a well-heeled Olympian on my arm.

Tweet that, Brenna Tucker.

"Care to go together?" I ask.

"Sure. Pick you up at seven?"

Smiling, I press my lips together thoughtfully for a moment, imagining him driving me home at the end of the night. If he drinks anywhere as much as he did at the wedding, I'd be smart to keep my own car nearby. "How about I meet you there?" I offer.

"Works for me."

"Great. See you then." I click back over to Kim and squeal, "I have a date with Dylan Sheridan!" My voice is sing-songy.

"Um… yes, you do."

I freeze in the middle of the happy dance that I'm sharing with Rascal on my bedroom floor. Glancing at the phone, I see it never switched back over to Kim. Infernal technology! "Oh, God."

His laugh is a low rumble, as sexy as his body. "Don't worry about it. I was about to call my brother and scream in his ear that I have a date with Princess Buckeye."

I sigh. "Sorry. I was on the other line when you called. Newton's Creek runs a little thin on the single scene."

"I know. I was raised here. Don't worry about it. I'll see you at seven."

I sink to the floor, unable to even make it to my bed. As Rascal crawls onto my lap, I stare at my phone for a second, tempted to send it careening through the air and let it crack it against the wall. *Just like a dumb model*, I'm sure he's thinking. *Can't even manage to work a cell phone.*

Switching the call back to Kim, I'm careful to wait till I see her number appear on the screen before speaking this time. "Kim? You still there?"

"Yeah, still here."

"Oh, God."

"What? Was that someone from high school calling to rub salt in your wounds?"

"No, worse. It was Dylan Sheridan."

"Dylan? How can that be bad?"

I swallow—hard—before I tell her how I just shrieked in his ear like a high school freshman getting asked to senior prom.

She's laughing on the other end.

"It's not funny, Kim."

"It *is* funny. Seriously funny. He probably thought that was cute. Dylan's really a nice guy, Cass."

No, I want to tell her. Dylan is *faking* that he's a nice guy. Alcohol is the great enabler. It shows how people really are. But seeing as the guy is going to become her brother-in-law in two weeks, I feel it's only right to let her discover that on her own.

We chat a while longer before I disconnect the call. Curious, I move to my laptop again and punch his name into a search line, hoping—praying—he's not doing the same for me.

I scroll through the images of him with countless women on his arms. I weed through the articles about him, scanning his transition from Olympic medalist to MMA fighter to gym entrepreneur. The guy has a website, a Twitter feed, a Facebook page, and even an entry in Wikipedia.

And he's got a date with *me*? Seriously?

One photo with him and it will be all over the internet, undoing any trace of damage done by Brenna Tucker, and maybe—just maybe—enabling me to go to my ten-year reunion in a few years with my head held high.

CHAPTER 4

- DYLAN -

I arrive early at the shelter in case Allie needs a little extra help getting things set up. But apparently, she has everything under control. A band is already playing and white-gloved servers armed with hefty platters of appetizers are wandering through an already packed crowd beneath a massive white tent on the front lawn.

Three local TV stations are covering this event and there are a few photographers, including one I recognize from the Associated Press. I shouldn't be surprised by the coverage—Allie's got the public relations powerhouse at JLS Heartland backing them. With so much money sunk into this project, JLS looks like a saint today, constructing this shelter for a bunch of homeless animals. That's something JLS doesn't get to enjoy often. Being a housing developer, they've got their fair share of adversaries.

The sun is sparkling as it tracks lower to the horizon, and

I'm anxious for it to set permanently. It's hot, and I'm trapped in a suit for the evening, grateful as hell that Allie didn't take my advice and make this a black tie event. She was right; even though this is the biggest thing to happen in this area, it's still a small town. In fact, I doubt anyone within a thirty-mile radius even owns a tux, barring those with the Sheridan name.

We never did fit into this small town—which might be why I was so anxious to leave it.

As an adult, though, I see something in this town that I had never fully valued as a kid. There's a sense of community, of sincerity, that I just don't feel much in my sterile high-rise condo overlooking Lake Michigan. I probably would have been smarter to get a brownstone in Lincoln Park or up near Wrigley Field if I'd wanted to experience the real character of the Windy City.

Squinting against the setting sun, I spot Cass arriving in a practical-looking Mazda, her blonde hair giving her away through her open window.

Immediately, my protective side flares up—the same part of me that got me into a few too many fights in school, always when some jackass was trash-talking a girl.

I don't normally make it a practice to punch the names of women I date into a search engine. But when Logan had mentioned she was a model, well, I couldn't resist.

Then I spotted about a dozen fresh posts on Facebook and a few other social media sites made by some witch named Brenna Tucker, and a posse of people who apparently are still clinging to their high school cliques even though they are fast-approaching the quarter-century mark.

After reading their snide comments about Cass's job as the Buckeye Princess, my teeth had grated together so hard that my jaw locked up temporarily.

I can't even imagine how Cass will feel when she discovers their posts.

But I'm on it now, and I know just how to put people like Brenna Tucker in their place. The PR department at JLS pales compared to what I can pull off.

When she parks, I stride toward her car just in time to open her door for her. I'm rewarded with an eyeful of leg; the calf-length red dress she has on boasts a slit up to her mid-thigh. Suddenly I'm feeling like a tongue-tied teenager.

"Hi, Dylan." She greets me with a smile that makes the brilliant summer sun look lackluster by comparison.

"You look gorgeous," I say, extending a hand to her and helping her out of her car. "I hope you don't mind a lot of press tonight. The PR machine at JLS must have been working overtime to pull this off."

Her grin only builds from my statement. "I don't mind a few cameras."

With a smile like that, I can see why. "So where are you from, Cass? And don't tell me it's an enchanted kingdom. You're out of your dress now." Damn, just saying the words *out of your dress* has got me half-chubbed. This woman is so hot I could grill a burger on her buns.

Taking my arm, she laughs. "A Kansas City suburb on the Kansas side."

"A Midwestern girl. So Newton's Creek should feel like home to you, I'll bet."

"You know, it kind of does. I hated the town I grew up in so much. The kids were stereotypically cruel. You know, there were the kids born on the right side of the tracks, and then there was me. But looking back, it was the kids I hated. Not the town. New York City is so—"

"Cass!" Allie's voice interrupts her as she walks toward us with open arms.

I almost want to flag her away; I was enjoying learning a

little more about the girl behind the crown. But Allie steals Cass into a hug and a few cameras snap in response.

That's not the type of photo that will put that Brenna Tucker woman in her place.

Logan steals Cass for an embrace, and I immediately thump on his shoulder and shoot him a glare. "Hands off my date, big brother," I warn, offering him a smile and a tightly coiled fist six inches from his face as I tug Cass next to me, resting my other hand on her tiny waist.

That's the type of photo that the press likes, as Logan lets out a hearty laugh and I glare at him mockingly with Cass snug at my side.

And, of course, the photographers eat it up.

Ryan approaches, shaking his head, knowing full well I'm hamming it up for the cameras. He always calls me an attention whore, and he's not too far off the mark. But it's easy for him to keep things on the down-low. Unlike me, he was handed his career at JLS Heartland on a silver platter, and never had to use the media to build a brand like I did with my gyms. I'm not saying he hasn't worked hard to keep JLS thriving, but it's a hell of a lot easier to thrive when you're already starting off on top.

We share in our usual brotherly banter and Allie, Kim, and Cass chat, sipping their champagnes and mingling through the crowd. I'm feeling jealous as everyone seems to get a chance to talk to Cass except me. I manage to steal her away from Allie at one point when a reporter starts asking me questions. I know Cass needs her face in that camera more than I do right now. So I keep her at my side and tolerate their intrusion till they move on to a couple of the guys from the Bengals who came to the event tonight.

"Allie and Kim really pulled it off," she says to me in a brief moment when we're not surrounded by others.

"Kim? Did she help plan the event, too?"

She nods. "She works at the shelter doing fundraising now."

I frown momentarily at how little I know about the woman who is going to become my sister-in-law in two short weeks. Even though I've made a point to visit Newton's Creek often since my dad's diagnosis, I still haven't managed to keep updated on what's going on in my family's life like I should.

I steal a bacon-wrapped shrimp from a server. "Well, they did a great job. The place looks phenomenal," I comment, extending the shrimp toward Cass's lips. She takes it into her mouth, and the nanosecond that her lips touch my fingers sends a signal to my groin that has rendered me momentarily speechless.

"It looks even better now that the sun has set," she remarks, her eyes tracking from mine toward the tiny white lights that are twinkling in the trees surrounding us, making the area around the tent sparkle like the holidays.

My mouth hitches upward. "Everything looks better when the sun sets."

"Especially with champagne," she adds, lifting her eyebrows and raising her glass.

I wouldn't know. I avoid alcohol like the plague at events like these. I'm a lightweight around booze. And I'm a rotten drunk.

Wrapping my arm around her waist, I savor the feel of her body close to mine. For the hour and a half we've shared together tonight, we've barely said a word to each other. Yet I can't help noticing how incredible it feels to have her near. "You say that, but I can't help noticing, you've been holding the same flute of champagne all night while barely taking a sip."

"You're sharp. It's a prop. Photos look more candid if you're holding something."

Smart girl. "Am I a prop too, then?"

"I could ask the same question to you," she challenges.

Very smart, indeed.

"Well, I won't argue that you do attract the cameras, Cass."

She tilts her head. "I think that's all you, Dylan. Do they always follow you like this?"

"Only at events like this. I can't complain because I've kind of fostered it. Every time my photo appears somewhere, it's publicity for Sheridan Gyms."

"You really like to promote your gyms."

"Building my brand brings in more memberships, which brings in more money, which enables me to do the things I really want to do." My mind wanders to the new gym I'm planning on building near Walter Reed. The place will drain the coffers for a while; the kind of specialized equipment I'll be bringing in there is top-of-the-line. But sometimes it's better to do something simply because it's the right thing to do.

I spot the photographer from the AP perusing the room, looking for something worthy of a few clicks of his camera.

"Want to be make some headlines?" I ask.

"Love to," she replies, her eyes sparking with delight.

So I whirl her into a dip, and lay one on her. It's only meant to attract the photographer. I hadn't expected my knees to nearly buckle when I feel her lips full against mine. She opens them slightly, an invitation I gratefully accept, tasting the spice of the shrimp I had hand-fed her only a few minutes ago. The feel of her slick tongue against mine sends a jolt into my heart and then tracks downward, gathering heat in my loins that will make for a hell of a photograph if I don't put a stop to this kiss right now.

At the bright pulses of a few camera flashes, I know I've attracted the attention she needs—there's no need to prolong this—but she's so responsive, purring low and seductive. It unleashes the alpha in me, despite the camera on us right now. I should pull away, fire off a smile as though we've been "caught," but I can't stop my tongue from sliding along her teeth as she threads her fingers into my hair and pulls me closer, deeper.

My lips devour her, hot and urgent, marking her as my own. Our mouths joined, I steal a breath from her as my hand cradles her back, aching to stray and feel other parts of her supple body.

But then, unmistakably, I feel the eyes of my brothers burrowing into the back of my head, and my mind clears.

Lifting my face an inch from hers, I watch her eyelids open slowly. *Sweet Jesus*, her eyes are bluer than the waters of Grace Bay in Turks and Caicos.

"Look at me, and smile for the cameras," I say quietly enough to be heard by her and her alone. She takes my direction and flashes a smile worthy of the cover of *Vogue*.

I set her vertical again, still keeping my fingers woven into her long princess tresses possessively.

She's glowing, and while I'd like to think it's from the aftereffects of my kiss, I know the truth. It's the attention she's savoring. She's as much of a ham as I am.

"Well, if that doesn't give my career a boost, I don't know what will," she says breathlessly.

Her honesty is refreshing. The last several women I dated loved to attract the cameras, but refused to admit they were doing it for their career. Even the dramatic break-ups that would inevitably follow I'd swear were staged—at a moment when a reporter just happened to be around.

"I hope I wasn't being too forward," I tell her.

She lets out the cutest snort. "I should say you were. And you can be forward like that anytime you want."

I laugh, despite the glare I'm getting from Ryan across the room.

"I think I better run and check my lipstick," she says, brushing her two fingers against my own lips to wipe me free of the smear of pink from her lips on mine. It's another moment that makes the cameras flash in our direction. I can't help feeling annoyed with them this time, because the motion of her fingers gently stroking my lips feels somehow more intimate even than the searing kiss we just shared.

"I'll be right back," she says, and just like that, I can see my brothers closing in on me like wolves.

Logan's biting back a grin, but there's nothing but fury in Ryan's eyes. He looks like he could rip my head off my torso and eat it for dinner. And wouldn't that be a hell of a photo op?

"Watch it with Cass, Dylan," Ryan warns.

"Watch what?" I ask innocently.

"That stunt you pulled in front of the cameras."

"What—the kiss? That was for her, not for me."

Ryan crosses his arms in front of his chest as though it's the only way to keep from strangling me. "Oh, really? You arrogant ass."

"No, I'm serious. I looked her up online yesterday after we made the date. Seems some of her classmates from high school are talking trash about her."

Ryan's eyes change from refrigerator-cold to deep-freeze. My brothers are a bit on the protective side like I am.

"What kind of trash?" Logan asks.

"Oh, some aging Homecoming Queen saw her working at her princess job at Buckeye Land yesterday. Posted the photo on Twitter, Facebook, everywhere she can, dissing Cass."

"Dammit."

"Yeah. I guess Cass had told everyone back in high school that she was going to be a model in New York. So now people are pouncing on the fact that she's stuck in Ohio working at an amusement park."

"I hate social media," Ryan mutters.

"Well, it can also turn things around for her. I figured if I can get our picture out there, it might shut them up a bit. Don't tell Cass, though. I don't want her knowing I saw those posts."

The rage leaves Ryan's eyes. "Good call on the kiss, in that case, then."

"You know me. I'm a whiz with publicity."

"Just don't break her heart," he adds. "She's Allie's and Kim's best friend, so she's pretty close to being family."

"I won't," I assure him.

"You won't sleep with her then?" Ryan specifies.

My face contorts. "What? Hell, I never said I wouldn't do that. Why the hell can't I?"

"Family, bro. I just said she's *like family*. Treat her that way."

"Screw you. I think she's the only single woman here tonight, and you're telling me I can't sleep with her?"

"That's exactly what I'm telling you. Your record for breaking hearts is pretty bad, Dylan," he says, reflecting the same sentiment I'd heard from Logan yesterday.

"Hey, the last one cheated on *me*," I say defensively. "Not the other way around. I don't cheat. Never will. And I never lead a woman on. I make sure they know I'm not looking for anything permanent." I gaze at Cass across the room as she chats with Allie en route to the restroom in the shelter adjacent to the tent. Her eyes meet mine for a moment and my cock perks up at the site of that red dress hugging her curves in the most seductive way. "If I choose to sleep with her—and that's still an *if*—she'll know I'm not looking for a picket fence and minivan filled with kids."

Logan stands up poker-straight, bringing his height a

little taller than my own six feet. "Cass is a nice girl, Dylan. You might be smart to get to know her before actually jumping in the sack with her. Might be refreshing for a change. You'd be lucky to have a girl like her."

"Yeah, and I'd be luckier if I could pursue her without Thing 1 and Thing 2 cockblocking me." I send them both a glare before I walk away.

CHAPTER 5

~ CASS ~

Since I barely managed a C in high school Chemistry, I don't exactly consider myself an expert on the subject. But until about five minutes ago, I would have bet my princess paycheck that there was no chemistry between Dylan and me. I mean, we'd barely said a handful of words to each other, and both of us seemed more focused on attracting cameras than attracting each other.

Till he laid that kiss on me.

Now, my girl parts are still humming and my lips feel hungry for more. Even though I know my purpose tonight had nothing to do with a roll in the sack, I'm wondering if it would be totally wrong for me to follow him back to his hotel and end this sexual drought I've been in.

As I glide on Jell-O knees across the massive tent on the front lawn of the shelter, I search the room for my friends. I exchange a few words with Allie as I pass her. But she's in a conversation with the mayor of our small town, so I can't exactly pull her into my internal debate about whether or not I should have wicked sex with her brother-in-law tonight.

Looking for Kim, I frown when I see Ryan without her, talking to Dylan at the other side of the room. Kim probably left early with her son and her soon-to-be stepdaughter, Hannah, I'm betting. A couple kids wouldn't last long at an event like this.

I give Dylan a quick glance as I leave the tent and head toward the building where the restrooms are. Just seeing him in the distance makes my knees weak again. He flashes me a brief, knowing smile that I swear should be listed as one of the seven wonders of the world.

Just outside the restroom door, my eyes meet those of Dylan's dad, Mr. Jacob Sheridan himself. He grins at me. "Good evening," he says cordially.

Damn, he's good-looking for an old guy, with those unmistakable Sheridan eyes and sculpted chin.

I extend my hand. "Mr. Sheridan. I'm Cass, Kim's housemate."

He gives me a baffled look momentarily, but then nods. "Jake Sheridan."

"You must be so proud of the opening tonight. I know Allie and Logan have been excited for months about this."

"You know my son?"

"Yes. You must be really proud of him."

He gives a curt nod. "I'm proud of all my boys. Are you his teacher? I apologize for the ruckus he made during recess last week. Not the way Sheridans should act, and you have my word it won't happen again."

My mouth opens, but I'm silent for a moment, confused. "No. No, I'm not his teacher. But he's really great," I finish feebly, my voice suddenly small, afraid of saying the wrong thing.

I don't know much about vascular dementia—only that it's a little bit like Alzheimer's. Logan told me once about a time when his dad disappeared, driving all the way to another state, convinced he had to pick up his son at an airport, even though his son wasn't flying anywhere that day.

My heart rate quickens, worried that Mr. Sheridan might be having some kind of a spell like that right now.

What am I supposed to do in a situation like this?

"Well, if he can manage to stop those fights at recess," he replies, giving a slight nod at the restroom door. "If you don't mind, would you ask my wife to hurry in there? There are some people I need to introduce her to."

I smile uncertainly, feeling a hint of relief at hearing that his wife is nearby. I extend my hand again. "I will. It was so nice meeting you, sir."

Pushing the door open to the restroom, I spot Mrs. Sheridan washing her hands. Our eyes meet in the mirror and I can tell she recognizes me. I've met her a couple times when she's taken her granddaughter to Buckeye Land.

"Cass, right?" she says.

"Yes. Hi, Mrs. Sheridan. I'm surprised you recognized me out of my princess costume."

She wipes her hands on a paper towel and gives me a hug. "Of course I would. And please, call me Anna. When people call me Mrs. Sheridan, I still turn around and look for my mother-in-law, God rest her soul. And that woman scared the life out of me."

I laugh. She just doesn't seem like the wife of a billionaire corporate mogul.

"I'm glad you could make it to Allie's big opening," she continues.

I nod. "It's going so well out there..." My voice trails, thinking about Mr. Sheridan on the other side of the door.

41

"Um, I saw your husband outside the restroom and he asked me to tell you there are a few people he'd like you to meet."

"Always in a rush, that one, even at his age." She rolls her eyes. "Thank you, Cass."

I reach out, lightly touching her arm. "He seemed—I don't know—a little confused."

Concern washes over her face. "Thank you, Cass," she replies, hastily making her exit, not looking nearly as carefree as she did even fifteen seconds ago.

My eyes follow her out of the restroom, but I can't erase her look of distress from my memory. They always shock me, somehow—these couples who still love each other so deeply after decades.

I've watched my friends take a chance on having a love like that. Hell, I've even encouraged them to do it. Yet for me, the risk seems too great.

I was raised on the front lines of when love falls apart, with too many memories of sitting on the top step of the staircase, hearing the arguments. Waiting there, my skinny arms wrapped around my stuffed bunny, listening for reconciliation—that moment when my parents would look at each other and remember the love they once had for each other and know that their marriage—that our *family*—was worth saving.

Hell, it happened in the old movies I watched with my grandma every weekday after school. It was bound to happen in our house. It was only a matter of time.

But the years came and went. Just like my dad finally went... out the door.

These couples like the Sheridans seem to have some secret that ordinary people like my parents never quite grasped. So, even as my heart breaks for Anna Sheridan as she watches someone she loves slowly lose his memories, I can't help feeling that she is somehow still lucky to have experienced a love like that in the first place—a kind of love that apparently is not in my genetic code.

With a sigh, I give the restroom a quick perusal, noticing I'm alone. Leaning against the wall, I pull my phone out of my purse and text Kim.

"Did u leave early?" I type in.

I'm not even able to touch up my lipstick before my phone buzzes with her reply. "Connor doesn't last long at those things. I took him and Hannah home with me. He's asleep. She's still wired for sound, tho," she's written back.

I bite my lip thoughtfully a moment, glancing at myself in the mirror. I swear my cheeks are still flushed from that kiss Dylan and I shared. I know it was all staged for the cameras. He made that pretty clear. But my reaction to it was anything but staged. "Remind me again why I shouldn't sleep with Dylan," I tap into my phone.

It only takes an instant before she replies.

"So I take it u like him?"

My mouth curves downward, thinking of our conversation at the wedding a few months ago. Do I like him? Ugh. Do I really have to like him? "I like to *LOOK* at him," I type back.

"That's it?"

"He's not exactly a deep guy, Kim."

"Pot? Kettle. Kettle? Pot," she texts, adding a smiley face.

Touché. "LOL. K. Then I guess I'll sleep with him."

"I didn't say that!"

"What SHOULD I do?"

"Don't sleep with him."

I frown. "Y not?"

"Because u wouldn't be texting me if u thought u should!"

She has a point.

"But it's been soooo long! If I don't come home, will u let Rascal out for me in the morning?" I type in, thinking about my foster dog who possibly won't appreciate how much I need to get laid.

"Yes. But don't be EZ."

Easy? Easy for Kim to say. She's got a kid to wear her out during the day and a hot fiancé to wear her out at night. Single life in Newton's Creek is pretty bleak. If I don't take this opportunity to sleep with Dylan, I might not get to have sex again till I return to New York.

I smirk, tapping into my phone, "EZ does it."

I grin at myself in the mirror, knowing my friend is right now shaking her head. She and Allie are the romantics. Not me. I'm looking for a good, short burst of fireworks rather than a slow burn that might last forever.

Sliding my phone back into my purse, I touch up my makeup quickly and return to Dylan who conveniently is talking to a reporter I recognize from the Cincinnati six o'clock news. I'm moderately surprised at how much press is here tonight. I know the Sheridans are billionaires, but this is still puny Newton's Creek.

Dylan extends his hand toward me, almost as if he knows instinctively why I so desperately need to be seen with him tonight. I can't help being grateful for it—grateful enough that I'm considering asking him to show me some of those wrestling moves naked in his hotel room tonight.

As I take his hand, he pulls me to his side possessively, even as he talks to the reporter. Then, as soon as he answers the reporter's last question, he leans in to kiss me as the camera is still rolling.

I try not to look surprised, but it's hard. The feel of his lips on me, even lightly, scorches me, making my breath catch as though I just smacked my hand against a hibachi grill.

Fuck chemistry and conversation skills. This man kisses like a professional.

Lifting his face an inch from mine, his eyes twinkle as he introduces me to the reporter. I feel like I'm in a movie; this is really as close to fame as I'll probably ever get aside from being recognized as the Halton's Used Car girl on the subway a couple times. I feel dazzled by the magic of the evening.

Looking around me suddenly, I start to realize the scope of the Sheridan wealth. They're like nobility here in the Midwest, all so strikingly handsome and charming that it's no wonder the press comes out in droves when the Sheridans snap their fingers.

Leading me through the tent, Dylan dabbles in one casual conversation after another until his mother touches him on the shoulder.

She looks paler than earlier. I don't even know her that well, yet my entire body goes into high alert.

"Dylan, I can't find your father," she says, her voice low.

"Could he be in the restroom?" Dylan asks.

"No. I already asked someone to check there. I checked outside, too. And our car is gone."

"Shit," Dylan curses softly, glancing around, his eyes searching. "We need to call the police. Have them put out one of those silver alerts."

Mrs. Sheridan quickly shakes her head. "No. Don't do that. It would embarrass your father. Especially with all the press here."

"Mom, we have to do something."

"Give the man his dignity, dammit." Her eyes flash at Dylan, and I'm betting that this woman has cursed about three times in her life, for the power that single word seems to have over her son.

"Okay. We'll find him ourselves. Did you try accessing that tracking app on his phone?"

"I did. But he must have turned his phone off. Or the battery ran out."

"Well, there's a way you can use the app to find the last location of his phone before it got turned off," he tells her. "Let's grab Ryan and talk in the parking lot without the press watching."

"I'll get Allie and Logan," I offer.

"No. I don't want this to ruin Allie's big night. Your father would be devastated. I'll tell Logan, but not Allie," his mother says. "And I'm having him stay with her. We can find him on our own."

My eyes move to Dylan. If he disagrees with his mother, I don't think he'll utter a word of it right now. "I'll meet you out front," he tells her, and we head in Ryan's direction.

"Hey, bro," Dylan greets him with a smile, and then says softly, "Mom can't find Dad. She doesn't want the press to know. Meet us in the parking lot. And don't tell Allie. Not till we find him. Mom's orders."

Revealing nothing, Ryan gives a nod.

My heart is racing as we gather in the parking lot. Dylan pulls out his iPhone. I watch him tap in a password to access an app.

"Well, it's showing that his phone's last location was just north of the shelter," he says, the slide of his fingers zooming in on the map on the phone. "Right near Danvers Street. But we can't assume anything. Mom, I think you should check at home."

She nods. "Logan gave me his keys. I'll head there now. And I'll check the JLS parking lot on my way there."

"Good idea. Ryan, you take the area west of Newton's Creek and I'll take east. It's mostly likely he's around here. It would seem the most familiar to him."

"I'll check around Pop's and the new development down by the river, too. Those places would a natural for him to go to," Ryan adds before jogging to his car, leaving Dylan and me alone.

"Cass, would you mind looking in this area over here?" He points to a section of the map on his phone. "And then if you see nothing, just keep going north... I guess. Dammit." He shakes his head, watching his mother's and brother's cars pull out of the parking lot. "I'm trying to sound like I know what the hell I'm talking about, and I'm clueless."

I take his hand. "Where did he go last time he disappeared like this?"

"He was in Pennsylvania."

"Jesus."

"Yeah. He was trying to find a construction site for one of his developments, but drove right by it because the damn project had been finished fifteen years ago." He lets out a pained breath. "Maybe we should call the police."

"Your mother said not to."

"My mother thinks too much about what my dad would want."

That's what people do when they love each other, I can't help thinking. "Give us an hour to try to find him. Then we'll call."

I have Dylan give me a description of his parents' SUV and I climb into my car, barely taking a moment to breathe before I pull out of the parking lot.

The streetlights whizz past me as I drive toward the area where Dylan wants me to go.

Are you his teacher?

I feel my forehead crease sharply as I remember what Mr. Sheridan had said to me in that brief conversation we had tonight. His teacher? Is he thinking about his son's school? Should I check the schools in the area?

No, no. That doesn't seem right either. I drum my fingers on my steering wheel as I merge onto the highway.

Are you his teacher? He must have thought that his sons were young again.

Wait a minute! Glancing in my mirror, I change lanes and then exit the highway. Spotting a gas station, I pull in and put the car in park.

So, he thinks we are at a different point in time. A time when his sons were in school. What was his life like then? Thoroughly focused on work, I'd gather, from the way the Sheridan empire grew so quickly when his sons were young.

Dylan's mother probably will find him at JLS, I'm betting, wishing my phone would ring bringing me this news.

But where else would he have gone back in the days when his sons were in school? Job sites? Isn't that what Dylan said he was doing that time he was found in Pennsylvania—looking for a construction site?

I pull my phone out of my purse and pull up a mapping app. Typing in "JLS Heartland Community," I hold my breath. There are two JLS developments within ten miles of where my car is right now, appearing as red dots on the map. I ponder which I should go to first.

I tap on one of the red dots and let my GPS start guiding me to the closest one.

My eyes narrow on every car I pass on my way there. At a stoplight, when I pull up behind a dark Lincoln Navigator like Dylan had described, I let it take me off my route, following it. Straining my eyes, I try to make out the figure behind the wheel. I hear my phone buzzing in my purse, but ignore it, locking my eyes on the SUV in front of me.

It turns into a residential community that doesn't have the JLS logo on the sign at the entrance and I'm immediately questioning myself. There are plenty of Lincoln Navigators, and it could be anyone. Yet still holding out on the hope that it might be him, I continue behind it as it takes two more turns. I tail it closely, wishing I could just pass it safely so that I might get a better glimpse of the driver.

Dammit. Another turn comes pulling me further away from my intended route, and my phone buzzes again next to me. Finally, the SUV pulls up beside a house and I have a chance to pass it, just as the passenger side door opens and a pregnant woman steps out.

Cursing quietly, I pull into someone's driveway to turn around as I see the driver, a man about forty years younger than Mr. Sheridan.

Frowning, I pull to the curb to scan the incoming texts from Dylan, which were copied to his brothers. "Mom called. Dad is not at JLS or the house. Anything there?"

"Nothing here," Ryan has texted back.

My heart sinks. *No, nothing here either*, I'm thinking. *And I just wasted five minutes following a man and his pregnant wife.*

But instead, I simply text back, "No luck yet."

I look at the GPS app again, feeling time ticking by too rapidly.

They need to call the police, I can't help thinking. Every minute we waste could be taking him further from us.

Thanks to my futile detour, I'm equal distance from both the JLS communities I've pulled up on my map now. I click on the links to both, to try to figure out which I should go to first.

One appears to be the newer community of the two, built sometime during the housing boom of the late nineties, by the opulent look of their façades. The other, a more modest development, I'm guessing was built earlier than that.

Recess, he had mentioned. Something about Logan having a problem at recess. Since Mr. Sheridan seemed to think his sons were in school—at a time when there was still recess— that would push back the clock earlier, to about when the older development was built.

I hear my phone buzz next to me again, and at a stop sign, I take a quick glance. Ryan has written, "He's not at the new development. Checking Pop's and the stores on Anders Street next."

I sigh, taking a turn. I have no idea where I am right now, and if my battery on my phone gave way, I'd end up as lost as Mr. Sheridan is right now.

Finally, I see the JLS logo on a sign welcoming me as I turn into a community. I slow my car to a snail's pace, eyes searching for his dark SUV.

It's not even a minute before my eyes rest on one, pulled alongside one of the first houses in the community. I bite my lip, almost thinking it's too good to be true, until I see the older gentleman sitting in the front seat.

It's him. Oh my God, it's him.

I feel my breath expel from my lungs and I press in Dylan's number.

"I found him. I found him, Dylan." I'm almost in tears as I say it.

"Oh, thank God. Where?"

"At an old JLS development. What do I do? Should I just approach him, or what?" I've never dealt with someone who was going through something like this. I have no clue what his reaction will be.

"Yes. See if you can get him to get in your car and you can take him back to my mom's house. I'll text you the address."

"What if he won't go with me?"

"Uh, ask him if you can stay with him till I get there and you can text me the location of the nearest house. Just please don't let him out of your sight."

"I'll do my best," I say, uncertainty in my voice.

"Thanks, Cass. God, we owe you for this. You have no idea."

I hang up the call, and slip my phone into my clutch.

Swallowing hard, I approach his car slowly and tap on the window. His bewildered eyes greet me, and he lowers his window.

"Hi, Mr. Sheridan. Remember me? I met you tonight."

"Of course. You know my son."

"Right. Logan. You seem a little lost."

Slowly, he nods. "I—I thought I had some business here. A meeting or something. But…" He falls silent.

"It's a beautiful development you built."

He nods again. "It is, isn't it? Always topping the last one these days. But they put this one up so quickly…"

His head shakes as his voice trails, and I know that it's a shock for him to see it completed. My heart is breaking for this man.

"You know, sometimes when I'm really tired, I get confused, too. How about I drive you back to your house so you can catch up on some rest?" I try to sound casual, even though I can hear my voice quiver.

He gives his head a shake. "No, no, dear. That's unnecessary. I can make it home on my own just fine."

My brain presses the panic button. I know I can't let him drive off on his own. I could try to follow him, but I might lose him. "Would you mind driving me back there, too? I don't live too far from you, and I'm a little too tired to drive right now."

He looks somewhat perplexed by my statement, but answers, "Hop in."

Walking around the car, I text Dylan quickly, "In his car. Going to your mom's."

I climb into the car. "I really appreciate the ride, Mr. Sheridan," I say, even though I'm wondering if he should even be behind the wheel of a car in this state.

"Not a problem at all."

"Do you know where we're going?"

"Of course," he replies, and I can only hope he's right. "So how is it that you know Logan?"

"We're friends. I rent a room two doors down from where he used to live."

He looks confused and I immediately bite my tongue. This man is seeing Logan as an elementary school student, not a married man who just moved into a new house with his wife. I clamp my mouth shut so that I don't say anything else wrong.

His brow furrows sharply. "Logan. He's a big boy now, isn't he? I get confused these days. My mind..." He taps his finger to his temple. "It's not all working the way it used to be."

I smile. "People say the same thing about me because I'm a blonde."

He lets out a laugh, breaking the tension. "Being blonde has nothing to do with smarts, young lady. My son Dylan was towhead blonde till he was about eight years old when it darkened up a touch, and he's the smartest of all my boys."

"He is? Why do you say that?"

"He takes after me. The others—they'll fall into line at JLS one day—take their positions in our company. But Dylan? He's too smart for that. He'll make his own way in the world, not ride on the Sheridan coattails."

"Oh, I don't think any of them are riding on your coattails."

"It'll happen, believe me. But not with Dylan."

Wondering how he'll react when Dylan greets him at their house fully grown, I consider whether I should coax him back to the present year somehow, or if that's even possible. I wish I knew something about dealing with dementia patients. "So that development back there... did you really build it?"

He chuckles warmly. "No. I hired people to build it for

me. That's where my own father went wrong with JLS a while back. He wanted to actually be the one doing the hammering and sawing. That's not the way to grow a company. You need to hire the right people to do it for you."

"Do you have any other developments?" I ask, hoping to God that he might mention a few more recent ones.

"Of course. Our first one after I took control of JLS was about twenty miles south of here. We built about a dozen more here in Ohio since then." He pauses for about a minute, his eyes looking thoughtful, as though he's recollecting something for the first time. "Our first one in another state was when the boys were in elementary school. That's when business really took off," he eventually continues.

Noting how he mentioned elementary school in the past tense, I watch him expectantly, wondering if he's noticing the passing of the years very quickly. And then I see a glimmer of awareness.

"We have developments in thirty-two states now," he finishes.

A sigh of relief escapes me. Welcome back to the twenty-first century, I congratulate him in my head. "Really? That many?"

"Absolutely. We just opened one in Hawaii this past winter. I took my wife there to see it. I think she'd make me move there permanently if all our boys weren't settled in the Midwest."

Exiting the highway, he doesn't hesitate in making several turns into an opulent neighborhood. He flicks on his signal and turns into a long, paved driveway lit with wrought iron lampposts.

I spot Dylan, Ryan, and their mother sitting on the front porch waiting for us. Glancing over at Mr. Sheridan, I see him frown at the sight.

"I've worried my wife again," he says and I can immediately tell he realizes now what happened.

"She worries because she loves you."

"I'll find some way to make it up to her," he says quietly, putting the car in park.

I watch his gaze follow her as she approaches. There's more love in his eyes for her in this one moment than I saw between my father and mother in eighteen years of their marriage.

He lets out a pained breath. "There's little dignity in growing old, young lady. I thank you, for making sure I made it home all right. So, you said you know my Logan?"

"His wife is one of my best friends."

"Allie," he states and winces. "Dammit. I was at her opening, wasn't I? For her shelter."

I nod.

"Did it go well?"

I see him hold his breath for my answer. "Phenomenally well," I assure him.

"I didn't—" he pauses, concern in his eyes, "—disturb it at all, did I?"

I smile and shake my head. "Not in the slightest. Besides, you would have made your way home just fine on your own."

"I wish I agreed with you there."

Anna Sheridan swings open her husband's car door. "Jake, you scared me to death." She hugs him fiercely after he rises from his seat, her eyes pressed together in relief before she shoots me a grateful look.

"Cass, I will never be able to thank you enough," she says before escorting her husband toward their door.

Ryan reaches me first, pulling me into an unanticipated hug. He usually intimidates the hell out of me, so the warm greeting isn't quite what I expected.

"We owe you for this, Cass," he says, and I can tell from

the weight of his tone that it's not a statement he takes lightly.

Uncomfortable, I wave my hand through the air. "You don't owe me anything."

"We do," he says, backing away toward the door to his parents' house. "See that she gets home all right, Dylan. And remember what I said. *Like family.*"

He says the last two words as though they're a code of some kind—or possibly a threat, considering the way his eyes are glaring at his brother as he walks away.

"What does he mean by that?" I dare to ask.

"What?" Dylan asks innocently.

"What he said about family. He looked like he was about to throttle you as he said it."

"It was nothing. Ryan says everything like a mild threat. You get used to it in my family."

I smile, staring at the immense fortress of a home that somehow manages to exude warmth, despite its size. "I think you should feel pretty lucky to have a family like yours."

"I do," he says, then repeats thoughtfully, "I do. And you're a damn hero to ours right now. Come on." He extends his arm my way and leads me to his car. "I'll take you back to your car."

Still holding my clutch, I slide into the passenger seat, savoring the feel of imported leather against my thigh that is partly exposed by the slit in my dress.

I never believed in love at first sight, till I sat in Dylan's car.

"I'm in love," I whisper just as he sits in the driver's seat next to me.

His eyes widen at my statement. "Pardon?"

"I'm in love," I repeat unabashedly. "What kind of car is this?"

He laughs. "A McLaren Spider."

"McLaren Spider," I repeat reverently, my breath catching as the engine comes to life and we pull out of their driveway. Leave it to a Sheridan to find a car I've never even heard of. "Lord, have mercy."

"It is nice, isn't it? I keep this here at my parents' since I fly out to visit family and check on the progress on my new gym so often. It's a lot more fun to drive than a rental."

"I'll bet."

He flashes me a quick smile. "Want to take the wheel?"

I scoff, "You're joking right?"

"Not joking at all." He flicks on his turn signal and pulls to the side of the quiet road. "You're the one who knows where you left your car, anyway."

I practically have to stop myself from clapping my hands like a little kid. "Yeah, but behind this wheel, I might need to take a few detours."

"Take as many as you want. I've got all night."

I leap out my side of the car before he can even open my door for me. Chuckling, he glances down at me as he stands next to the driver's side door. "I have to say, Cass, you look like you were born to drive one of these."

Unable to resist, I glance at myself in the rear view mirror. "I'd have to agree with you. But show me someone who *doesn't* look good in a car like this."

As he sits in the passenger seat, I send him a perplexed look. "Um, how do I shift?"

"It's got a rocker shift paddle on the steering wheel."

"Okay, uh… let me say right off that you're not getting me out of this seat just yet. But I should tell you that I've never shifted that way before."

He grins, and his hand brushes against me as he reaches over. "You can switch it to auto right here. No shifting necessary."

The light touch of his hand against my forearm sends a

prickle of heat from my heart, right down to below my belly. Throw in the low vibration of the car's motor as it hums beneath me, and the experience is nothing less than erotic.

Holding back a squeal, I pull onto the residential road, resisting—just barely—the urge to flatten the accelerator.

The power of the car has my heart tap-dancing as I turn onto the expressway. "Why don't you keep this car with you in Chicago?"

"In my high-rise, there's secure parking. But a car like this really needs a private garage."

"So it just sits here when you're not visiting your parents?"

"Pretty much. Sometimes my brothers take it out for a spin. My dad doesn't. He thinks it's ridiculous. Too showy. He says that the sensibilities of his family diminished with each successive son."

"What does he mean by that?"

"Well, think about it. Logan's the first-born. The guy drives a truck most of the time and every once in a while you *might* catch him in his pretty basic BMW. Then there's the middle child, Ryan. He's got an impressive Mercedes and had a Jag that I think he just donated to someplace—"

"He could have donated it to me," I can't resist interjecting.

He laughs. "You should have said something. But anyway, he's in his SUV most of the time now. Then there's me, the youngest and completely insensible third son. I've got the McLaren. So Dad's theory is right." He pauses thoughtfully. "But if you toss in Ryan's plane, then actually he beats me. There's nothing sensible about a private plane. The damn thing can't even fly to California without refueling. I never could understand the logic in it."

"Nah, you've still got him beat. He uses that plane to fly sick kids to hospitals. Pretty practical to me."

57

"You're right. I guess that puts me back in the lead, then."

In my peripheral vision, I catch his mischievous grin. "And you like being the insensible one, don't you?"

"I like letting them *think* that I'm insensible."

"So, you're not?" I ask in disbelief.

"There are layers to me, Cass, that no one seems to want to peel away."

As I flick on the turn signal when I see the JLS development where I spotted Dylan's dad, I can't help thinking how I'd like to peel away some of his layers later tonight. Especially that layer of silk blend that is blocking my view of his ridiculously cut chest.

"How the hell did you find him out here?" he asks, shaking his head as I pull up behind my parked car.

I tell him about the brief conversation I'd had with his father that gave me a clue to where he might be, and the internet search for JLS developments that led me here.

He gets out of the car and comes to my side to open my door for me. I let him, just because it's something I'm not used to from men, and I want to savor it while I can.

Anna Sheridan raised her boys right.

He takes my hand and eases me out of the driver's seat. I almost weep; I've grown attached to his McLaren on so many levels I can't describe.

I turn to the car and plant a kiss on its bold trim behind the windshield. "I'll miss you," I whisper to it as he laughs behind me.

His hand wraps around my waist to the small of my back and he pulls me closer. "I hope you'll miss me in the same way," he murmurs, his mouth close to mine.

I inhale his thoroughly masculine scent as his lips caress me ever-so-lightly before I pull back, smiling coyly. "I don't know. It's a pretty impressive car."

I love the way I can feel the vibration of his laughter low in my belly, with him still pressed up against me.

"It would have destroyed Dad if the police had to show up at Allie's big event, Cass. You have no idea how much pride that man's got. I can't tell you what it means to me that you found him."

"I just got lucky." And I'm hoping I'll get luckier, I suddenly realize, lost in his blue eyes. I don't want this evening to end just yet.

Every nerve in my body is screaming for satisfaction, especially a particular bundle of nerves just south of my navel.

As his lips touch mine again, I try to remind myself that he only sees me as a dumb model—even though he just doesn't seem to be treating me that way at all. My body eases closer to him, stealing his heat, feeling the ridge of his erection pressing against my dress.

Damn, he's not lacking in that department either.

What *was* it that he'd said that night that angered me so? My mind scurries to remember, even as his lips move to my cheekbone, and then downward to the hyper-sensitive skin on my neck.

Something about models being dumb. Yes, that was it. Dumb and out to use him.

Out to use him.

Holy shit. I'd conveniently forgotten that part.

I pull back from him sharply, my eyes wide.

"What is it?"

"Oh, God, Dylan. I kind of have to tell you something."

"What?"

I can barely look at him as I say this. "I—I kind of had some ulterior motives for going out with you tonight. I sort of needed some… well, good press, I guess you could say. There's this woman I went to high school with—"

"Brenna Tucker."

My eyes snap to his. "You know?"

"Yeah. I guess I have a confession, too. I did an internet search on you after we talked the other night."

"Oh, God." *He knew.* "Is that why you kept pulling me in front of the cameras?"

"The first kiss was definitely for the benefit of the press. But the rest were all for me." His fingertips trace along my jawline up to my ear, and he tucks away a lock of hair tenderly. "I can be pretty selfish that way."

I lower my eyes. "I'm sorry. I used you. You even said that models all just want to use you, and then I go and do the same thing."

Curving a finger beneath my chin, he lifts my face upwards toward him. "When did I say that?"

"At Allie's wedding."

"I talked to you at Allie's wedding?" He's slack-jawed for a moment, his eyes confused.

"Yeah. You were just this side of conscious though."

"Oh, no."

"Yeah. You really don't hold your liquor well."

Dropping his arms to his sides, he shakes his head. "No. No, I definitely don't. Comes from spending too much time in the gym—"

"I've noticed," I interject.

"—rather than hanging out in bars like the other guys my age. So I've never built up any kind of tolerance, I guess. After Allie and Logan left, some of his SEAL brothers started doing shots, and that's the last thing I remember."

I can't help the smile that hitches up my face. "So, Dylan Sheridan, MMA fighter, Olympian wrestler, and all-around beefcake is actually a lightweight."

"Guilty as charged. I turn into an asshole around liquor.

It's why I rarely drink. God, I hope I didn't say anything rude to you."

Smiling, I mentally click "delete" on my entire first meeting with Dylan Sheridan. "Nothing you didn't completely make up for tonight."

"Good," he says, sounding unconvinced. "I'll follow you home."

I press my lips together, wishing for another taste of him so that I could show him just how little I want to go home right now. "You don't have to do that. Kim's home now. She'll keep an eye out for me."

"I'll follow you home anyway. I'd like to make sure you're back, safe and sound."

"I can text—"

"Hush," he interrupts, quickly pressing his mouth against mine. The sensation of his lips on me makes my belly tingle.

Take me back to your hotel room, I silently will him, parting my lips and I'm greeted by a smoky taste, something close to the essence of a charcoal barbeque, with a hint of spice.

Splaying my hands against his back, I savor the slide of his muscles beneath my fingertips, and delight in the feel of his pecs against my breasts through the fabric of our clothing.

Inhaling sharply, he pulls back from me. "I knew I'd have to kiss you to get you to stop talking. I'm following you home. No more arguments."

Oh, really?

"Wait," I say. "You don't need to—" And just like that, his lips are on me again, just as I'd hoped. He spins me slightly, sending my head reeling, and presses me up against the side of his car as his lips entangle with mine. I'll argue with him all night if that's what it takes to keep feeling the pressure of his body against mine. His hands glide along my dress, thumbs barely caressing the side of my breasts and I all but cry for more. I feel his arousal against me, and my body instinctively arches toward him, craving more pressure just there.

Again, he pulls back from me, and I nearly fist his shirt in my hands and pull him back to my mouth.

"Or I could follow you back to your hotel," I offer.

Yes. I can see the answer in his eyes, the primal need to mate coursing as thick in his veins as it is in mine right now. *Thank God.*

He stands there, frozen for a moment before he finally opens his mouth. "Dinner."

My eyebrows hike up a couple inches. "What?"

"Dinner tomorrow." His words are almost breathless.

"You want to go to dinner tomorrow?"

He cracks a smile. "Why, yes. I thought you'd never ask." He skims his hands down my sides, not in a passionate gesture this time. It's more like he's straightening my dress.

His eyes lock onto my perplexed gaze for a moment, and I see a debate brewing in his eyes. "And I'm following you home now," he says, pulling his body away from mine, making me nearly scream in dispute.

I bite my lip awkwardly as he opens my car door for me. I'm not quite sure what to make of his dinner invitation, or how to interpret the first time I've ever been turned down for sex.

Dylan Sheridan is playing hard to get.

Son of a bitch.

CHAPTER 6

- DYLAN -

Son of a bitch.

The entire drive back to Cass's townhouse last night, I was silently cursing my damn brother and his "she's like family" speech he gave me for the second time as we waited for her and my father to arrive.

And the seven hours that followed, I continued to curse him, as I lay in my bed, with a raging hard-on that would never be placated with Rosie Palm and her Five Friends. Good Lord, am I back in high school?

Now, with the late afternoon sun striking my eyes, the chimes on the door jingle as I leave Henderson's Five-and-Dime on Anders Street in downtown Newton's Creek. It's the last of my errands today, and the only one that isn't somehow linked to my brother's impending nuptials.

I'm surprised they had what I needed in there, even if they did have to search the back room for five minutes to find everything. There's something pleasant about waltzing into Henderson's to get what I need rather than going to some big, generic store up in Jeffers, the sprawling suburb north of here.

I went to high school with Mr. Henderson's two grand-sons. He knows my name, remembers some of my escapades in high school, and cheered me on in his living room when I was fighting for a medal at the Olympics. And he always asks about my dad, not to be nosy, but in a sincere way that pretty much epitomizes small town living.

I miss that. In my condo in Chicago, I don't even know the names of the people I share walls with—something I plan on rectifying when I head back there after Ryan's wedding in a couple weeks.

Spotting Cass across the street, her long legs striding toward Pop's with a sense of urgency, I give her a shout-out. "Cass!"

She stops cold and looks at me as I jog across Anders Street toward her.

"Hi, Dylan. What are you doing here?"

Her eyes look a bit pink, and I can hope it was from staying up all night thinking about me. But the smeared mascara makes me think otherwise.

Something's not right here.

"Picking up some plaster of Paris and a metal pipe for a project I'm working on with Connor."

Her alabaster forehead creases. "What's the project?"

"We're building a foundry."

"A foundry?"

"Yeah. You know, kind of like a super hot oven that you can melt metal in."

She blinks exactly twice before she responds. "Why would you want to melt metal?"

I cock my head. "Because it's cool."

Pressing her lips together, she gives me the same look I get from Hannah right before she informs me that boys are weird.

"Sounds a little dangerous," she comments cautiously.

"I won't let him too close. He saw a video of someone melting aluminum cans into metal bars on YouTube. I'm showing him how it's done. Thought a homemade metal bar might be neat for his first show-and-tell in kindergarten this fall."

"Oh," she says quietly with a hint of surprise, as though she never pictured me working on a project with a five-year-old.

"Are you still up for dinner tonight?" I ask.

She smiles—a forced smile, which I don't think bodes well for our plans tonight. But then she nods. "I was just going to go home and change first."

"Why change? You look great just as you are."

"Really, I—"

"Come on." I angle my body, offering her my bent elbow in invitation. "Let's just grab something at Francesca's. Unless you were headed someplace else and I interrupted you," I say, suddenly remembering the very determined stride she had before I called her name.

"Oh, no. Not really. I was just going to bury my sorrows in a couple chocolate donuts."

I can't help it when my eyes track down her slim model figure, the kind of body that makes me want to get her a good juicy burger and fries. She's not one to bury her sorrows in food often, by the look of her, so this must be pretty bad. "What's wrong?"

"Just a rough day."

I feel a sense of achievement when she slides her hand into the crook of my arm. "Bad day at Buckeye Land?"

"No. That was the easy part, actually. I had the early shift, so didn't have to deal with the late afternoon crowds today. But then I had to take Rascal to his new home."

"Rascal?"

"My foster dog."

"You have a foster dog? Even with the shelter now open?"

"*Had* a foster dog, yes. Allie thought it would be smarter for all of us with foster dogs to keep them in our homes till they got adopted. It would be hard on them to change from sleeping in someone's bed to sleeping in the shelter. But this is our last batch of fosters. All the future dogs will stay in the shelter."

"And you'll miss having a dog around the house." I say it like a statement, since I still go through that myself. We always had lots of pets growing up. That's something I can't have, traveling as much as I do, with my only "real" home base being a high-rise that doesn't allow animals.

"Yeah. But I've said good-bye to a lot of fosters. I mean, Rascal is maybe my tenth because I did it all last summer when I was here for my first season at Buckeye Land. And then there were three just this summer."

"So you should be used to this."

"I should be." She gives her head a shake. "I *am*. I really am so glad to see him go. He's got a great family that will love him. But there's just… something more to it than that."

I push the door open to Francesca's and tell the hostess we'll be having dinner for two on their new rooftop terrace. It's one of the recent changes I've seen downtown since my brother opened a new JLS community just adjacent to downtown. Some of the houses are already occupied, and with the new residents and people visiting the complex's bike trail and playground, these businesses are starting to invest and expand.

I like seeing it. It's like JLS Heartland gave this town the jolt of caffeine it needed. It makes me proud to be a Sheridan, even though that pride is somehow tainted with a bitterness I rarely admit to, since my family has kept the inner workings of JLS far out of my reach.

We walk up the steep steps and I pull her seat out for her as we find a table under the stellar blue sky this evening. The sky matches Cass's eyes perfectly, a thought I can't let distract me right now.

"So why does it upset you so much, Cass?" I ask. If I'm going to commit to this get-to-know-her thing, now's the time to start.

She stares at me momentarily, almost skeptically. "It's nothing. Silly, really. I should be happy. The dogs in the shelter will get adopted a lot more quickly now than when they were in foster homes just because people can come meet them a lot more easily. She'll be able to save a lot more dogs that way."

I can't help noticing she says, "she'll save" rather than "we'll save." Realization sets in. "But *you* won't be doing the saving then, will you?"

She shrugs. "Yeah, I guess that's it. I'm not really needed anymore."

"I'm sure Allie will still need volunteers at the shelter. And Logan even told me that you're the one who takes all those cute pictures of the dogs for the website."

"You saw them?"

"Yeah. I couldn't resist looking. You're a good photographer."

"Oh, anyone can take dog pictures." She bats a hand through the air. "And yeah, I'll still do that. But there's something about actually taking in a dog who would have been killed otherwise. It's like—I don't know. Have you ever seen that old holiday movie, *It's a Wonderful Life*?"

"Was it black and white?"

She nods.

"Nope. Didn't see it. I never watched anything that wasn't in color as a kid."

Her eyes widen dramatically. "Seriously? You were missing out. I love all the classics. The highest compliment I ever got was when an agent said I looked like Grace Kelly."

"Is she another model?"

She stares at me blankly. "*Dial M for Murder. Rear Window. High Noon.* You really need to see those." Slowly, she shakes her head in disbelief. "So anyway, *It's a Wonderful Life*—"

"That's the one with the three spirits, right?" I toy with her.

She gives me a diminishing look. "No, that's *A Christmas Carol*. You seriously didn't know that?"

I hold my hands up. "Sorry. My winters were filled with ice hockey as a kid." I actually *did* know that. But I can't resist riling her up like this. Her eyes flash in the sexiest way, making every ounce of testosterone in me flood my brain... among other organs.

"Well, it's the one with Jimmy Stewart—you should really watch it sometime—and he plays this guy who is going to jump off a bridge—"

"This is a holiday show?" I interject when the waitress comes to take our drink orders. I order Cass a glass of wine. She looks like she needs it.

"So you were saying something about jumping off a bridge?" I say with a smile after the waitress leaves.

She narrows her eyes on me. "Anyway, this angel comes to stop him, and he shows him what the world would have been like if he hadn't been born. And there's this huge differ-ence, of course, just because he saved his brother from drowning and stopped a pharmacist from poisoning some kid, and helped all these townspeople buy homes. And without him, his wife would just be working at the library."

"Oh, God, no! Not the library." I feign horror.

"Yeah, okay, I'll agree that was kind of lame. But the other stuff really affected me as a kid. I always wanted to be like George Bailey. To know that the world actually somehow was changed just because I was in it."

I get what she's saying, and I like the nobility of it, but something's not adding up. "But you wanted to be a model."

She raises her eyebrows at me.

I hold my hands up from the table. "I don't mean any disrespect to the profession, but it's generally not a business that humanitarians flock toward."

She shrugs as the waitress sets down her glass. After we place our entrée orders, she says, "My looks are all I had. I wasn't smart—"

"I'll argue that point," I interrupt.

"No, seriously. I wasn't good in school. I was a B and C student all the way. I didn't have money, so I couldn't afford college full-time. I got a local commercial for a barbeque restaurant in Kansas City when I was seventeen and that gave me my way out. I figured I'd make it big in New York, and then use my fame and money to do something good. Something big."

"Like what?"

"I don't know." She stares into her wine, then shakes her head. "No, actually I *do* know. Like build Allie a shelter like JLS did. Or maybe build a community center in a neighborhood like where I grew up. Or give scholarships to kids who didn't get straight As, but still want to go to college like me. Or donate money to cancer research so kids like Kim's brother won't die."

I snap to attention. "Kim's brother?"

"Yeah. You didn't know that? He died from leukemia when he was fourteen."

My shoulders sag. Yet again, I'm faced with something huge that I didn't know about my future sister-in-law. Do I really spend that much time away from my family that I'm not up on these things?

She sets her glass down. "You see, *you* don't have to think about those things because you can just do them. You just write a check, make a difference, and move on. You're a Sheridan. You get to be George Bailey by default."

"I've never touched my family's money for things like that," I point out, feeling slightly defensive.

"Okay, that might be so. But would you have been able to get the training you needed to become an Olympian if you weren't a Sheridan?"

I frown. "If you're trying to knock my ego down a couple notches, you're doing a good job."

Her face softens. "I didn't mean it that way. God, I really didn't."

She brushes her fingers onto my forearm before grasping it lightly, and I swear all the blood in my brain just rushed to my groin.

"I just mean that for average people like me, it's a lot harder to get that feeling like I'm making a really big difference. I mean, I give to charities when I can—which isn't too often—and try to be a nice influence, a good friend, and all that. But these dogs..." Her voice trails as she shakes her head. "Dammit, taking them in was the first thing I did that gave me that feeling. If I didn't exist, Rascal would have been euthanized. And Ranger and Skylar and a lot more. And, it's like an addiction. I don't want to give it up."

"So, don't. Keep fostering."

She shrugs hopelessly. "They just don't need me anymore. The shelter is big enough to handle all the dogs our county has on the 'kill list'—you know, the dogs slated to be euthanized that week. And they'll get placed in homes a lot faster. People will be able to meet them six days a week rather than just at our few adoption events each month."

I can't help the eye roll as I pull out my phone and tap a button. "Search high kill shelters in Ohio," I tell it.

"Searching high kill shelters in Ohio," it repeats back in its robotic female voice.

I put the phone in front of Cass. "There are always more dogs to save, Cass."

Her face softens as she stares at the list on my phone. Her finger taps on a link and she reads silently for a moment. "Sweet Jesus. This one has a fifty-percent kill rate."

I scoot my chair closer to hers and look at the article she pulled up. "And it's only a couple hours from here. Go save another dog."

She nods, ever so slowly and pauses, long and thoughtfully. "When I mentioned I wanted to keep fostering to Allie, she talked about expanding later and transporting dogs from other places. That's what a lot of other organizations do. But there's a lot of work to running the foster program. She just wanted to focus on getting the shelter up and running first. And Kim—she's so absorbed in her fundraising for the shelter right now. Toss in a kid to raise and a wedding to plan, and she's not up for it right now."

"Can you take the lead on it? I mean, Allie did it while doing another job, right? So it's not like it would be something full-time."

"Actually, she was working *two* jobs when she first started. So, no, I wouldn't have to give up my job."

"How many foster families did you guys have?"

"About ten," I reply.

"That's a lot more dogs you could save."

Taking an extra long sip of her wine, she stares at my phone, silently mulling my words for a minute. Then she gives her head a quick shake. "What am I thinking? I'm supposed to go back to New York this fall," she says, her voice seeming a thousand miles away—or six hundred miles to be more precise—just as the waitress arrives with the appetizers I ordered.

I'm annoyed by the interruption. I'm enjoying this—discovering that the most fascinating part of Cass doesn't have a thing to do with her perfect features and model proportions.

"Do you *want* to go back to New York?" I ask when we're alone again.

"I feel like I'm supposed to say yes, just because moving to New York was all I talked about in high school. I mean that *literally*. But I'm 24 now. That's pretty washed-up for a model. I mean, there are older models out there, but they had to make a name for themselves while they were young. I'm too short for runway. I bite my fingernails and wear a size eight shoe, so even hand and shoe modeling are out. Catalogs are my bread-and-butter, at this point, unless I get lucky and land another commercial or two."

"Is that why you came back for a second summer as the princess?"

"One of the many reasons. I know it might sound weird, but I like it here. I love my friends. I love the dogs. I love being able to hang my purse on the back of my chair right now without thinking it's going to disappear. And I live for so much cheaper here. I've been able to use the money I save to take some college courses online."

I can't help laughing.

"Don't laugh at me," she admonishes.

"Oh, I'm not laughing at you. I'm laughing at me. I kind of had you pegged wrong."

Setting her elbows on the table, she rests her head on her entwined fingers and gazes up at me. "Well, I guess we were both wrong. I thought you were a rat bastard when I met you at the wedding."

"Since I was drunk, I'm guessing I *was* a rat bastard when

you met me at the wedding." Staring at her now, I wrack my brain for the memory of meeting her that night. But it's all too much of a blur, as if the image is there somewhere, yet just out of my reach.

"True. But I should have cut you some slack. I just never thought a guy as—well—*big* as you wouldn't be able to handle his liquor."

"Now you know my secret," I say, lifting my soda glass and tapping it against the side of her wine.

CHAPTER 7

~ CASS ~

"I had a really nice time tonight," I tell him as we arrive at my car parked three doors down from Pop's Donuts on Anders Street. The words seem so stale as I say them—the same words I say after any halfway-mediocre date.

But there was nothing halfway-mediocre about this evening with Dylan Sheridan.

Never had I suspected I'd walk away from a date with Dylan feeling energized in a completely unexpected way, with my mind wandering to those dogs in that shelter he found on his phone. The sadness I had felt earlier in the evening has dissipated into the humid summer air.

Dylan reminded me that I'm in control of my future. I may only have a short time left in Newton's Creek, but I can save a lot of dogs in three months, and hopefully get this program up and running well enough so that someone can continue it after I leave.

"I had a great time, too," he answers, taking both my hands so tenderly it makes me tingle inside.

I tilt my head toward him slightly, encouraging him, and he responds by touching his lips to mine. His mouth is soft—it must be the only soft thing on his muscular body—and he leans into me so that I can feel his chest against me.

Uh, yep. *Definitely* his lips are the only soft thing on his body, I discover at the feel of him against me. A charge crackles through my nerves at the idea of him wanting me like this.

For the years I spent fantasizing about him as a teen, it was always the power of him that I craved, the way he moved those expansive muscles to overcome a foe. And I'd wondered—like every other woman in America, I imagine—what it would be like to be dominated by a man like that, to feel his strength taking over my body while I let myself give in completely.

His fingers on one hand lightly trace the contours of my shoulder, up to my ear and then thread into my hair, pulling my mouth even closer to his. I don't need any encouragement to comply, I'm his completely tonight, ready to do anything, everything with this man.

His full mouth feels potent as our tongues glide against one another, exploring, tentatively at first and then unabashedly. A torch at my center radiates its fire throughout my body as his arms encircle me.

Like last night, I find myself leaning against my car, with his hard body sandwiching me between flesh and steel. The need to get horizontal is all-consuming, as I ache for his touch right here in public, right here on our town's version of Main Street.

He moves his mouth from mine with a pained sigh.

"You are…" he pauses, as though he is summoning control

over his body once more, "simply extraordinary, Cassidy Parker."

So, invite me to your hotel room, I want to tell him. But I won't. I offered last night and got shot down. It's his turn to put his ego on the line and proposition me, not the other way around.

A girl has her rules.

I skim my lips against his as I murmur, "You're pretty extraordinary yourself, Dylan Sheridan."

And he is, I think as I slide my tongue across his teeth, a contented hum vibrating through my body. The Dylan I met at the wedding a few months ago has completely redeemed himself, and I'm regretting throwing away the scrapbook-shrine I constructed for him in my teen years.

His hands move from my back to my sides, and I can tell they want to venture elsewhere, the way they massage me through the fabric of my shirt. But in small town America, public groping is generally frowned upon, especially on major thoroughfares like Anders Street.

Invite me to your hotel room, I silently command him. *Now.*

He pulls his face back again, almost with a gasp and my entire body sings with the knowledge that the invitation is on its way, with first-class postage and a big red bow on it.

"I'm headed out of town tomorrow," he says. "To the DC area on business."

I stroke my fingers along his sharp jawline as he talks, watching his ice blue eyes dilate more with every cell I caress.

I can feel the pulsing of his erection against me, and I know I'm not too long from the moment when I'll get to feel him inside of me.

Damn, this is going to be a hell of a night.

His hands squeeze my hips, my flesh seeming to simmer under his touch. "I'll be back in a couple days. I'd love to spend some more time with you before I head back to Chicago after Ryan's wedding. How about dinner Wednesday?"

For a split second, time stands perfectly still. My mouth freezes in the shape of a tiny o.

Dinner? Wednesday? Is he seriously blowing me off again?

Only inches from his, my face is chilled, suddenly not feeling the rush of heat I once was. There's no faking that pressure I feel against my belly. So why isn't he inviting me back to his hotel room?

But I'll be damned if I'm going to ask. My ego feels battered enough in this moment, shot down for the second time by Dylan Sheridan.

"Okay," I say, even though my hormones want to stage a *coup d'état* against my brain, and tear his clothes off right here on Anders Street. I give a little nod, more to myself than him, and pull my body from his.

"I'll call you," he says when he opens my car door for me.

I give another feeble nod before mumbling, "Thanks again for dinner."

Then he flashes one last smile—and it's one that will haunt me all night, I'm certain—just before he shuts my car door.

I don't dare glance at his broad form in my rear view mirror as I pull away. I might weep.

Just outside of downtown Newton's Creek, I pull to the side of the road, my body still thrumming from the full body contact of Dylan not five minutes before. I call Kim, completely ready to pull her away from anything for a chat tonight. If I wait till I get home to talk to her, I'll have to censor my words with Connor nearby. And I'm not up for it. Not now.

"Hey, Cass. How'd it go with Dylan tonight?"

"What's his problem, dammit?" I bark at her. Okay, I'm not exactly tactful, especially considering he'll be her brother-in-law in two weeks, but I just don't care.

"What do you mean? Did he do something wrong?"

"Well, *yeah*. He completely blew me off after a freaking off-the-charts kiss."

"I'm not following you."

My shoulders rise and fall with frustration. "We had a great time, you know? And then he kisses me and it's... absolutely incredible. And then, just when I think he's going to invite me back to his hotel, he asks me to dinner on Wednesday after some trip he's going on."

"Yeah, he's headed to the DC area to buy some property for a gym or something."

"So how am I supposed to interpret this?"

There's a long pause. I know I sound like a raving lunatic, but I don't care.

"Um, well, I'd say he likes you if he wants to see you again."

"If he likes me, then why didn't he invite me back to his hotel? I mean, does he just like to *eat* with me? I thought all men wanted to have sex with me."

Kim chuckles. "You have a pretty high opinion of yourself, don't you, Princess Buckeye?"

"No. I just have a pretty low opinion of men."

Kim sighs. "Look, he's just trying to take it slow with you. Ryan's been on his case about that. You're like family and—"

Like family. I remember the words spiked with threatening undertones from Ryan last night. *Son of a bitch*. "Well, tell your fiancé to butt out of my sex life. Geez, Kim, I haven't had sex since I moved back here in May. I'm a starved woman here. And you're telling me that Dylan is being coerced to take things slow?"

"It's more than that, Cass. He wants to get to know you. It's sweet."

"Says you. You're the one who's probably getting laid tonight, while I'm just going home to pick the spinach out of my teeth from the salad I ate. What's his room number?"

"410. The Presidential Suite, I think. Why?"

I narrow my eyes on the sprawling cornfields in front of me, my fingers tightly gripping my steering wheel. "You know why," I tell her, hitting the red button on my phone, and quickly flicking off the ringer. I'm in no mood for interruptions.

He wants to get to know me? Fine. He can accomplish that in thirty seconds.

The drive to Bergin's is a ten-minute blur as a surge of hormones makes my foot flatten against my accelerator.

I pull into the lot and make a beeline past the front desk to the elevator. Inhaling a deep breath for courage, I lean against the mirrored elevator walls as I wait for the fourth floor to arrive, and then charge down the hall toward him.

I thump on the door, and am greeted by an eyeful of man candy when he swings open the door, now shirtless.

Holy crap.

It's the first time I've seen his chest in the living flesh and it's just a hell of a lot more impressive than they could ever capture in a shaving ad, believe me.

"Cass," he says with surprise. "What are you doing here?"

"You want to get to know me?" I nudge myself through the doorway as he steps backward, a mix of amusement and shock on his face. "My favorite color is pink. My favorite flower is a red rose. My favorite movie is a tie between *Vertigo* and *Casablanca*."

When I hear him shut the door behind me, I tell him, "And my favorite position is missionary which probably surprises the hell out of you because I'm otherwise not a very conventional kind of girl. But I just like the feeling of being dominated by a man. I love kids, but probably won't have any because I have no plans on ever getting married. I don't do long-term with men. It tends to get messy."

"We have a lot in common, then," he interjects.

I cock my head coyly. "You don't do long-term with men either?"

He chuckles, stepping closer to me. "No. And not with women either."

My smile edges upward, knowing I've got him where I want him. "I'm right-handed, but for a year I tried to write with my left hand in middle school because I thought that would make me more interesting. I'm an only child. I was raised in a lower middle class family in an upper middle class suburb. My parents are divorced. I'm a Taurus, if you believe in that sort of thing. And if there's anything else you'd like to know about me before having sex with me, I suggest you ask me right now."

His mouth opens slightly, devoid of emotion only momentarily till I see a slight smile creep up his face. "Favorite car?"

"A McLaren Spider, as of yesterday."

"Favorite vacation destination?"

"I haven't traveled much, but I like anyplace with a water view."

His hand reaches for me, touching my waist lightly and I move toward him in response.

"Favorite holiday?" he asks, his face nearing mine.

"Christmas."

His mouth touches my neck as he murmurs, "Me, too."

The whisper of breath against my skin makes all the tiny hairs on my back stand upright.

"I told you we have a lot in common," he adds. "Favorite food?"

"Anything fried."

His eyebrows rise as his hand strokes my belly from my waist… downward. "And the last time you had something fried?"

"Last summer."

"Do you always deprive yourself of the things you want?"

"I'm here now, Dylan. So, what do you think the answer to that question is?"

His lips turn hot, sizzling against my neck as his hand touches me where I need it most through the thick fabric of my shorts.

My hands reach for my zipper, needing to free myself from my clothing, but he bats them away.

"That's my job," he says in between kisses. "I thought you said you like to be dominated."

My heart sings at his words as his fingers toy with the waistband of my shorts briefly before unbuttoning the button and then slowly, so slowly, unzipping the zipper. His mouth moves to my neck, and I feel a faint nip just above my collarbone before he touches my breasts, cupping them in his hands and making my nipples pebble as he kisses the cotton that separates me from his mouth.

Kneeling in front of me, his fingers breeze past the bottom of my shirt and he lifts it slightly so that just my navel is exposed to him. I feel his tongue dip inside its hollow as he pulls down my shorts and panties at the same time, revealing each inch of my flesh slowly, as though I'm a package he's been dying to open all night, and he's deter-mined to savor the experience.

My eyelids flutter at the feel of his warm breath against me as I stand in front of him. With my knees weakening, I'd move to a wall where I might be able to lean, but I don't dare move, except to step out of my shorts when he moves my legs slightly, opening them.

Oh my goodness. The feel of this man kneeling in front of me, my body so exposed to him in the harsh lighting of the small foyer in his suite makes me so wet, that I'm almost embarrassed when his fingers move to me, finding the tiny pearl of my arousal. His tongue lightly strokes me there and I whimper at the sensation. Instinctively, my hands move to his head to pull him closer as I ache for more pressure.

Giving his head a shake, he pulls his face away from me. He takes my fingers in his and moves my hands to behind my back. As he leaves them there, my fingers intertwined with each other, he grabs the flesh of my ass in his hands and nuzzles his face against me, murmuring low and deep. The vibration tickles me and sends a fire through my core, extending up to my breasts and down to my toes.

Just as I nearly beg for more, his finger slides inside of me making my breath shudder. First one, and then another, and he gazes up at me with those eyes that have haunted my fantasies for so long now.

"So, you really want this, Cass? You don't want to take our time? Get to know each other better?"

What I want to tell him—if I could manage to form words while his fingers are moving inside me—is that he's already gotten to know me better tonight than any man I've ever been with. I've never confided in a man like I have in Dylan tonight, making me feel like whatever this is between us is already on a completely separate level than my previous relationships.

The truth is, I've never had a man sit through a dinner with me and actually show genuine interest while I prattled on about George Bailey, or my dogs, or the online college classes that I take with such pride any time I can, or the fact that I'm not even sure I want to be a model anymore.

There's not a soul on this planet outside of Dylan who knows that, as much as I complain about small town living, I actually find myself longing for it every night in New York when I click the five bolts on my front door of my apartment or strap my purse across my chest as I walk down Madison Avenue headed to my fifth go-see of the day.

And I've never thought any man would think I'm anything but mildly delusional for daring to think that I might actually be able to make some kind of a tangible difference in the world.

Lover or not, Dylan Sheridan knows me better than any man I've known in my life. And I want to know him, every inch of him, and to feel intimacy with this man in a way that only sex can provide.

"I want this," I finally manage to utter—and forming the words is a painful task as my body feels like it's being lifted onto a new plane of reality, the heat inside me building, the pressure to explode under his touch so close that I can barely breathe, much less speak.

The flick of his tongue encourages me up a long spiral of desire, and his fingers penetrating me make me realize how desperately I want more of him inside me than just this.

My eyes shut, the image of him kneeling in front of me, pleasuring me, still so sharp in my mind that it's enough to make the fire inside of me flare lightning-hot as I shatter against his mouth.

He stays with me till the last aftershock trembles through me and my knees wobble. Then he stands quickly, sweeping me off my feet just as I'm ready to drop to the ground in a heap.

He carries me to his neatly made bed and sets me down. I reach for the bottom of my shirt to pull it off, but he grasps my hands and gives his head a shake.

"For a girl who says she wants to be dominated, your hands are entirely too busy," he says with a grin, lifting my shirt for me, and then unclasping my bra.

His hands slide past the lacey fabric to where my nipples are puckered, hard, and aching for his touch. Taking the strap in his teeth, he pulls the bra off my body as he lowers my back to the soft duvet cover.

"God, you're a beautiful woman, Cass." The words seem to carry more weight coming from him than from any other man who's laid eyes on me.

The fullness of his mouth moves over my breast, sucking it in, leaving me damp. He reaches for one of the chocolate mints left by housekeeping on the pillow. I watch him, mesmerized, as he unwraps it. Then he moves it to my breast, lightly tracing a dark chocolate streak around my nipple, making me giggle as it tickles my skin.

I feel a smile on his lips as he licks it off.

"I've never appreciated turn-down service quite like I do right now, Cass."

My laughter bubbles up inside of me, and then dissipates into a gasp when he draws a dark line of chocolate down my belly and his tongue chases the streak, all the way to my curls. I see the last chunk of chocolate in his hands just as his mouth hovers above where I ache for his touch, and he reaches up, putting the sweet candy in my mouth.

Honest to God, I don't think I'll ever eat a chocolate mint again without remembering the feel of his tongue on my skin.

His hands grasp my ankles as he parts my legs, leaving me so open to him that I feel a tinge of shyness sweep over me. But just as I feel the urge to reach for the lamp and switch off the light, my body goes completely limp when he takes me in his mouth. His tongue glides around my entry as his thumb presses against my nub, and then I feel him enter me, his moisture meeting my own, and I come undone immediately.

A chill sweeps over me when he moves away from my body momentarily. I want him close again, closer still than

I've experienced with him so far tonight. I want to feel completely fused with him, in such a way that I can barely tell where his body ends and mine begins. Nothing less than that will placate me tonight. So my body rejoices when I see him reach into a pocket and pull out a condom, then tossing it on the bed beside us, knowing that I will finally get what I've been craving from Dylan all night. *No*—what I've been craving from him for years.

He strips himself of his jeans and briefs with one quick movement and my vision practically blurs at the sight of him, fully erect and jutting out from the base of the tight V of muscles below his waist.

I reach for him, wanting to wrap my fingers around his length and slide him into me, but he grabs my hand. "Am I going to have to tie you up, sweet Cass?" he says, and I wonder if I should feel as aroused by the idea of that as I am.

He gently grasps my hands and moves them above my head, holding them in his. "Now, behave yourself," he says, amusement in his warning as his eyebrows rise. "I'm trying to give you what you wanted."

"What I want is you," I reply.

Leaving my hands above me, he reaches for the condom, sheathing himself swiftly, and then lowers his chest so that his body warms me again. His deltoids bulge as his arms prop himself over me, and his knee nudges my legs open further. "So why do you like missionary style again?"

I feel his erection toy with me, brushing against my wet opening, and my heart rate quickens. "I'm hoping you'll remind me why," I tell him with a smile.

"I think I can do that," he murmurs as he takes my mouth against his, plundering me, letting his tongue explore me. As he slides inside of me, I gasp as the full length of him plunges into my most sensitive depths. Moisture spills from me as my body vibrates.

"Is this why you like this position?" His eyes are locked on me as his groin presses hard against the center of my arousal with him fully joined with me. The pressure of it has my breath quickening, as I arch toward him involuntarily.

"Yes," I cry out, my hips thrusting as he begins to move inside me. He is all control, and I am all instinct, grinding myself against him each time he's at my innermost depths.

Climbing up on a sensual spiral again, I feel a spike of fear inside me—fear of how completely addicted I've already become to the feel of his hard body fused with mine. The sensation of his muscles stroking against my flesh consumes me. And I feel the prickles of pleasure as his hands grip mine again above me, allowing me only to receive pleasure rather than give it.

My eyes journey to the point where we're joined. His muscles, so sharply defined, seem to almost shiver beneath his skin. And I desperately want to touch them—to feel the sensation of his power quaking beneath my fingertips. But I yield to him so willingly, giving in to the feel of being completely overpowered by a man who makes my body experience carnal pleasure I never thought possible.

He moves in a slow, seductive rhythm, each thrust caressing me where I need it most, and jarring against my depths. I've had a healthy handful of lovers in my life, but none as big as Dylan. Yet my body, so slick and pliant under his ministrations, seems to adjust to his size, only wanting him deeper, only wanting him more.

I sink further into the bed linens, further into this feeling of being completely possessed by him.

His eyebrows rise as I try to move one of my hands.

"I want to touch you," I plead, my fingertips aching to feel him.

The grin he offers me is pure devil. "Ask nicely."

I giggle at the mischief in his eyes. "Pretty please," I offer in my coyest tone.

"You're lucky you're irresistible," he says, his eyelids slamming shut as my fingertip touches the point where our bodies meet. As he moves himself in and out from my entry, my finger slides along his length, and then when he thrusts again, my finger is left at his base.

I watch the tiny creases in his forehead deepen as his eyes remain shut, pleased that my touch seems to have as great an impact on him as his does on me.

"Oh, God, Cass," he groans, his speed increasing as I feel the pulsing inside of me becoming more intense.

My channel tightens around him as I ascend again, within arm's reach of a climax. I gasp at the sensation.

"That's it, Cass," he coaxes me as I chase the pleasure he offers.

The slide of his skin against mine awakens every nerve in my body. My hand moves upward from his cock to the ripples of his chest, savoring their sharp hills and valleys beneath my touch.

Reaching his pecs, I feel the thundering of his heartbeat beneath my fingertips, and I'd swear it's in perfect unison with my own. Its rapid cadence excites me even more, knowing that he's feeling as desperate as I am as we float over every wave of sensation together.

His hand lifts my one leg higher up on his waist, and I respond doing the same thing with my other leg, then interlocking them behind his back as he takes me from a new angle, making me even more vulnerable to him.

Then, just before I'm about to shatter beneath him, I feel him slowly pull himself out of me, only the tip of him still remaining inside my entry.

"I promised myself I'd take it slow with you, dammit. But

I have no control around you," he says, his words ragged, and dark with reprimand against himself.

"I don't want you to show control around me." I arch my body, angling myself so that he'll have no choice but to sink inside of me again. "I just want you to take me, Dylan. Completely. Now."

My harsh demand is his undoing and he plunges into me hard, deep—so much so that I can't help the scream that escapes my lips as spasms rock my body. I tremble, feeling him come undone along with me with a final thrust.

Still heaving from release, he moves himself to my side, still joined with me.

Like mine, his eyelids are at half-mast.

"Cass, I need to tell you something."

My heart feels a quick blast of panic at his solemn tone, until I see the smile creep up his face.

"You completely dominated me," he says, and I laugh, taking his lips against my own.

CHAPTER 8

- DYLAN -

I've always been an early riser, usually at the gym before the sun even peeks over the horizon. So it didn't come as a surprise to me when my eyelids flew open long before dawn.

The surprise was my heartbeat pounding in my ears as I stared at the woman beside me, sleeping so peacefully, and this feeling that I wanted to wrap my arms around her and never let go.

I blame Ryan. I blame him, and all the damn wedding talk around this town. Every day the past week, he's had me running on some wedding errand or another. Isn't that what they hired a wedding planner for? And every time I run into someone on the street that I know (which happens on a continual basis in a small town like Newton's Creek) while running the aforementioned errands, I'm assaulted with questions about the wedding.

Will there really be pony rides for all the kids in the

town? Did they really spring for four bouncers? Is it true about the fireworks display being open to the public?

After those questions comes the inevitable, "So, your brothers are both going to be married now. When are *you* going to settle down?"

Then there's the added burden of having to look at my brothers completely besot with the women in their lives—utterly, hopelessly in love.

And happy about it.

So that *must* be the reason that right now, as I lie in my warm bed next to Cass, holding the room service menu and listening to the soothing sound of her breathing next to me, I'm having a hard time even leaving the room to call in my order. I don't want to be five feet from her, as though there's some bungee cord that wrapped itself around my wrist and hers, and we're indelibly joined.

Mine. The word just keeps springing from the depths of my soul as I look at her. *Mine.*

I shake my head and slowly force myself out of the bed. I'll have to head to the airport soon and I want to make sure she has a good meal in her before I leave. I understand the reason she needs to be rail thin for her career, but Lord, I can't help wanting to feed her.

I pad into the small sitting room in my suite and pick up the phone.

"Hi, this is Dylan Sheridan in the Presidential Suite. I'd like to make an order for room service."

I ask for a pot of coffee and just about everything else they've got on the menu, having no idea what Cass prefers.

I wish I had time to take her to Pop's for some donuts. That would probably be more of a temptation to her than anything this hotel could whip up at this hour. But there's a plane bound for DC with my name on it this morning.

Stepping back into the bedroom, Cass's open eyes greet me.

I smile as I watch her blink away the last remnants of sleep. She almost looks like she might doze off again, and I'd love to see her do it. I stole plenty of sleep from her last night and I can't even feel the slightest remorse over it.

"Go back to sleep, princess."

"No," her voice murmurs, vibrating the sheet tucked high near her chin. "I'm awake." A soft sigh escapes her. "I really should get out of here. You've got to catch a plane, right?"

"There's no rush. I ordered some room service. It should be up here soon."

"Oh, I usually skip breakfast."

"Why did I know you were going to say that?" I reply, sitting beside her.

Her lips curve into a smile, and I lower myself toward them, unable to resist.

"You know, I'll take it as an insult if you don't eat something because that would mean I didn't do enough to work up your appetite," I add.

"Okay, maybe I can handle a few bites."

"Now there's an offer I can't refuse," I say, my mouth meeting hers as I give a gentle nip. She tastes glorious to me in the morning, better than a salted caramel donut at Pop's chased by a cup of java. I could wake up every morning happy if I could have a taste of Cass to start my day.

She yields to me, moving from her side to her back, her long blonde tresses fanning out on the pillow. I deepen my kiss, our tongues entwining, searching and exploring. The sheet falls away from her naked breasts, and my hand instinctively moves there, caressing the supple skin and feeling her nipples bead at my touch.

Kneading the soft skin, I savor the moan I feel gathering

in her throat. My hand nudges the sheet lower, venturing down her belly.

Oh, God, I love the feel of her beneath my fingertips. I want to memorize every curve, every freckle, every subtle texture of Cass Parker. My fingers thread through her, finding the nub of her arousal, just as a knock at the door in the foyer makes me grimace.

"Room service," I hear someone call through the door.

"Damn their promptness," I mutter through my teeth.

She giggles quietly, tucking the sheet back under her chin.

I leave her side again, the act as painful to me now as it was earlier this morning.

What's happening to me? I can't help wondering, and feeling that a few days away from this temptress might snap me out of the fevered stupor that has fogged my sensibilities. I should be happy to have an excuse to break away from her. Yet I can't feel anything but unsettled by the idea of being pulled away from Cass Parker.

Twelve hours later, my mind is still five hundred miles away in Newton's Creek, as Mick Riley makes another attempt to flag down the bartender from his stool at the long mahogany bar at O'Toole's just off Main Street in Annapolis.

It's hopping here tonight, filled mostly with tourists according to Mick. It's not until the Wednesday night sailboat races that locals start to migrate toward the impressive pub scene that this historic city offers.

"I'm buying," Mick says as he tugs the check from the bartender's hand after he approaches us.

"No way. I still owe you for all the help you gave me with the gym plans."

"Bullshit. You paid me back in full and then some, sparring with the Group up at Meade. I'm the only Navy guy at AWG right now, so you made me look good."

"How long will you be there?"

"Two years unless they figure out somewhere else they need me." He frowns. "This liaison post is just temporary. The Navy's having a hard time finding a place for me since my injury. I'll probably end up in Military Intelligence next. How's that for a joke? Putting a guy with a brain injury into Intelligence?"

I laugh. "There's nothing wrong with your brain, Mick."

"Well, they fixed me up pretty well at Walter Reed. And Intelligence might work out since it would keep us in the area. We just bought a little townhouse on Spa Creek. Lacey's fixing it up."

"I wish she could have joined us."

Mick shakes his head. "Can't stand the sight of oysters and the smell of beer while she's pregnant."

"Pregnant?" My eyes bulge. This is a shock.

He grins, pulling out his wallet and showing me a small black-and-white ultrasound that looks like an alien in a sci-fi film. "It's a boy."

"Holy crap, Mick. Congratulations. Now I definitely need to buy the drinks." I snatch the tab from him.

Handing the bartender my credit card, I finish off the last of my soda—which Mick needles me about unapologetically, since last time I saw him I was throwing back shots like a college kid at Logan's wedding.

"You're a lot better at conversation when you're conscious," he comments as we tug the antique brass handles of the old historic pub and open the doors to the view of Ego Alley. The narrow waterway is jam-packed with boats tonight.

I'm pretty familiar with Annapolis since I visited a few times while Logan was in school at the Academy, and then when he was stationed here a while back. It's a city, but still has that small town feel like Newton's Creek. In place of the Midwest's vast cornfields, Annapolis boasts sparkling waterways leading to the Chesapeake Bay.

It's one of those cities that whittles its way deep into your soul, whether you want it to or not. So anytime business takes me to DC, I prefer to stay in Annapolis for the nights, just a half hour from our nation's capital.

"Can I stop by tomorrow after my meeting at Walter Reed and take a look at the townhouse?"

"Of course. Lacey would love to see you. I'll throw some steaks on. Just watch out. She might try to sell you the place."

"But you just moved in."

"She's flipped our last two homes for a profit. She's getting to be a bit of an addict. I always thought the Navy moving us around would be hard on her, but she's turned it into a little side job. Hell, not even a side job. Between that, and her income as a real estate agent, I think she's made more than I have the past two years."

"Does it bother you?"

"Hell, no. I'm proud of her. But I'm starting to think she married *down* when she married me," he jokes. "What about you? Still dating that model? Lacey said she read you'd been dumped on your ass again. You can't trust those magazines in the checkout line, though."

I'd normally steer clear of this topic. But tonight, I don't. "Lacey was right. But it turned out to be a good thing. I met someone else. Another model."

He shakes his head. "Dylan, do you ever learn?"

"Nah, Cass is different." My eyes wander, picturing her, remembering every instant of last night, and especially how hard it was to say good-bye to her this morning when I had to leave for my plane. As hard as I've tried to let the miles between us somehow lessen the intensity of the feelings I have for her, they are still there, simmering in the back of my mind.

At Mick's silence, I finally glance over to him.

He raises his eyebrows at me.

"Seriously, she's different," I say. "She's a friend of Allie's. She fosters dogs. Actually, she's looking to take over the foster program now that Allie has the shelter to focus on. Hopefully, they'll be able to start bringing dogs in from other counties. Maybe other states."

"A do-gooder, like you."

I chuckle at the thought. "I've never been called a do-gooder before. Attention whore, yes. Do-gooder, nope."

"Sometimes the two go hand-in-hand. I still say you should call Vi and get her to pull some strings at CNN to pump up your gym. I mean, she just talks finances on air, and only part-time now. But she knows people there. She'd find someone to cover it who wouldn't turn it into a circus like you worry about."

"You sound like Logan."

"Well, it's a fact. The more press you get, the quicker you'll be able to build the same kind of gyms elsewhere. We've got wounded veterans all over the place these days, not just near Walter Reed. We could use some gyms like you're building in other parts of the country." He gives a nod in the direction of a candy shop on Main. "You should pick up something for your new girl while you're here."

I glance at the display of at least fourteen different flavors of fudge in the window. "Did you not hear the part about Cass being a model? She'd kill me if I brought her fudge."

"If you want to make things last with a woman, I always say chocolate is the way to make it happen."

"Who says we want to make things last? She's already made it clear that she's doesn't want to settle down, and God knows I've never felt that way myself. We'll see how things go," I say, masking an odd pinch of hope with indifference.

"Yeah, well, watch out or you'll be skipping the fudge and heading straight to the jewelry shop to buy a ring. Logan's married now. And Ryan's getting married, right?"

"In a couple weeks."

Mick nods sagely. "Exactly. You're next in line. That's just what happens."

"It won't."

"It will. I'm always right about these things."

"You're a cocky son-of-a-bitch."

"Goes with the SEAL trident." He grins, extending his hand and giving my shoulder a swift thump as I shake it. "Call tomorrow morning and let me know what time you'll be stopping by for dinner."

Mick breaks off of our path up Main Street to head to the parking lot, and I walk toward the bed & breakfast I'll call home for the next two nights. It's cozier than Bergin's, and a lot friendlier. It makes me think that maybe with the new trickle of life in downtown Newton's Creek, our town might be overdue to open a B & B like this one. I read in the local paper that a few more restaurants are opening on Anders Street this fall, as well as an antique store. Now that Ryan has the riverside project complete, with its park, nature preserve, and bike paths, I can really picture people coming to our town for a weekend getaway.

Our town. I slow that train of thought momentarily, my back stiffening as I walk up the stone staircase to the B & B.

It's the first time I've thought of Newton's Creek as being *my* town in a long while. When I left for college, I turned my head and never looked back. It had stung when my father didn't ask me to come on board at JLS Heartland, and the wound deepened last year when Logan started working there to help take some of the load off Ryan.

I've been happy to be anywhere *but* Newton's Creek, a town that survives solely because of a company that is completely enmeshed with my family heritage, yet hasn't got a damn thing to do with me.

Despite that, it seems to be creeping its way back into my heart. I wonder if it has more to do with the town, or with the woman who is temporarily residing there.

Feeling a buzz in my pocket, I stop in front of the spiral staircase that will lead to my room, and pull out my phone. A smile touches my lips when I see the message waiting for me.

"How did your meeting today go?" Cass has texted to me. I start to tap in my reply, but the need to hear her voice is crushing. So I call her instead.

"Hi." There's surprise in her voice as she answers the phone.

"I was going to text you back, but I needed to hear your voice," I say, turning the key in my door, and feeling the bite of shock that I let the truth slip that way to her.

"I'm glad you called. Did the meeting at Walter Reed go well?"

"That's tomorrow. Today I just caught up with a friend who helped me put the gym plans together, and did a little sparring on the mats with some of the guys on base at Meade."

She laughs. "Wish I was there to see that."

"I can re-enact it with you when I get home, if you want," I offer in a shameless tone, thinking how much more fun it is wrapping my legs around Cass than an opponent on the mats.

"It's a date. So what time are you coming home on Wednesday?"

"Can't remember. I'll double-check and send you my itinerary." Geez, since when do I send the woman I'm dating my travel itinerary? I stretch out on the fluffy bed crowded with eight superfluous pillows. "How about dinner?"

"I'm working till four Wednesday. I usually cool down in the break room for a while afterward. It's so hot now. But I'll probably be back at my place by around five. Does that sound good?"

"Five o'clock for dinner? You're becoming too accustomed to Newton's Creek. You'll go into shock back in New York where no one eats before eight."

She laughs. "Hey, I wasn't saying I wanted to *eat* at five. I thought we'd otherwise occupy ourselves till a more appropriate dinner hour," she says using a suggestive tone.

"I love it when you talk that way. Five it is."

I pause, thinking this is normally when I'd cut the conversation off with a woman. Plans are made. No need to prolong this. But I don't want to hang up.

"So did you make it up to that shelter to see some dogs?" I ask, adjusting one of the pillows beneath my head.

"I couldn't. I had the early shift, and then there was a birthday at the pavilion at Buckeye Land. I needed to make an appearance. I didn't get out till too late. I talked to them, though. There's a hound mix they said is really mild-mannered. Hopefully good with kids, so it would be fine here with Connor. And they've got a lot of other dogs on their last days there. I still need to okay this with Allie. But she's been in Cincy with Kim who's getting her dress fitted. It just came in this morning."

"Kim got her gown fitted *today*?" Even as a guy, I know she's cutting it close.

"This is Kim we're talking about here. She only bought it a month ago, so she's lucky they could even get it to her before the wedding. For months, she kept saying that she already picked something out, so Allie and I thought that she'd actually ordered it. Turns out that her idea of picking something out just means clipping a photo from a magazine."

"That's not good."

"Yeah, but the crazy part is that she had already ordered the flower girl dress for Hannah, and the little tux for Connor a month before she even got something for herself."

"Typical mom. Always thinking about the kids first," I comment with admiration I can't hide. My mom is the same way. "Well, don't worry. If she drops the Sheridan name, they'll magically get any last-minute alterations done for her by the time next week comes."

"You think?"

"Yep."

She sighs. "Nice. What's it like to live in your world, Dylan?"

She says the words as a joke, but I feel compelled to tell her how much I'd like to show her.

I don't, of course. I'm not completely insane. I've only been out with her a couple times. But this feeling I get when I'm around her is like an avalanche burying me, completely consuming me. And that should be a bad thing. Yet for some reason, I'm liking it.

I remember what Mick said a few minutes ago, but shake it off. Just because the other two Sheridans have claimed their lifelong mates doesn't mean I'm ready to.

"So you're really thinking about doing it? Taking over the foster program?" I ask, feeling myself drawn again toward the enjoyment of learning more about what makes Cass Parker tick.

"I really am..." she begins, as my muscles relax into the duvet and I let her sweet voice soothe my consciousness.

Two nights without her is two nights too long.

CHAPTER 9

~ CASS ~

I'm staring into the soulful eyes of a hound mix, feeling the smile touch my lips just as urgency weighs on my heart.

He looks to have some basset in him, maybe some beagle. And a touch of something else—who knows what? But he's 100% love, I decide as I scratch the soft fur behind his ears.

He rests his head wearily in my hands, and I'm a goner.

"Will you be a good boy if Connor pulls your tail?" I ask him, and he wags furiously in response. Kim said to go with my instinct when I talked to her about getting a dog. I'm surprised she said it, since she's pretty protective with Connor. But this dog seems sweet as pie.

"Pie," I say, remembering the scene in *National Velvet* with a very young Elizabeth Taylor. "That's your name." I laugh, knowing that with me picking out dogs now, we'll have more names in homage to the silver screen than we can handle.

"He's on the kill list for this week," the county worker behind me informs me, saying the words in a way that suggests she hates to see this dog get euthanized just as much as I do.

I can't imagine working here, having to do that. People always give these high-kill shelters such flack for doing what they do. But no sane person wants to kill these dogs. If there's no home for them, and no room to take in more, then that's just the horrible reality.

A reality I suddenly feel committed to changing, one dog at a time.

"Not any more, he's not. I'll take him," I tell her, and watch a smile ease up her face when I do. "I've got some foster families that will take some more. My friend just opened a big shelter last weekend. But I'm taking over our foster program so that we can take on dogs outside the county."

"That shelter in Newton's Creek?" She snaps her fingers in recollection. "Hey, I thought I recognized you. I saw your picture at the opening. You were all over the news."

A blush touches my cheeks when I remember how Dylan kept those cameras aimed at us. "That was me."

"You were with that Sheridan wrestler guy. Damn, he's *hot*."

"I'll have to agree with you there," I say, planting one last kiss on the hound's forehead before the leash is attached to him again.

"Come on. I'll show you the ones we need to get placed by the end of the week."

She takes me from the exercise area to the long hallway filled with sad eyes and barking mouths, pointing out the dogs that have run out of time. I snap their photos with my phone. I'll take better ones of them later, but I need to show our foster parents the dogs as best I can so that I can convince them to keep taking in dogs.

"What's this one's story?" I ask, pointing to a shepherd mix.

"She was found in a dumpster with her pups. The pups got adopted, but no one wants her."

"What's wrong with her eye? Cataract?"

"No. The vet says she was probably hurt a while back. Trauma to her eye. Someone probably kicked her or threw a rock at her. She's blind in it now."

Blinded by cruelty, left behind in a dumpster to try to fend for her little pups. Damn, with Kim's knack for fundraising, Allie could build a new wing on her shelter from that story alone. "We'll take this one, too. I'll find a spot for her. Can you give me till Thursday to get back up here? I need to talk to my fosters. Make sure they're on board."

"Done. Any others you want?"

That's a trick question. I want them all. I walk further through the hallway, suddenly struck by how many more dogs there are.

God, how did Allie do this for so long? No wonder she was ready to give up everything to build that shelter. How do I choose among them, deciding which ones will live and which will die?

"Just show me the ones who are on their last days. I'll try to place them as quickly as possible. And call me before any others get euthanized. I'm going to try to dredge up some more foster families this week. I work till four every other day, so can't make it all the way out here too easily before you close, but—"

"Hon, if you're taking dogs off my hands, I'll hang around late till you get here," she says with a grin.

A comrade in arms, I think. Just what I need to pull this off.

I load my hound into my car and catch myself dialing Dylan before I pull out of the parking lot. My heart is racing with the adrenaline rush of actually taking the lead on this. I bury away the question in my brain about what I'll do at the end of Buckeye Land's season when I'm supposed to return to New York, and accept a grateful lick on my neck from Pie. *Right now* is all I'll focus on. Because right now, I just saved a dog's life and I'm feeling high as a kite from it.

I grin when I hear Dylan's voice and switch it to speaker-phone. We'd talked long into the night last night, but it still wasn't enough for me.

"I got a dog, Dylan. A sweet hound mix. Connor will love him," I practically chirp.

"That's great, Cass. What'd you name him?"

"Pie," I say, not even bothering to tell him the backstory of the name since, if he hadn't managed to see *It's a Wonderful Life*, there's no way he saw *National Velvet*.

"Like in *National Velvet*?" he asks.

Will wonders never cease? "You saw the film? It's black and white. How is that possible?"

"No, I read it to Hannah while I was visiting a couple years ago. She loves anything with horses. Well, horses and singing. Those are her two great loves. So I guess if they made *National Velvet* into a musical, you could bet she'd make me watch it with her."

"So you hate old movies, but you might have a weakness for musicals?"

"Hell no. I have a weakness for Hannah."

As usual, my belly feels the flutter of butterflies when he shows his soft side, which is surprisingly often. "That's sweet," I respond quietly, and laugh when Pie lets out a howl as someone passes our car.

"That's him, I take it?"

"That's my boy."

"Logan and Allie will be happy they moved out of the townhouse next to you, with a howl like that. Hope some dog-friendly people moved in to replace them."

I bite my lip thoughtfully for a moment. "Actually, yeah. They've really liked the foster dogs of ours they met. I might try to convince them to foster one, come to think of it."

"Is Kim getting another foster?"

"She said she wants to wait till after the wedding and honeymoon to get another. She and Connor will move in with Ryan and Hannah then, of course. And they've got Lollipop as their permanent dog, remember? They need some time to settle in as a family."

"Agreed. What about Allie and Logan?"

"I'm pretty sure they'll take one or two. They have Kosmo, of course, but that dog gets along with everyone."

"Want me to call some of the guys I went to high school with? There are a few who still live in Newton's Creek. We don't really do much except email every once in a while, but it's worth a shot."

"Dylan, that would be fantastic."

"No problem. I'll tell Ryan and Logan to do the same, if they haven't already."

A girl could fall in love with this guy. Not that *I* will, of course.

"I adore you," I feel comfortable enough to say instead. Adoration is safe. It doesn't lead to heartache and abandonment.

"I'm adoring being adored by you." He pauses. "Just don't tell my brothers I said that. They'll say I sound like a pussy."

"It's our little secret. Where are you now, anyway?" I ask, feeling the need to be able to draw up a picture of him in my mind to ease my loneliness. How can I miss him this much, this quickly?

"Headed to dinner with Mick and his wife. We're having steaks on the grill."

Just like that, I conjure an image of his broad form filling out the small driver's seat of a rental car—something not up to his usual standard, I'm guessing, now that I've seen what he likes to drive. He probably has some heavily caffeinated drink at his side, just like I do, seeing as I kept him up pretty late describing the many things I'd be doing to him in that hotel bed if I had been with him.

"I miss you. Wish you could be here to join us tonight," he tells me, surprising the hell out of me.

"I'll see you soon. When is your plane taking off tomorrow? I can't remember what your email said."

"Noon. I have to get there early because security's a bitch at Reagan National. Logan says I should have flown home out of BWI. Live and learn. I envy Ryan and his private plane right now."

"I thought you said it was totally impractical."

"As impractical as my McLaren. So I want one. Lacey told me about an airfield for small aircraft just a few miles from Annapolis."

I can't help the surge of jealousy I feel. "Lacey?" I ask carefully.

"Mick's wife. She was at Logan's wedding. I'd tell you whether you met her that night, but my memory is a little foggy."

Feeling relief, I laugh.

"She's a real estate agent. Thinks my brothers and I should get a vacation property on the water out here. Logan would do it in a heartbeat. He lives for the water. And I've been sold on Annapolis since Logan was at the Academy. But Ryan's more of a Midwestern guy, through and through. With an airfield he can fly right into, though… I'm thinking that's a good selling point."

"Sell Kim on it, and he'd do it in a heartbeat."

"You're right. Damn, why hadn't I thought to go through her? Hell, Connor would love crabbing off a dock somewhere or having Logan teach him how to sail. You're brilliant, baby."

I feel a warmth touch my cheeks, thinking of him sitting in his car driving through Annapolis, complimenting me.

Me.

How the heck did a second-rate catalog model get this lucky?

He chats with me for about a quarter of my drive home till he arrives at his friends' house. I envy the picture I draw up in my mind of him grilling steaks with this couple sitting by the water's edge on… Spa Creek, I think he called it. Geez, even the name sounds like a vacation. I don't remember meeting Mick at Ryan's wedding any more than I do someone named Lacey. But there were so many men in uniform there that they pretty much blended into one ultra-sexy amalgam.

Not nearly as sexy as the wrestler I get to see tomorrow night, though.

When I open the door to Kim's townhouse, Pie immediately darts through a bunch of papers on the floor in front of Kim, who is spread eagle on the hardwood with a pen behind her ear.

"Damn. Sorry, Kim."

"No worries. It's just wedding stuff. I'm trying to find the contract I signed with the caterer. I'm positive I offered a vegetarian option, but I can't remember what it is."

"So, call the wedding planner. She'll have the information."

"I don't want to bug her again today. I've already called her three times this week."

I shake my head. Kim is the exact opposite of a bridezilla. "Hon, that's what she's there for."

But Kim is already distracted from wedding minutia by the bundle of fur that is now enjoying a good scratch behind the ears. "So you're our new doggie?" she asks, grasping his face and giving him a kiss on the soft fur on the tip of his head.

"Kim, meet Pie. Pie, this is Kim," I say, watching them on the floor together.

Connor races down the stairs at the sound of paws on the hardwood floors.

"A dog!" he cries and immediately leads Pie out to the backyard for an exhausting game of fetch while Kim and I put a frozen lasagna in the microwave.

When Connor goes to bed, I pull out my phone and show Kim the photos of the other dogs I met today.

"Did you contact the foster families yet?" she asks, looking all misty-eyed after hearing the story of the mama dog who is blind in one eye.

"I did. And they're all on board except for one who just found out she's pregnant. Just doesn't want a dog when she's dealing with the joys of her first trimester, I guess."

"Can't imagine why," Kim says sarcastically with a chuckle, her eyes telling me she still has vivid memories of *her* first trimester. I can't even imagine going through what she did when she got pregnant, and so alone at the time. It brings a smile to my face to know I'll see her happily-ever-after in less than two weeks. God knows she deserves it.

"Well, if you are still short another house, I can take one on, too, you know. Ryan wouldn't mind. It's not my first choice with my life in chaos right now, but I don't want to see any of these sweethearts get put down."

"You're not needed. I mean, you're *always* needed. But I

think I've got them all covered this time. And you really should wait till you get through the wedding and honeymoon first. It's stressful."

"No kidding. The wedding planner is taking care of everything. She's incredible. But I'm still so stressed about it. And then there's everything that comes *after* the wedding that's keeping me up nights."

"You mean having a daughter? Hannah already adores you. And she and Connor get along. It's all like it was meant to be."

"No, not that. It's just that I'll be…" Her voice trails.

"A Sheridan," I finish for her. "Yeah, that's got to be intimidating as hell. They're like the Midwest's version of the Kennedys. And Ryan's kind of like the head of them these days."

"Exactly, and I'm just not a Jackie O, you know? Even my parents are freaking out about this, as if they're somehow expected to rise up to some kind of Sheridan standard."

I bite my tongue. I've never cared much for Kim's parents. I think they could only improve by holding themselves up to a higher standard like the Sheridans.

While she sips her therapeutic wine, she updates me on the latest wedding plans which have blossomed from an intimate gathering in JLS's new riverside park in downtown Newton's Creek, into an entire festival for the town.

The wedding and reception will be invitation-only, but there will be plenty of activities for the entire community in the area adjacent to the park where Kim and Ryan will say their vows.

It sounds a little over-the-top, in my humble opinion, but they wanted everyone to feel a part of the festivities since so many of the people in our small town work for JLS.

I pour her another glass of Chardonnay before she retreats to her bedroom.

"Drink it," I order her when she hesitates. "I'm on call if anything happens with Connor. And you really need to get some sleep."

She hugs me before she retreats to her room, and then I wander to my own, holding my phone in my hand and fighting the urge to call Dylan again.

Just as I sit in my bed, I feel it buzz in my hand.

"Lonely bed here," he texts.

I smile. "Lonely bed here, too," I tap in. "How was dinner at your friends'?"

"Great." He texts me a photo of a narrow waterway with a bridge in the distance. There's a heron in the forefront, standing tall in the water as though it loves to get its photo taken.

"Pretty," I type.

"That's their backyard."

Wow, I think. Even living in a town named after a creek, you just don't get water like that around here. "Nice," I tap in. "How were the steaks?"

"I loved mine. Lacey couldn't stomach hers."

"??" I type in.

"First trimester."

I laugh. "Kim and I were just talking about that."

There's a pause before I get his reply. "Hold on. She's not pregnant? Is she?"

"NO!" I write back, adding a smiley face. "We were talking about one of the foster families who is expecting a baby." But it won't be long till she *is* pregnant, I ponder as I wait for his reply. I can definitely picture Ryan and Kim expanding their already full family tree very soon.

"Lonely bed," he types again, adding a frown this time.

I laugh. "U said that already."

"How are u for sexting?"

Pressing my lips together, I feel a little flutter down below. "Never tried it."

"I'll go first: I'm totally naked right now."

Giggling, I glance down at the t-shirt and shorts I have on. "Me 2," I type.

"That's always a good start…"

CHAPTER 10

~ CASS ~

Taffeta sticks to my sweat-soaked skin like cellophane as I retreat to the character break room trailer to peel my golden-tipped slippers off my aching feet.

My shift is finally over, and I'm eagerly anticipating the cool cascade of soda down my throat after telling hundreds of little girls to have a sparkly day.

Emitting a long breath, I turn the knob to the trailer and am surprised by the scent of roses that greets me.

Then I see him, six feet of formidable muscle and a boyish grin that makes my heart melt, holding at least two dozen red roses in his hands.

I've missed him desperately—no, pathetically—these past two nights. But it's not until I actually rest my eyes on him that I realize just how much I've wanted him near.

"You said red roses were your favorite," he greets me.

"Dylan! What are you doing here?"

He pulls me close and his lips are hot against mine for a glorious few seconds before he replies, "I got back to my hotel an hour ago and I couldn't wait till five to see you." His hand cradles my chin and he bends to kiss me again, covering every inch of me with goose bumps. "Hope you don't mind. I slipped the guy at the gate a fifty to show me where your break room is so I could deliver them myself."

"I don't mind in the slightest," I say, my eyelids fluttering shut when I feel his hands against my breasts. Even through the tight bodice, the pressure of him against me sends shockwaves of lust through my body. "I've missed you," I whimper as his lips move from my mouth to my ear, nibbling slightly. My mind wanders to our late night texts, the memory of his words making me purr all over again. Something about this man turns me feral, thinking only of my most basic instincts —even with forty pounds of shimmering material weighing me down.

His hands lock together at the small of my back, arching me toward him, as his lips track from my ear down to my neck, and then to the bare skin just above my bodice.

"God, you are gorgeous in this dress, Cass."

I inhale sharply, feeling his tongue dipping into my cleavage. "You want it with the dress *on* sometime, my handsome prince?"

"Sweet Jesus, don't tempt me," he growls.

My mouth curves upward, laced with desire. I need him in me now so desperately it nearly pains me. "Well, I think I told you no one ever uses this break room."

His eyes look up toward mine, hungry and needy. "Ever?"

I take his hand and lead it back to my breast, needing more of the pressure. "It used to be for all the characters. There was a prince, a dragon, and a witch. But they all got their pink slips at the end of last summer due to budget cuts.

I'm the only one left." I take an earlobe in my mouth and give him a playful nip.

"I'm glad the prince is gone. I might have gotten a bit jealous of the guy."

"No need to be jealous. He's got a great boyfriend named Louis and they're both in *Seven Brides for Seven Brothers* right now at the dinner theater about ten miles away." I brush my hand along the hard ridge beneath his shorts and ponder how long I'll have to wait before I feel him inside of me. I can't wait till after dinner. I can't even wait till we get out of Buckeye Land. He is six feet of pure, unadulterated sex god, and all I can think is that he's mine for the next several hours.

Why waste time, then?

Digging my fingers into his short hair, I tug him along with me, lips still locked together, to turn the bolt on the door. Just in case.

"You're serious. Right now?" His eyes light with mischief.

"Unless you have a problem with that."

"Cass, I'm problem-free right now," he says, his lips nuzzling the compressed flesh from my tight bodice as he lowers his hand, tugging my skirts upward.

Then I feel his hand against me, cupping me tightly, slipping his finger past my panties and into me, and I shudder.

"Oh, God..." I murmur. The uncomfortable fabric scratches at me, yet somehow that only arouses me more, making my skin crave the softness of his hands on me.

His thumb toys with my clit in tiny circles as his mouth pushes past the tight bodice till my nipple feels the moisture of his tongue. I cry out, my pelvis thrusting against his, aching for more pressure till I see stars explode behind my eyes.

I tug at his shorts, finding the button first, then the

zipper. Without even bothering to strip him bare, I pull at his boxers till I feel his length in my hand, so hard and ready.

"Sofa," he murmurs into my mouth, his breath entering mine in heated gasps.

"I can't wait," I demand, just as he reaches into the shorts still hanging loosely from his hips and pulls out a condom. My hands are shaking as I tug it from him, tearing off the wrapping and sheathing his length myself, so eager to feel him inside of me. I lock my fingers around the breadth of him as he devours my exposed skin above the low neckline with his mouth.

"We don't need to rush," he says, yet his words somehow lose their meaning as his breath tickles me, making my nipples tighten into hard nubs. My desire multiplies.

"Speak for yourself," I respond, and he spins me around so that my back faces him. Sighing, knowing that I'll finally feel what I need, I bend slightly over the small kitchen counter as he lifts my skirts.

After nudging the thin fabric of my panties aside, the crown of his cock touches the moisture at my slit and his hand reaches around to my belly, moving slowly downward till his fingers lace into my curls. Finally, I feel the penetration as he enters me, fast and hard.

I'm so slick around him it's almost stunning, and my body seems to cry out in relief as though it's been ages since I'd felt him like this.

The width of him stretches me as he thrusts deeper, his movements slow at first, entering me a little more with each thrust, till I feel the pressure against my G spot. I cry out from the sensation, my body quaking against the counter.

Lips still pressed against my neck, his hands venture to the tiny buttons on the back of my costume. I feel his hands slide past the constraining fabric, splaying across my back and moving toward my breasts. His skin feels so soft compared to the rough fabric of my bodice that I get chills from their caress, and he cups the mounds in his hands possessively and massages me slowly, sinuously, the rhythm mirroring the movements he makes inside me. The combination of sensations amplifies awareness in every cell of my body. Every touch, every stroke seems so deliberate, designed just to make me needier, more desperate.

His tongue cascades along my spine as I feel him throb inside of me just as I had imagined so many times these past days in his absence. Yet this is more powerful than any dream could possibly be. Once again, the reality of Dylan Sheridan is so sharp to me—so refined and crystal-clear that it shocks my senses.

One hand moves from my breast downward, cupping the soft flesh of my bottom, and then moving forward till his thumb makes a perfect circle around my center with each thrust. I'd swear I am flying right now, climbing up to a height that thrills me.

My heart rate hastens, and I can hear it echoing in my ear drums as the blood flow to my brain seems to set my head spinning.

"That's it, baby," he coaxes as my channel grips him harder with each thrust. He whispers in my ear as I feel my body reaching for a climax barely out of its grasp.

Harder he thrusts, whispering heated words, coarse and just crude enough to make me blush in my heavy dress. They're words that somehow fit the heat of this moment, as we grab whatever sexual gratification we can, without even taking the time to tear the clothing off each other.

That's how desperately I've needed him, I realize. For days, my desire's been building, and now I'm poised to explode.

I bend a degree further, almost hugging the counter in exhaustion as my feverish breath escapes me.

"You okay, baby?"

I murmur my response, not even sure what I just uttered. All I know is that if he stops right now, I might very well die.

His fingers move adeptly, pinching my clit gently, making me cry out as he quickens his pace. I'm submerged in sensation, drowning in it, yet I don't want it to end. Without being able to see him—only feel the thrusts of him inside of me, his lips on me, his hands squeezing me—somehow this seems more erotic, wilder, thoroughly unbridled.

"Harder," is the only word I manage to say coherently, and he obliges.

I whimper at the feel of his teeth teasing the skin on my shoulder as the cadence of his movements quicken, pounding against my innermost depths, till I feel the orgasm overtake me. My soul feels like it's in a free-fall and my breath catches in my throat as my body seizes up around him.

Both his hands fill with the flesh of my hips as he plunges one last time inside of me, the urgency consuming him just as it does me.

He shatters inside of me just as the last aftershock of climax leaves my body.

His torso folds over mine, heaving breath upon breath. "Holy, shit, princess."

A laugh escapes me. "Right back at ya, handsome prince."

In unison, our bodies breathe as one, and my eyes shut at the feel of his strong arms encompassing me, cradling me so tenderly that it seems completely incongruent to what we've just done—mating like a couple of wild animals.

When I can see straight again, I manage to straighten my dress while he retrieves that soda I'd been longing for so desperately just minutes ago. I crack a smile, realizing that sex with him is the only thing that I could ever crave more than a cool soda at the end of a workday at Buckeye Land.

After I eventually catch my breath enough to change, I

turn down his offer of a picturesque walk in the riverside park in downtown Newton's Creek and dinner at Francesca's. I'm not feeling like I want to share Dylan with the public. I only want him alone. So I follow him in my car back to his hotel, opting for room service.

As soon as he opens the door to his suite, I find myself charging into his bedroom and diving head first into his bed, tugging my t-shirt off and feeling the cool sheets against my skin. He joins me, pulling off his polo shirt revealing a chest so expansive it covers two zip codes.

Damn, I'll never tire of that sight.

After tugging off his shorts, he stretches out like a cat on the bed. He only has his boxers on, and I decide I'd like him better with them off. So I move my hand down his firm abs and let my fingertips slip beneath the elastic.

My head rests on Dylan's chest as I stroke him from his base all the way up to the crown, then fingering the tiny speck of moisture I feel at the tip. I love listening to the synchronicity of our breathing as we lie next to each other like this. His heart beats, slowly and hypnotically, despite the fact that the firmness I grip in my hand right now tells me he's anything but relaxed.

"Shouldn't we order something to eat?" he murmurs with a hint of reluctance. His torso barely moves as he flops one arm in the direction of the phone on the nightstand.

"I'm not even hungry."

"Well, I'm feeding you, anyway. I don't want you running out of energy this early in the night."

I smile. "Then you should have thought of that an hour ago when you showed up in the break room with two dozen roses." My eyes widen. "Damn. I just realized I left them at Buckeye Land."

"Don't worry. You can get them tomorrow."

"I have tomorrow off," I inform him.

A grin slides up his face. "That's the best news I've heard all day. I'll buy you two dozen *more* roses if you say you'll spend the day with me."

"It's a deal. Any plans in mind?"

"Anything with you. We could go to Cincinnati. I could show you my new gym there." He scrunches his face. "No. That's boring as hell."

"I think it sounds nice."

He shakes his head. "No. Hey—we could take a last-minute flight up to Chicago. Grab a pizza, check out Navy Pier. Take a walk in Lincoln Park. We could spend the night in my condo there and fly back the next morning. What time do you have to be at work?"

"Nine."

He frowns slightly. "It's do-able. I can charter a private jet and we'll avoid security."

It sounds almost magical—a last-minute, whirlwind trip like that. But there's something I want to do more with my day off.

"Actually, I was planning on driving up north again and picking up the dogs for my foster families. It's not Chicago, but we can pick up a pizza somewhere, I'm sure." I bite my lip, waiting for his reply.

He pulls me close and the feel of his bare skin against me soothes me. "That sounds like an even better plan."

Eagerly, I grip him hard again, wanting to show him what *else* I want to do on my day off.

Ounce by ounce, I feel my soul getting wrapped up in him completely, daring to think past today, past this week, and into that *other* F word: future.

It terrifies me because it breaks one of the rules I live by. *Never dare to think about a future with a man* is right up there with my Holy Grail of rules, *Never be the first to say I love you.*

So I fight the feeling—even as the heat inside me builds

and I find myself straddling him, savoring the feel of him beneath me.

My cell phone rings and I groan.

"Ignore it," he growls, flipping me over so that I'm underneath him as he parts my legs with his knee. "I'm begging you to ignore it."

"Let me just make sure it's not Allie or Kim." Some friendships are worth postponing sex for. But it's a stretch.

I pull my phone off the nightstand and see the number. My shoulders fall, deflated. "Shoot. It's work. If they're changing my schedule tomorrow, I'll have a fit." I tap the green button. "Hello?"

"Cassidy Parker?"

"Yes."

"This is Ms. Flanagan in Human Resources. Security informed us of a situation in the break room that breaks the terms of your contract."

I sit up sharply. "What are you talking about?"

"Ms. Parker, one of our security cameras revealed that you had a non-employee visitor in the break room."

No, no, no. My heart is racing. Where was the camera? It *had* to be outside. That's all. I've worked there for nearly two summers. I would have heard if there was a camera in the break room.

Dylan sits up, probably noticing all the color washing away from my face. "What is it?" he mouths silently to me.

I give my head a quick shake in answer. "I'm sorry. I didn't realize I wasn't supposed to have non-employees in the break room."

"That's not why you are being dismissed."

My stomach drops twenty feet to the floor below ours. I hear the blood flow in my brain, hammering, and I'm nauseous as I listen to this woman tell me that I'm being fired for having "sexual relations" in the break room, and in full costume.

Oh my God.

"There's a camera in the break room?" The words fall from my mouth like lead weights, each with a terrifying thud. I think I stuttered the last two words, and I know immediately that Dylan knows what's being said on the other end of the call when I see the daggers in his eyes.

"Yes," she says so damn calmly I have to wonder how many Princess Buckeyes before me grabbed a quickie in the break room. "There is one camera for security purposes in the break room. We have the legal right to have cameras in common areas."

"It's a break room. A break room only I use. I thought I'd have a little privacy in there." I teeter on a razor-sharp edge between fury and humiliation.

"The camera is in the kitchen area of the break room. Not the changing area."

My breath starts coming in short gasps, and I fall silent, just barely holding the phone to my ear. Dylan reaches his hand out and, not knowing what else to do, I instinctively hand it to him. I'm incapable of speaking now.

"This is Dylan Sheridan. To whom am I speaking?"

I listen to him pause as she speaks on the other end.

"According to laws in most states, Ms. Flanagan, employers are not allowed to put cameras in areas where employees should expect some degree of privacy. I believe a break room would fall under those constraints." Again he pauses. His tone is different from what I've ever heard from him before, smooth and deadly. "Ms. Flanagan, I'm sure you're familiar with the Sheridan name and we're certainly more acquainted with the laws protecting employees than you are. You'll be hearing from my lawyers in the morning."

My eyes are wide, blurred with unshed tears, as I watch

him touch the end button on my phone. I just stare at the phone silently as he sets it on the nightstand, feeling his eyes on me, but unable to meet his gaze.

Someone saw us having sex. Someone *watched* us?

I press my hand to my mouth charging from the bed toward the bathroom. I'm going to throw up. I'm sure of it. I can taste the bile in my mouth, but nothing comes as I kneel in front of the porcelain god and let the tears fall.

I hear Dylan's voice behind me. "Oh, baby, I'm so damn sorry. So, so damn sorry."

I stare into the bowl, wishing it would bring me some kind of relief. "They *watched* us? God, I feel so... violated. And so stupid. So damn stupid." Sobbing, I finally look at him. "I swear to you, I had no clue there was a camera in there. I don't know where the hell it was. I've been in there so many times, Dylan. Jesus, I've *changed* in that room sometimes just because I'm so damn hot at the end of the day, I can't make it twenty more feet to the changing area. You'd think they would have mentioned something *then*, don't you?"

"We'll sue those bastards. They don't stand a chance against our lawyers."

"Great. That'll be good press for the Sheridans. Sheridan housing development empire sues a kiddie amusement park. You don't need that, dammit."

He reaches for a glass of water and hands it to me. "Here. Sip this. And don't worry about the Sheridan name. Jesus. This is my fault, Cass. I'm the idiot who showed up there unannounced. I didn't see a camera, and I'm sharp with noticing things like that. It was definitely hidden and that makes it completely unethical."

"Are you sure?"

I watch him press his lips together thoughtfully.

"That it's unethical? Hell, yes. That's a no brainer, Cass.

But I'll have the lawyers check on any precedence in Ohio that would allow it. Security cameras are a sketchy area. We've dealt with this in some of my gyms where we've had thefts. But our cameras are always in full view."

I sit back, leaning against the cold, tiled wall, unable to stand. I'm wordless and numb. Even as he sits next to me, draping his arm across my shoulders, I can barely feel it.

Every time I play over that time I spent with Dylan in the break room, it sickens me to think that someone was watching us.

"We'll get through this, Cass. I'll call our lawyers. I'll have them write up what we need to get our hands on any recordings they've got. We'll see exactly what they saw or didn't see. It's probably not as bad as you're picturing. Believe me, they'll be apologizing to you by the end of this."

CHAPTER 11

- DYLAN -

They'll be apologizing to you by the end of this, I had told her.

I'd wanted to believe it was true. Video surveillance is a vague area of law, at best. And even though I know our lawyers will have them begging for mercy by the end of this, it's not going to make up for the tears I saw pour from Cass's eyes last night as I drove her home to Kim's.

It *is* my fault. I should have known better than that. What is it about that woman that has all sense and reason leaving me the moment I rest eyes on her?

As I walk into the lobby at JLS, I catch a strange look from the receptionist as I make my way to the elevator. Ryan called me in here first thing—and first thing for him is just past seven in the morning now that he's got a nanny for Hannah and Connor for the summer.

I'm in a fresh polo and I managed to pull a comb through my hair this morning. But compared to everyone else here at

JLS at this hour, I pretty much look like something the cat dragged in.

My eyes burn with fatigue. I didn't sleep a wink last night.

Half the night I was pounding my pillow, out for blood, wanting some kind of revenge on Buckeye Land for hurting the woman I care for.

And the other half of the night, I was awake, scared shit-less by just *how much* I care for her.

Knowing that my actions, my poor judgment, caused her pain is like ramming a knife into my heart and twisting sharply 180 degrees.

I nod to Ryan's assistant and she gives me a smile, as always. "Your brother's waiting for you," she says.

"I'll bet he is," I mutter. I knew Ryan would catch wind of this when I drove Cass home to Kim's around ten—if not from his fiancée, then definitely from the tribe of lawyers I was talking to for at least an hour last night.

Time to stick my tail between my legs and grovel.

I don't see Ryan at first when I walk through his door, till I follow the sound of fists pounding into the heavy bag he keeps in the back room of his office. Never a good sign.

"Ryan," I greet him tentatively, and as he hears my voice he gives the bag one more impressive blow. He turns to me, his face pink and pissed, a total clash with the refined suit he's wearing.

"You son of a bitch," he snarls at me.

I hold my hands up. "I know. I fucked up. Literally. And I'm sorry I had to pull our lawyers in on this, but they're the best in the state."

"What the hell did you think you were doing?" He storms toward me, like he's going to pull my heart out through my throat. Then he freezes momentarily, checking himself, and blows out an exasperated breath before retreating to his desk.

I'm happy to have a piece of furniture in between us because I haven't seen Ryan this furious since—well, *never*.

"Screwing her in a break room? In *costume*? Jesus, Dylan. I've known you to do some pretty stupid things, but this takes the cake."

"I know it. Okay? Look, it's bad enough I had to see Cass crying half the night—"

"And Kim saw her cry the second half of the night. Dammit, we're barely a week away from our wedding and you've just got to upstage everyone."

"I know. I'm sorry. We sure as hell didn't mean to have it happen. Dammit, haven't you ever had sex someplace... questionable?" I shake my head. This is my responsible brother I'm talking about here.

"No, of course. Not the esteemed Ryan Sher—" I start, and then stop cold, seeing the guilty look in his eyes. "You *have*. You have, dammit, and yet you sit there judging me. Well, be pissed at Buckeye Land. It's a break room. A break room that no one ever uses except Cass. Cass says she's even changed there and no one ever said a thing to her. My guess is that some asshole in security is jacking off to the sight of her while she's on break every day. So I'm suing those assholes so that it doesn't happen to the next poor woman stuck in that job. We'll get the footage from them. We'll get Cass out of that job. And I'll take her to the islands for a while to get her mind off of it."

He stares at me motionless for a moment. Still like a statue, as my niece always says. With eyes locked on me, he barely blinks.

"What?" I finally ask him.

"You don't know."

My fists coil instinctively. "I don't know what?"

"The video was leaked Dylan."

"*What*? When?"

"Sometime last night. It's all over the internet."

Staggering to a chair, my stomach roils. "Are you serious?" I glance at him, and from the look on his face I know he's dead serious. "You've seen it?"

He scowls. "Yeah, I've seen it. I had to know what we're dealing with here. But I sure as hell closed my eyes at certain parts. I mean, sweet Jesus, Dylan..." His voice trails.

I rake my hands through my hair. "What's it show?"

"You want me to pull it up on my computer?"

The thought of my unintended sex video playing on a JLS computer sickens me. "No. Not here. Just give me the bad news."

"Well, it wasn't as bad as it could have been. I mean, shit, Dylan, you didn't even take the time to take your clothes off. There was a kitchen counter blocking a lot of it, and well, hell, there was crinoline everywhere. I think I saw a little flash of—"

"Don't say it, bro."

"Right. Well, it kind of looked like two college kids trying to make a bad porno or something."

Rolling my eyes, I toss my head backward, staring at the ceiling. "Does Cass know?"

"I don't think so. Kim just called me. Cass was up till about four. Finally Kim gave her two shots of bourbon and she's sleeping it off now. Kim'll tell her when she wakes up."

I rise from my chair. "I need to be there."

"Dylan, no offense, but don't you think you've screwed up her life enough? Kim's her friend. She'll be there for her. You—"

"Fuck you, Ryan." I cut him off, knowing what he was going to say. That I won't be there for her. That this thing we have won't last for more than three months. And he might be right. That's pretty much my norm.

But I'm here now.

"I need to be there," I say again and bolt from his office, giving a quick nod to Ryan's assistant as I tear toward the elevators.

———

Wordless, Kim gives me a withering look as she opens the door.

"She's awake?" I ask, my voice low.

Saying nothing, she steps to the side so that I can pass. If it's possible to piss off my future sister-in-law more than I have, I'd be damn surprised.

"She's in the kitchen," she finally responds. "I'm going to pick Connor up from your parents' house. I took him there last night because I figured Cass needed a night to cry it out." She raises a single eyebrow, accusingly. "And that was *before* this morning's news."

I step into the hall and behind me, I hear Kim close the door. My stomach twists as I walk toward the kitchen to see Cass sitting at the counter, staring at a laptop, face ashen and streaked with tears. Pie is up on his hind legs, stretching out with his front paws on her thighs. His droopy hound eyes are filled with an abundance of sympathy.

She doesn't even lift her eyes from the screen to acknowledge me. The only movement from her is in one of her hands as she rubs Pie's head unconsciously. The silence between us is suffocating until she eventually speaks.

"It's everywhere, Dylan," she says, still staring at her computer.

"Ryan told me." I want desperately to reach for her. But I fear she would recoil at my touch right now, and I certainly wouldn't blame her.

"Did you see it?"

"Not yet."

Her face looks so pale, so weak, it's disturbing.

"Oh, I have," she mutters dejectedly. "Twice. Which apparently is fewer times than most Americans have seen it by now. That's what I get for sleeping in."

I search her eyes, wondering if she meant that to be funny. From the look on her face, I'm thinking not.

"Well, I guess the upside of this is that we were so horny that we didn't bother taking our clothes off. There's this one point when there's a little flash of something that one commenter called 'definite nipplage,' but it's not nearly as bad as it could have been." She sighs painfully. "We've added a new word to the American lexicon. *Nipplage.*"

From the bite in her tone, she seems somehow a little stronger than last night. But I think she has just surpassed that point when things look so bleak, she might be assuming she's caught in a surreal nightmare.

I dare to touch her, sliding my hand across her shoulder and to my triumph, she doesn't pull away.

Words escape me as I sit next to her. I screwed up. Big time. And I need to make this right.

A single tear drops from her eye, tearing me in two.

"I'll never live this down. I mean, look at it, Dylan. If it wasn't me in it, I'd be laughing hysterically. It's so absurd—it's comical. Look at us."

She pushes the laptop closer to me and hits play. There's no sound. But a hell of a lot of action. Crinoline tossed around... her crown, lopsided on her head... and a look of wild fury in both our eyes that almost makes it look like we're faking it. I press my hand to my forehead, the cold chill of it soothing the ache stretching across my skull.

I watch myself struggle with her ball gown. "Damn, that's a big dress," I can't help commenting, watching layers of taffeta and satin fly upward as I lift her skirts. The counter blocks most of the action, just like Ryan said. And I see that moment Cass mentioned—the "nipplage" in question—and can picture every horny thirteen-year-old boy replaying that split-second again and again this morning.

I hate the internet.

Then she sinks to the counter after we're done, her breasts nearly falling out of her bodice and a look of complete sexual satisfaction on her face.

"This probably isn't what you want to hear," I begin cautiously, "but you do look pretty damn hot."

To my relief, she bursts out laughing, my statement coming just as I watch her head fall to the side on the video, cheek resting on the countertop, and the tiara falls to the ground.

I don't even remember her dropping her tiara.

I almost join in laughing—it really does have a humorous side to it—until I see the tears pouring from her face as her laugh turns to a sob. She's reached that point of sheer hysteria, I'm betting, as I glance around the kitchen wondering where Kim keeps that bourbon Ryan mentioned.

"I'll never escape this. Oh, God. It's a *kids'* park, for God's sake. I'm going to get picketed by every conservative group out there. I'll always be that whore that defiled the Princess Buckeye costume." She tosses her hands upward. "Geez, and I was upset about Brenna Tucker putting my picture on Facebook? That just doesn't hold a candle to this, does it?"

No, it definitely doesn't. And what kills me is that she's right. I'll bounce back from this unscathed. *Dylan Sheridan can't keep it in his pants*, they'll joke and then give me a thump on the shoulder and move on.

But the public isn't so forgiving of women. The comments will be more along the lines of *How could Buckeye Land let that woman around all those innocent children?* They'll crucify her until some other distraction comes along. But it will be a while before something happens more attention-grabbing than this.

Unless…

I lean back in the counter chair. "What we need is a distraction."

Her head now resting in her hands, she doesn't even look at me. "What do you mean?"

"Social media—it's all just a series of distractions. We're trending now, and we'll stay there until something better comes along to talk about."

"It'll be a while till someone tops this."

I stand up, wringing my hands together in thought. "Okay, you're right. So let's top it ourselves."

"What do you mean?"

"I mean, they want a show. Let's give them one. My publicist already called while I was on my way here this morning. Everyone is hoping for a statement or a press release. I'll give them better. I'll give them a fucking interview."

She cocks her head, incredulous. "And say what? Sorry we offended you, America?"

"No." The idea pops into my head as I stare out her window, and I keep my mouth shut momentarily, hoping it will get replaced by something better. But it's all I've got. "We'll get engaged," I blurt.

"*What?*"

"Just for show, Cass. A distraction. They want a spectacle? We'll give them one. I'll ask you right there on live TV. You'll cry, laugh, we'll kiss, they'll cut to commercial and America is suddenly planning our wedding."

"A fake engagement?"

"Yeah. Why not? Look, right now you're known as the girl who, well, essentially made a sex tape in a princess costume. Not good. But if we get engaged on TV, people will eat it up.

You'll be the girl who snagged a Sheridan and looked pretty hot doing it."

She looks perplexed, but deep in her eyes I see something that wasn't there five minutes ago. I see hope.

"Okay. But what then?" she asks.

"We drag it out a while. Hell, Cass, we're having a great time together anyway, right?"

Her brow twists. "Well, yeah, up to last night, but—"

"I'm here till the wedding is over next week. I go back to Chicago. You go back to New York. We let a little time pass. Then you dump me."

"*I* dump *you?*"

I'm pacing now, the plan seeming more plausible as it unfolds in my brain. "Right. You can say I cheated. No, wait." I shake my head. "Then people will go right back to something like 'she deserved it.'" I know how people think. I've been on the receiving end of unintended publicity before—not quite doing something as extreme as this, though.

I take a few more steps toward the window, and rest my arm against the warm pane of glass. The sunshine gives my brain that extra charge it needs. I snap my fingers. "We say I wanted you to give up your career."

"*What* career?"

"What career? You'll get at least a couple commercials off of the publicity we'll get. At least. You'll be on *Dancing with the Stars* if you want it."

She curls her lip. "I don't want it."

"What do you want then?"

She frowns, that overwhelmed look returning to her face as I see the tears welling up in her eyes. "I just want to pick up my foster dogs today, and go back to the way life was before yesterday," she says, her voice small. "But I feel like I can't even leave the house without people pointing at me."

"Cass, I'm going to fix this. Look at me." I cup her cheeks

in my hands. "I'm good at this. This, I can do. I won a lame silver in the Olympics and walked away with two multimillion dollar contracts off of it. I put a spin on things so well I should have been in politics." I plant a kiss on her lips—God, I missed her and it's only been a matter of hours.

"This is completely insane. We can't do this."

"You got a better idea?"

Biting her lip, her eyes look lost as she stares at me. "No, I guess I don't."

I nod, finalizing the details in my head. Didn't Mick have a sister-in-law with connections at CNN? Maybe she'd be a good one to call. I could get any network to cover my interview. But I need someone I can trust on the inside so that I'll have the right person doing it. The last thing we need is a hard-hitter turning the interview into three minutes of Cass and me defending ourselves.

I pull my phone out of my pocket to call Mick, glancing briefly at Cass. "Will Kim take care of Pie for a night or two?"

"Probably."

"Then pack a bag with something suitable for a TV interview while I make a few calls. And hurry up. We've got some dogs to deliver to foster families, in the meantime."

She withers in her seat. "Oh, God, how am I going to show my face today?"

"Well, the dogs won't judge you," I say, grinning at Pie as he gives Cass's leg a lick of affirmation.

CHAPTER 12

~ CASS ~

I should talk him out of this. I should talk *me* out of this.

I'm sitting here on a newsroom soundstage, which is every bit as intimidating as I thought it would be, sweating bullets beneath my cream silk blend sheath dress.

I'm going to pass out any minute, and I just hope it's after they break for commercial.

I've never been to Washington, DC, and certainly never imagined visiting our nation's capital under these circumstances. But the moment Vi Owens-Shey, the sister-in-law of Mick Riley, greeted me, I knew we were in good hands.

"You're being interviewed by Meredith Esslinger," she'd said in a brusque manner that somehow fits her as she walked us down the long hallway. "She's easily our softest on-air personality. That's why I insisted on her. She won't push any kind of agenda on you or participate in some kind of public flogging. She just does fluff pieces. So when he pulls out that ring, I guarantee she'll get all weepy. She's overly emotional—it's kind of her shtick. And when she gets weepy during an interview, her publicist will make sure it goes viral. Considering the outcome we're going for, she'll be just what we need."

I had been surprised that Vi had been told the truth. Dylan told me that Logan, Mick, and he decided we should have reinforcements out here who know the truth just in case our plan goes "FUBAR" as Logan called it, which I thought was a military technical term until I found out it stands for Fucked Up Beyond All Recognition.

Like her sister Lacey, Vi is married to a SEAL. According to Logan, that makes them as good as blood.

I can't say I feel comfortable with any of this, but I'm in no position to argue either. In fact, I'm not even in a position to breathe right now, having to remind myself to inhale and exhale every few seconds.

The hot lights glaring down on my face on the set of *Wake Up, Washington with Meredith Esslinger* aren't that different from the ones I've faced during my mediocre modeling career. But it's a whole different ball of wax when I'm expected to actually open my mouth and *talk* rather than just smile for the cameras.

Dylan, however, is a really good talker.

"It's upsetting to me that companies feel like they can put cameras wherever they want, and then leak the video saying it was an accident," he's saying. "In this day and age, when things go viral within minutes—and I think we certainly proved *that* point—companies need to be culpable for their actions."

"So you're saying that the entire thing was staged to make a point?"

Dylan laughs, a low rumble that somehow soothes me. "Well, I'd never say *that* since that would mean I wasn't capable of giving my girlfriend the look of satisfaction that all of America seems to be talking about."

Meredith chuckles in response, and Dylan takes my hand to give it a reassuring squeeze.

"And that's not what I want the public to learn from this," he continues.

"What is it you'd like people to take away from this experience?"

I look at him, just as Meredith does. I'm seriously curious as to what he'll answer. The guy talks more like he's ready to run for President.

"I want companies to remember that we live in a different era from anything our nation has ever experienced. They need to question where and when they use cameras. The goal of surveillance and security should be to keep people safe. Not to catch people at inopportune moments, so that some rogue employee can make some kind of profit by releasing unauthorized footage. In this age, it spreads too quickly and can't be undone. I've got a webpage, a Facebook page, and 1.1 million Twitter followers. As Dylan Sheridan, I have the chance to set the record straight, to change the public's opinion of me, to tell our side of the story. Other people aren't so fortunate."

Meredith cocks her head. "There are some people who are saying that this was all a publicity stunt."

He holds a hand up slightly. "I won't address what people are saying because people are going to believe what they want to believe. But my bottom line is that companies need to be held responsible for their security decisions now more than ever before."

"Your own company, Sheridan Gyms, as well as your family's development company, JLS Heartland, uses security cameras. Do you want to comment on that?"

"Of course. Our cameras are in full view, because I think

their presence deters crime. And our security personnel go through a rigorous background check. Bottom line: we stand behind our employees. We're here to protect them. We're a family-owned operation and they are part of our family."

He says it in a way that tugs at my heart. Damn, he's good.

"How are you holding up through all this, Cassidy?" she asks me.

I knew she would, because Vi warned me. And I've practiced what I'll say in response at least a hundred times last night. I know my speech verbatim, every word of it written by Dylan.

But I'm reminded now of my fifth grade play when I only had one line, but I still blew it.

My heart is hammering behind my ribcage as I open my mouth, but then I flash my well-practiced smile—the same wholesome one that won me the Halton's Used Car commercial. And I feel some measure of control from it. "I'm holding up pretty well. But all the things that are being said about me online really make my heart break for other people who go through something like this—and there are so many who do—especially kids. They're bullied online, scared to go to school, scared to even turn on their computers to do their homework. And they're innocent kids. I think if I wanted anyone to take something away from this, it's that you can't let what some cowards are saying about you online ruin your life. You just have to move on and not be bothered by it. That's probably why I love working with dogs. They love you no matter what people are saying about you."

Phew. I'm done, leading right into the segue Dylan concocted.

"Cass heads up the foster program at a shelter my family's company just opened," Dylan interjects, just like we had planned.

Hey, if we're going to do this, I figured we might as well put in a plug for our dogs.

"In fact, we've brought a few pictures if you wouldn't mind us sharing," he continues, and I watch a photo of our half-blind foster appear on the monitor in the distance. "This one we named Rooster."

"Rooster?" Meredith laughs. "Funny name for a dog."

"Cass has a thing for old movies. Rooster is named after John Wayne's character in *True Grit* because she's blind in one eye, like his character. The vet says someone either kicked her in the eye or threw a rock at her. They're not sure. She was found in a dumpster trying to protect her pups."

"Ohh…" Meredith reaches for a tissue.

"And this one is Pie."

I watch the photo switch to my foster hound and see the contact information for Allie's shelter scroll at the bottom of the screen as Dylan tells the stories of another few dogs.

I relish the thirty seconds that America is not looking directly at me. But then I see that pesky light come to life on the camera in front of us again and my stomach hits the floor.

But Dylan's still the star of this show, I console myself as he continues, "When my family's company opened the Newton's Creek Animal Shelter last week, Cass volunteered to take over and expand the foster program so that we can start helping dogs in other counties. Eventually, she'd like to take in some from other states."

"How wonderful, Cass." Meredith dabs her eyes with the tissue she reached for at the first mention of a half-blind dog.

It's her shtick, I remember Vi telling us, bringing a smile to my face. I can't resist briefly glancing past the glare of the lights to see Vi standing nearby, a knowing smile on her face.

"That's why Cass is so special to me, Meredith," Dylan says as he turns to me. "She's always doing things like that—

137

inspiring me to try to make a difference in the world, every day. And I'm hoping that she'll be there at my side for what's ahead…"

He pauses for dramatic effect, just like he did when we rehearsed this, and I find myself swallowing. Hard.

Here we go.

"…but not as my girlfriend," he continues, pulling a velvet box from his pocket and getting down on one knee.

"Oh my goodness," I hear Meredith say over the swooshing sound of the blood rushing to my ears as I watch Dylan in front of me. Somehow doing this now, on live TV, is a hell of a lot different from when we practiced it last night at Kim's house.

Cameramen rush across the floor to get a better angle and I hear the producer in the distance saying, "Get a reaction shot… We need a close-up of the ring … Her hands are shaking. Be sure to get that…"

And sure enough, my hands *are* shaking as he takes them in his own and presses a kiss to each one.

"Cass, we've been through so much together. Some good, some bad, but all of it I'm so grateful for—every minute. You bring light to my days and hope to my heart every time I look into those blue eyes of yours. And I can't imagine spending my life without you. So Cassidy Parker, will you do me the honor of being my wife?"

He opens the box and I see the pink pillow-cut diamond that he'd insisted I couldn't look at till this very moment.

"Ohh…" I hear Meredith murmur.

My face is motionless for a brief moment. I knew every word he was going to say, but I had no idea how effectively he'd deliver his line, somehow making all the cameras seem to disappear to me so that all I can see is him.

And a freaking huge pink diamond.

No one's ever asked me to marry him before. It should

depress me that the first time someone does, it's all for show. Yet it doesn't. I'd never planned on letting a relationship reach this point, anyway, and Dylan is so damn good at playing to the cameras, that he's got even *me* so convinced that tears are tracking down my face.

"Yes," I tell him and watch the smile—a fake smile, I remind myself—stretch across his face in response. He kisses me, long and hard.

"Wow. Well, I wasn't expecting that on live TV," Meredith says, blotting her eyes again with a tissue.

He pulls his face from mine, and tenderly traces his finger along my lips, fixing my smeared lipstick. I hear a couple *awws* from people on the soundstage in the distance.

His grin is triumphant as he turns to Meredith. "She said yes!" he says, giving Meredith a high five and hamming it up with a fist pump to the cameras.

He pulls both my hands into his own, and gazes into my eyes lovingly, syrupy sweet, and kisses me again, as Meredith closes the segment and cuts to commercial.

My lips feel cold when his leave mine and I stare at him, dumbfounded.

"Are we off the air?" I whisper.

He nods, leaning forward and whispering in my ear, "Just keep playing it up till we get to Annapolis. America is watching."

And that warm and fuzzy feeling that had resided in my heart just fifteen seconds ago dissipates completely.

We're just faking it, I remind myself. And considering I've never wanted to get married, that thought should calm me.

So, why doesn't it?

We drive our rental car out Highway 50 to Annapolis where Dylan has made reservations at a B & B.

"I really don't know why we're not just catching a flight home this afternoon." I don't mean for it to sound like a complaint, but I know it does. Somehow, I just feel the need to retreat to my normal life, my little room in Kim's townhome where I can hear the soothing sounds of Connor playing Clay Jam on his new iPad in his bedroom next to mine.

For all my bluster in high school about wanting fame and fortune, I'm starting to wonder if I'm even cut out for the fame part of that equation. But I'd never planned on acquiring it with a viral sex video and subsequent fake engagement.

"Honey," he begins, the endearment making my breath catch, "your house is swarmed with photographers right now. Kim and Connor are staying at Ryan's tonight."

"You're kidding me."

"Not in the slightest."

"Kim's going to kill me."

"Maybe. But Connor's already said he's going to spend the next twelve hours in Ryan's pool, so you've got him on your side."

"Connor's always on my side," I say with a smile. I love that kid. A sudden thought occurs to me. "Oh, God, what about Pie?"

"Ryan took him in, too. No worries. And Allie says they got a huge bump in donations this morning. Seems that little plug we threw in about the shelter helped."

"I'm glad." I expel a breath in relief. It's somehow heartening to know that something good might come from this mess. "You were... really good at that proposal thing."

I nearly tell him that he'll blow some lucky girl's mind when he decides one day to do it for real. Yet somehow I can't get the words past my lips because I feel jealous of her —whomever she is.

"I've had people tell me I should do some acting. You know, get a movie or something like the Rock did."

"Why don't you? You've got the Hollywood looks."

"Because I like business too much."

"Really?"

"Yeah. I like the challenge of it—expanding my franchise, making each gym thrive. I like the idea of the jobs I'm bringing to an area and providing a service for people that they really value."

"You're like your dad."

"I am. Though he's never looked at me long enough to realize it."

"What do you mean?"

"It was always Logan. Logan was going to be the one to run JLS after my dad. When Logan decided to go to the Naval Academy, Ryan stepped in. I was just fourteen then, but already I knew I wanted to be at JLS. I'd go there some-times after school and I loved it—loved watching Dad crunch numbers and plan projects and race off to meetings. I wanted it. But no one even looked twice at me. And I was young, so I never spoke up."

"And you still haven't?"

He shrugs. "Ryan runs that business well. I kind of thought once I started showing how good I was at building a business with my gyms, someone might ask me to play some kind of role at JLS. But even when Dad got diagnosed, it was Logan Ryan turned to. Not me. They just see me as a gym rat. Not a businessman."

"That's not true at all."

"It's definitely true. You just haven't hung around my family enough yet to see it."

"Well, maybe your brothers feel that way, but definitely not your father."

"Cass, it's sweet of you to defend him. But it's really fine. I'm cool with it. I've built my own company and it might not be the family empire that JLS is, but it's something I'm proud of."

"No, no, no. Listen to me, Dylan. Your dad doesn't think that at all. He told me so." That finally gets his attention.

"When?" he asks, brow furrowed.

"When he was having his—spell or whatever you want to call it. He said that his other sons would—how did he put it? Fall in line, that was it. They'd fall in line. But not you. He said you were like him. You'd make your own way in the world."

"You're serious?"

"I wouldn't kid about this. I remember it perfectly because I was so scared right then—really listening to every word he said, hoping he'd give some kind of indication that his memory was coming back."

"He said I was like him?"

"Yeah. Or that you took after him. I think those were his exact words."

Falling silent, he still looks incredulous as we exit off Highway 50 onto Rowe Boulevard and head over a narrow waterway called Weems Creek on a bridge dedicated to a fallen SEAL, Special Warfare Operator 1st Class Patrick Feeks.

The sign bearing his name seems more like a statement to me—not just a memorial to a brave man. But rather, a message that we're now entering a town that doesn't forget its military.

Where I grew up outside Kansas City, we were a few miles away from Fort Leavenworth, a huge Army base. But since I left, I'd kind of forgotten what it's like to be in a town that has such a strong military presence. It's as though the people in towns like this have a higher stake in the game than others. There are a few more flags flying. More people stand perfectly erect when they hear the *National Anthem* at a baseball game rather than sending a text or taking a selfie. And I remember the yellow ribbons—so many of them during my teen years—tied tightly and proudly around trees in our neighborhood.

I guess since I was so miserable in my hometown, I never really thought about the good aspects of living there.

We approach the State House with its classic symmetry and regal façade, and I'm already enchanted by this town. I hadn't quite understood why Dylan would insist on driving thirty minutes to stay in Annapolis when we could have stayed right in DC, until my eyes take in the brick-paved streets and historic buildings. Even the streetlamps look like they were plucked from a storybook and plopped in front of my eyes.

Then I see the water in the distance, and I'm sold. Being landlocked in the Midwest most of my life, I have an appreciation for the water that really can't be matched.

"Is that the Chesapeake Bay I see?" I ask.

"Actually that's the Severn River. But you can see the Bay when we get closer to the shore."

We pull into a parking spot behind a B & B on a quiet street that looks like a film set in Colonial times.

"We're just steps away from the Academy," he tells me. "I'll give you a little tour before we head over to Mick and Lacey's. They've got some Maryland crabs in your honor. And knowing Mick, he'll have some steaks on the barbeque, too."

"They really didn't need to go to any trouble. We could have gone out."

He shakes his head. "You have no idea how much our

engagement is trending right now. If we're going to get any peace while we eat, we'd best stick with eating at Mick and Lacey's."

I'm not sure what he means until we walk through the door of the bed and breakfast and the innkeeper beams, hugging us, wishing us her congratulations.

"That was the most beautiful thing I've seen on TV in a long time," the woman says. Mildred, I think she said her name was—but I couldn't quite hear it past the squeal she made announcing our arrival.

"You looked so lovely on TV, dear," she continues. "A classic beauty. Just like Grace Kelly."

I like this woman already.

"And you're pretty much marrying a prince, just like she did," she prattles on as we follow her up the stairway to our room.

I smile, sharing an amused look with Dylan as she opens the door, and knowing that with his ignorance of Hollywood's Golden Age, he has no idea what this woman is talking about.

CHAPTER 13

- DYLAN -

"She's nice." Mick tells me, cracking a mallet against the last crab on our paper covered table and peeling away a chunk of shell. "Are you sure this engagement is really fake? I mean, you guys seem to really get along well."

I watch Cass stretched out in an Adirondack chair down at the water's edge talking to Lacey while they enjoy the view of Spa Creek. My heart stirs with a now familiar feeling that I seem to get whenever I see her. I don't know what to call it. Possessiveness, maybe. Or just the innate desire to spend every moment I have with her.

The bridge is up in the distance, and a swarm of sailboats are headed our way returning from the Friday night "beer can" races. Our eyes meet briefly as she glances backward, and I somehow know she's talking about me.

I wonder what she's saying, and hope it's not regret she's confessing to the new friend she's found in Lacey. I've been looking in her eyes all day, wondering if she's already planning her exit strategy from this whole mess. She could let the dust settle this week and then break it off with me the moment I leave for Chicago after Ryan's wedding. She'd probably bounce back just fine at this point—or even better than before. She was a hit during our interview, with those sympathetic blue eyes of hers as she talked about kids dealing with bullies online. Throw in her work for the dogs and she's gone from the sullied princess to America's sweetheart.

I wonder if she knows it yet.

"She *is* nice," I finally reply. "But it's all for show. That break room sex thing—God, that was all my fault. I had to figure out some way to fix it."

"Taking one for the team, are you?"

I shrug. "I hardly can say pretending to be engaged to Cass is taking one for the team. She's pretty much everything I could ask for in a woman." I'm stunned that I said that out loud.

"Oh, *really?*"

"Well, yeah. She's pretty. Smart. Good with kids. Has a great heart—seriously, I've never met anyone who wants to help other people so much. And her commitment to those dogs…" My voice trails as I see her laugh at something Lacey says.

"Sounds to me like it's the real thing, then."

"It's not. It can't be. I've only known her—well, like a week now. In fact, yeah, if I don't count when I met her at the wedding—"

"Since I can't imagine you remember much about the wedding," Mick interjects.

"—then it's been exactly a week today."

"Hey, Lacey! It's their one-week anniversary," Mick calls out to his wife, who had to escape from the profuse smell of

Old Bay seasoning in the air from the crab feast on their back deck. He raises his bottle of root beer in her direction and she raises her can of ginger ale in response.

"I feel horrible making her sit out there." I frown.

"Don't worry about it. We had no idea the smell would set her off."

"Yeah, but she didn't even eat any crabs. You didn't have to get them if she can't eat them."

"We wanted Cass to get the whole Annapolis experience. You can't get that without cracking open a few crabs. Besides, she thought she could eat them while she's pregnant. That's what one website said. But then she saw another site that said she couldn't. And then another that said she could. And still another that said she couldn't. It's a pain in the ass. As soon as she thinks she's doing something right, then there's some headline that says she's doing it all wrong. It'll be easier after the baby's born."

I swallow my laugh, remembering all that Ryan's gone through with his daughter. But I don't dare warn him. Let Mick live in blissful ignorance for a few more months.

I toss a chin in the direction of his root beer, knowing he's more of a Sam Adams kind of a guy. "No beer for you while it's off limits for her?"

"If she can't, I don't really feel right drinking in front of her."

I crease my brow, glancing at the girls down by the water. "Do you think she minds that Cass is having wine tonight?"

"Hell no. That poor girl needs a drink or two. When you came in here, she looked completely shell-shocked."

"You noticed that, too? It's kind of a slam to my ego, you know? Is getting engaged to me really that painful?"

Laughing, Mick shakes his head as he wads up the thick brown paper stained with Old Bay covering their deck table. "You took one too many blows in the fight cage, Dylan."

"What's that supposed to mean?"

He mashes the paper into a trash bag and ties a tight knot at the end. "It means that her being shell-shocked is coming from all this attention. Not from the engagement. You're used to it. She's not."

"Nah. She was a model in New York."

"Oh, come on, Dylan." He disappears momentarily into the house and then reappears with a spray cleaner in his hand. "I'm not sure what she did or didn't do in New York, but it's probably hell-and-gone from what she's going through right now. Have you turned on the news at all today? I'd bet my paycheck that your little performance this morning is playing in seventeen different languages right now. She's just overwhelmed."

"You're right. I just kind of thought that since she wanted to make it big in modeling that she'd lap up this kind of attention." I tug a handful of paper towels off the dispenser and help him wipe down the table. I glance Cass's way again, thinking about how different she is from what I'd initially assumed about her, and just how much I like the woman she turned out to be.

"Take some time, Dylan, the two of you. And for God's sake, don't go staging some damn breakup till you figure out whether you might be right for each other. You've got that *thing* between you. It's unmistakable."

"That thing?"

"Yeah, that *thing*. In the military, I see a lot of couples come and go. High divorce rate, you know? But the ones that make it—I don't know—you can just tell. There's this thing between them. A spark. No, more like a certain energy between them." He shakes his head. "I don't know. It's just a thing. Like Lacey and me. Although with her short fuse since getting pregnant, I wouldn't be surprised if she's over there with Cass plotting my demise for something I've done wrong today."

"Ouch. That bad?"

"Yep. Hates me one minute, loves me the next, and crying regardless. Goddamn nightmare for her."

"And for you."

"Hell, I got the easy part of the deal." He tosses another wad of paper towel in the recycle bin. "Anyway, ask anyone and they'd tell you that they knew from the start Lacey and I were going to make it for the long haul." He turns to call out to his wife. "The place is scent free again, honey."

Cass rises first and extends a hand to Lacey to help pull her up out of the low chair. She's not really showing yet, but said she swears the extra pounds she's put on so far are making her back ache.

When she makes it to the deck, Mick leans in to kiss his wife. "Clean as a whistle," he tells her.

She takes a sniff of the air and gives an approving nod. "My hero," she tells him and turns to me. "I'm sorry I had to run off like that, Dylan. I never know what smells I can handle."

"Doesn't bother me in the least. Are you sure you ate enough? You barely had a bite of your steak."

"I'm fine. I'll grab a couple Pop-Tarts before I go to bed. They seem to be the only thing I can keep down these days." She glances at Cass. "So, Cass says my sister took good care of you guys this morning."

"The best. Vi definitely knew who'd do the right kind of interview."

"Added bonus that Meredith let us put in a plug for my dogs," Cass chimes in.

Lacey laughs. "Vi's had her own troubles with social media and things going viral in the past. I knew she'd make sure she found the right person to fix this." She swirls the ginger ale in her glass the same way she might a fine vintage of wine. "What are you guys going to do now?"

"What do you mean?"

"I mean, if Cass isn't working in Ohio anymore, maybe she'd be smart to get back to New York. She's a household name right now. Get back in her agent's face. Strike while the iron is hot, as they say."

I look at Cass. I hadn't really considered that she might want to head straight back to New York. Even though I had plans to return to Chicago, I'm having a hard time wrapping my mind around the idea of Newton's Creek without Cass in it.

"No, definitely not yet," she says, bringing me relief. "I've just started taking in new dogs. I don't want to leave until I have the program ready to be taken over by someone else. My agent left me a message this afternoon that my used car commercials are going to start running again. So I'll get some residuals off those. And I've got enough in my savings that I'll be able to cover my rent for a month or two without my princess paycheck."

I bristle automatically. "I'm not letting you tap into your savings, Cass. That's for those online college courses you said you take."

"And for emergencies. I think this classifies as an emergency," she replies with a shrug.

"Cass, I'll cover your expenses," I tell her.

Horrified, she looks at me. "Dylan, I don't want you covering my expenses. I don't take hand-outs."

"It's not a hand-out. You're my fiancée. You're a *Sheridan* fiancée, for God's sake. You don't need to blow through your money because I got you fired."

"I'm not your *real* fiancée, and you didn't get me fired. I'm the one who started it in the break room."

"And I'm the one who should have stopped it."

Lacey grabs Mick's arm and tugs it around her waist. "Isn't this cute, baby? Their first fight."

My eyes narrow at Lacey, pregnant or not. But then I let my expression soften figuring I need her on my side. "Will *you* tell her, Lacey? Maybe she'll listen to a woman."

She pats her belly. "And I'm definitely feeling all-woman these days. But really I wouldn't worry about the money, one way or the other. Cass, you're famous now. I could see you getting an offer for a dog food commercial off this because of that plug you gave your dogs today. Or maybe a jewelry ad— like Tiffany's or something—because wow, that's quite a ring you showed off this morning. I mean seriously, Dylan, a *pink* diamond? She's making mine look like it came out of a Cracker Jack box in comparison. No offense, honey," she finishes with a teasing smile to Mick, obviously trying to draw the ire of her husband.

He pulls her closer, wrapping both his arms snug around her waist. "Oh, I'm making you pay for that one," he tells her, planting a firm kiss against her lips while I roll my eyes.

"I hope so," Lacey murmurs against his mouth.

Cass and I look at each other awkwardly while their mouths are joined.

I silently count one… two… three… four…

"Okay, guys, if you wanted us to leave, you just had to say so," I butt in.

Still with his mouth securely affixed to his wife's, Mick waves us on.

I crack a smile. They've got that *thing* Mick was talking about. They've got it in spades.

CHAPTER 14

~ CASS ~

My coffee is piping hot when it touches my lips, as I listen to the clanging of the halyards from the boats docked in Annapolis Harbor a few blocks away. I can see the tips of their masts, moving ever so slowly back and forth in the breeze, as I sit here on the rooftop terrace of our B & B.

My mouth sinks into another bite of the cappuccino chocolate chunk muffin that I have on the table in front of me. I take great pains to not look at the butter shimmering on the bottom of the muffin, or the chocolate oozing onto the plate as I savor the taste of total indulgence on my tongue.

Do I always deprive myself of the things I like? Hadn't Dylan once asked me that? I remember it so clearly, like every moment I spend with Dylan. Well, I'm certainly not depriving myself now, even though I can picture every fat calorie going straight to my hips.

Surely Dylan and I have worked off at least a muffin or two these past several days.

Not last night, though. We had crashed into the lush bed coverings with crab on our breath and Old Bay seasoning still underneath our fingernails, and fell asleep in each other's arms fully clothed. I don't think either of us had slept much since that fateful call from HR, and even as I opened my eyes at the late morning hour of eight, Dylan still slept soundly. I watched him for more than an hour before I rose from the bed, my eyes becoming more and more accustomed to the sight of him sleeping next to me.

I felt myself wondering—wishing for something that I can't quite even name—till the smell of coffee brewing downstairs thankfully pulled me back to reality.

"I knew I'd find you up here."

I hear Dylan's voice behind me.

"Oh, no. Did I wake you up when I left the room?" I ask.

"No. It's not like me to sleep this late, anyway. Can I have a bite?"

"Mmhm. Cappuccino chocolate chunk made fresh this morning. I think I want to retire in a B & B."

I watch his mouth as it devours a small piece of it. His lips never fail to mesmerize me; they are so perfectly shaped for kissing, so faultlessly soft every time I feel them on my skin. He sits on the cushioned chaise lounge beside me.

"You're facing the wrong way," he tells me. "You can see the chapel dome at the Academy from here."

I turn slightly. "Is that what that is?"

"Yep. Here." He pats the cushion in front of him as he moves his legs to straddle either side of the chaise. "Come sit with me."

A smile spreads across my face, after hoping he'd give me some reason to join him there on that lounge. I sink into his embrace, his chest at my back, and look out at the dome in the distance.

"I can see why you and Logan love it here."

"The buildings are all so old and the history runs deep. You don't get that in Newton's Creek. But it's just similar enough—the people, the quaintness, the character of it—that it feels like home. And the water is gorgeous. I mean, I know Logan always says San Diego is his favorite city. But God, it's really hard to top Annapolis in my book."

"Have you ever been to San Diego?"

"Just once. When Logan was stationed there and he got some leave, Ryan and I met him there and we took the drive up the coastline together, up past San Francisco and then on to the Redwoods for backpacking. But we didn't really spend much time in San Diego. I mostly just remember the airport. If it's anything like the rest of the coast there, it must be pretty spectacular." He stretches his legs in front of him, while pulling me closer onto his lap. "Annapolis is a hell of a lot easier to get to from Newton's Creek, though."

I feel his deep intake of breath behind me and his lips caress the skin just below my ear. I purr unconsciously at the sensation, sinking more into his embrace, his thick arms wrapped around me so protectively it makes my heart heat from the inside out.

A seagull cries out in the distance, almost hauntingly, over the stillness of the morning.

Against my back, I can feel his heartbeat and it soothes me, like always. How is it that Dylan's presence seems to calm me and excite me at the same time?

"I could really see my brothers and me chipping in on a house together here one day, like Lacey suggested. Maybe coming out here every once in a while just to spend some time as a family away from the usual scenery. It would do us all some good. Force us to take some time away from work. Especially Ryan."

"What does your dad think of the idea?"

He shrugs. "I think he's like Ryan. The coastline just doesn't call to him."

"And your mom?"

"Oh, Mom would just love to see us get a place together, wherever it is. I think she worries now that Ryan and Logan are working together that they'll forget how to play together, you know? She thinks they work too hard."

"Like you do."

He sweeps my hair away from my neck with his fingers. "I don't think my family really thinks I work at all. They just think I'm doing bench presses all day or something." He brushes his lips against my neck, setting a million butterflies free in my stomach.

Hearing the sarcasm in his voice, I laugh. "I think a vacation home is a great idea. I can't imagine it, though."

"What do you mean?"

"You kind of live in a different world from the rest of us. Vacation properties aren't in my vocabulary. In New York, I was lucky to take the Long Island Railroad out to the coast for the day."

"You like the coast up there?"

"Sure. I like the coast anywhere. There's this place where I'd treat myself to a whale watching trip sometimes."

"In *New York City*? Whale watching?"

"I think mostly only locals know about it. It's in Queens— the Rockaways. People come to New York for things other than whale watching, I guess. But I couldn't get enough of it."

He lifts one of my hands to his lips, and tugs me closer till I feel the warm pressure of his forearms against my breasts. "I need to take you to Hawaii, then. When I was scuba diving off Maui, I could actually hear the whale song in the waters there."

I turn my head partway to look at him. "You're kidding me."

"Nope. Not kidding at all."

I fall silent, enjoying the fantasy that he might take me there one day, even though I know they are just words, kind of like someone might say "Let's do lunch" in passing to someone else. Nothing comes from it.

The morning sun strikes the ring on my finger and it sparkles. I know we're just play-acting. I tell myself that every few minutes so that I don't allow myself to get caught up in this fiction. If all goes well, this whole fiasco will die down in a few days and I'll be able to return to my life—whatever that might be now that I'm unemployed. And regrettably, he'll return to his, far away from me.

He must have noted how the diamond has caught my eye because he whispers, "Did I pick out a good one?"

A laugh escapes me. "Good isn't quite the right word for a diamond like this, Dylan. Overboard is more like it. It's gorgeous." I stop myself from thanking him for it, or even for having put any thought into it. I don't want him to think I have any trace of hope that I'll be keeping it.

"Well, I'm just a go-big-or-go-home kind of guy." He takes my hands in his, covering up the stone. "Have you ever been engaged before?"

"No. No way. I don't want to get married, so why would I get engaged?"

I feel him nod behind me.

"Ah, yes, I remember you said something about that before. Why don't you want to get married?"

I giggle. "Because I practically just met you."

"You know what I mean. And you're evading the question," he points out.

He has no idea how right he is. "Hmm... Why don't I want to get married?" I say, stalling. "My parents are divorced. I guess that's why."

I feel him shrug behind me. "So what? Plenty of people with divorced parents still want to get married. Why not you?"

"Maybe, but my parents didn't get divorced quickly enough, I guess. They just argued all the time. Nearly every night. And I'd sit on the top stair at night and listen to them go at it."

"I'm sorry."

"Oh, it's no big deal. Kids survive a lot worse, so I can't complain. If I'd been smart, I would have just gone to my room and shut the door. Ignored it. But I couldn't. I always felt compelled to sit there listening, night after night, year after year, because I was convinced that things were suddenly going to change between them. Like, all of a sudden, they'd look into each other's eyes and remember why they fell in love in the first place. I wanted to hear it." I shake my head, forcing a laugh. "I watched too many movies as a kid. Always a happy ending, you know?"

"You were a romantic."

"Yeah, I guess I was."

"Are you still?"

"Obviously not, since I have no intention of getting married. Look at the stats. It's pretty much a coin flip whether or not it will stick."

"You let your friends take the chance," he points out.

"Of course. Let them have hope." I let my back sink into his firm chest as I listen to the halyards clanging in the distance again. "So, what about you? You don't seem the type who's anxious to take the plunge either."

"God, no. For me, though, I think it's the opposite reason."

"What do you mean?"

"My parents stayed together. They had their share of arguments, but always managed to work things out. My dad was gone so much, but I'd bet my life he never even considered cheating on her. That's not what Sheridans do, you know? And same goes for my mom. She wouldn't have ever strayed. They made what little time they had together somehow count enough to stick it out all these years. Mom could have left him anytime and walked away with half of everything, but she never did. And now, with all he's going through, they're just tighter than ever, so damn determined to enjoy every bit of happiness they can before he slips away from us." His voice trails as he shifts in his seat, adjusting his arms around my waist.

"That should make you *want* to get married, I'd think."

"It should, yeah. But then I see the type of woman I always end up with."

"Watch it, buddy," I warn.

He laughs. "Before you, Cass. You know that. They've always had their eye on my bottom line. Always trying to get their faces in the press. Always dumping me in some kind of a way that will make headlines. Geez, the last girl cheated on me with the guy who beat me out for a gold way back, and went to the press about it before she even confessed it to me. It was all to get her name in the tabloids."

"'Natalya Goes for the Gold,'" I say. "Yeah, I saw that headline. That was pretty vile."

"And it happens every time. I think once they figure out that we're not headed toward the altar, they just decide to milk our dying relationship for what it's worth."

Frowning, a realization sets in. "And you want *me* to dump *you*?"

I feel his shoulders rise and fall carelessly behind me. "Sure. Why not? Everyone else does."

I shake my head. "I'm not going to do it. You're going to have to dump me."

"Cass, it'll be better for you that way. Believe me. I know the way the public thinks in these situations. Tell them I wanted you to give up your career. It's the cleanest way. And you'll be able to keep any gains you've made in your career."

I laugh at that thought. "You mean I get to see my used car ads running for the next ten years?"

His chuckle behind me vibrates against my back. "Oh, your phone will be ringing. Just wait till Monday, Cassidy Parker."

His arms wrap tighter, easing upward from my waist to my breasts again, making my breath catch from the alluring pressure of his forearms against me, so tight, so protective.

"Now let's stop talking about our break up and start enjoying our temporary engagement, Cass. You know, I've never been around someone who wasn't trying out the Sheridan last name after the first date. It's kind of refreshing."

"Cassidy Parker Sheridan. Yeah, I really don't want the same initials as Child Protective Services."

He laughs, and then falls silent as we listen to the tranquil sounds of the harbor for a few minutes of blissful peace. All thoughts leave me. All worries dissipate into the slightly salty air gusting in over the brackish water of the Bay.

"I don't want to go home."

His confession behind me somehow strengthens me, just knowing that he feels the same way I do.

"Me neither," I reply. "Things are so much simpler here in Annapolis." Barely anyone recognized me when we took a late night stroll down Main Street last night, and caught the water taxi over to Eastport for a quick drink at a pub on the other side of the creek.

Granted, Dylan and I were wearing baseball caps at the

time (they seem to be part of an unspoken dress code in this town). But in Newton's Creek, there will be no hiding from people, hat on my head or not. "I'm not sure what I hate more. Lying to people about our engagement, or the idea that half of them saw me have sex with you."

"Oh, don't worry too much about what people in Newton's Creek are thinking," he replies. "Everyone's going to be so focused on Kim and Ryan's wedding when we get home, they'll barely notice us. The damn thing's going to be bigger than their annual Buckeye Festival. Besides, we'll be busy with wedding stuff. We'll have dinner at my parents' tomorrow, last minute fittings, bachelor and bachelorette parties, rehearsal din—"

I hold my hand up. "Wait a sec. Did you say we're going to dinner at your parents tomorrow?"

"Yeah."

My chin tucks close to my chest. "You want me to go to dinner at your parents," I deadpan.

"Of course."

I shake my head. "Oh, God, Dylan. I can't do that. I can't face them right now."

"Why not?"

Turning, I raise my eyebrows at him.

"Cass, they didn't watch the video. I guarantee it. Seriously, they are so used to me being in the tabloids for things —most of which I never did, by the way. It all kind of rolls off of them at this point."

"It's not just that, Dylan. It's this." I lift my hand and waggle my ring finger at him.

"Don't worry. I told them we're just doing it to distract the press for a while. That's what you wanted, right?"

"Well, yeah. I told my parents the truth, too. But *your* parents must think I'm trying to trap you into marriage or something."

"They don't think that. Believe me, they've probably thought that about plenty of the women I've dated. But not with you."

"Why not?"

He laughs. "Because even though you have a knack for getting into trouble with me, it's pretty obvious your heart is in the right place." His arms squeeze me. "Look, I won't force you to go. But I'd really like you to go. And Allie and Kim will be there, so I know they'd want you there, too."

His body heat against me somehow mollifies me, lulling me into compliance. "Okay. You're a hard man to refuse."

He kisses my neck again. "Oh, really? I'm banking on that."

I giggle as I feel his fingers on my chin, turning my head. He adjusts himself so that his mouth can meet mine. Savoring the pressure of his lips, his kiss sears me, brands me as his and his alone, even though my mind resists the idea.

A rush of desire consumes me, forcing me to somehow acknowledge that I have never—nor will ever—experience this strong of a reaction to anyone else. After years of proclaiming I'd never hope for something lasting from a man, I should fight this undeniable feeling of addiction I have toward him. My soul should clamor against it. But just as it seems poised to, it simply melds with his, allowing myself to be completely owned by Dylan Sheridan.

"What time is our flight home?" I ask, reminding myself of the reality that awaits us. Up here on the roof, it's so easy to forget.

"Three o'clock. We're flying home out of Baltimore, so it shouldn't take long to get to the airport."

I glance at the watch on his arm. "Enough time to remind ourselves how we got into this mess?" I ask playfully, desperately wanting to enjoy the feel of his skin against mine again.

It's been too long, and with all that has happened since then, it seems even longer.

I feel him throb against my back the moment the words slip from my mouth.

"That can be arranged."

I follow him back to our room and sink into the bed coverings as he bolts the door behind us. The click of the lock sends a tingling down my spine, knowing how badly I want him right now.

I'm desperate to lose myself in him before we return to the reality waiting for us in Newton's Creek. I want to lose my mind to that heady blur of passion when he's inside of me, forgetting everything except how glorious it feels to be touched—to be taken—by this man.

I've stripped myself bare by the time he joins me in the bed.

"So, I don't get the pleasure of disrobing you this time?" he asks, mischief in his eyes as he cups my breasts and gives a gentle squeeze.

"Guess you're not quick enough," I tease.

In a flash, he's whisked me into his arms and has me in some kind of wresting hold on the bed, demanding my submission. "Not quick enough?" One eyebrow rises in challenge. "That's what I was told kept me from the gold medal."

"Aww," I say, raising my lips to the hard planes of his chest to kiss him through the fabric of his shirt as he holds me down. "Poor baby. I hope I didn't hit a sore spot."

I can feel his cock pulse against me at my core, and even though he's still fully clothed, my legs instinctively open.

"Not at all. I'll just have to prove you wrong."

I giggle as his hand wraps around both of my wrists, anchoring me to the mattress, as his other hand tugs his shirt half off. He switches hands, then pulls his body free of the cotton and I'm rewarded with an eyeful of chest. My mouth waters for him, and I stretch my neck upward to trace the outline of his pecs with my tongue.

His hand fumbles with his shorts now, pulling himself free of them and his boxers much more easily than he did with his shirt, and I can feel the hardness of him against me.

Moisture and heat pools between my legs, full of reckless desire, and my breath quickens as my back arches, legs lifting to his hips automatically.

Eyes slamming shut, I can only feel—not see—his mouth take in my breast, the suction of the sensation making my nipples harden. A moan escapes me, raw with need and I struggle to escape his hold, wanting desperately to reach for him—to slip him inside of me where I'm aching for penetration.

His mouth moves to my other breast as his cock presses against me. I thrust upwards, pleading for him.

I open my eyes when I feel his one hand move to the nightstand, reaching for a condom. I can't help the smile that slides up my face.

"You can't do *that* while you hold me down," I advise him.

His eyes flash with challenge. "Oh, can't I?"

I gasp as he lifts my torso slightly, bending my arms behind me and then locking them at my waist with his leg. Just to spite him, I try to free myself from his hold, and sputter when I can't. Damn, he's going to have to teach me some of these wrestling moves, I'm thinking as he sheaths himself easily now that he has two hands free.

"Impressive," I say when I find myself on my back again, his grip on my wrists as he plunges into me.

I angle myself to take him in fully, and then see a flash of weakness in him when I feel him throb inside me. I squeeze his cock with my channel, making his breath catch, weakening him further.

Seizing the opportunity, I slide my hands out of his hold

and push his shoulders till he's on his back beneath me. "But I have a few moves of my own," I laugh when his eyes widen with surprise.

"No fair."

"Completely fair. You got distracted," I tell him, riding him, seeing his face turn from resistance to complete satisfaction. A flood of sensation overtakes me as I fill myself with his length, watching the taut contours of his chest rise and fall beneath me as he breathes.

For all my talk about preferring the man on top, I'm second-guessing myself, enjoying the sensation of overpowering a man like Dylan. All his dominance and virility seem to be at my disposal as I slide him in and out of me, letting my breasts brush against him. My hair breezes along his shoulders, and I move my lips to his.

The kiss he offers me is ravenous, exploring me voraciously as I trace his teeth with my tongue, feeling greedy myself.

My movements quicken as he angles his hips upward, the point where we're joined teasing me each time I take him in deep. I hold him at my innermost depth, savoring the pressure of him at my clit, seeking to only satisfy myself. Selfishness assails me, my neck and back arching as I pull my mouth from his and whimper. My breasts thrust forward and he sucks my nipple hard into his mouth again, nipping me, his teeth grazing against my skin in the most tantalizing way.

Slowly, I pull myself off of him again, and instantly, the emptiness consumes me. I drop down on him, feeling the need for more of our complete joining.

The orgasm toys with me, just out of reach, and I grind myself firmly against him, rocking my hips—when he shifts suddenly. His cock slams against my G spot and I cry out, my muscles pulsing and chest heaving.

Fireworks blast in the darkness of my tightly closed eyes as my body exploits his, using every inch of his length inside me to fan the flames of my indulgence till I sink on top of him, satiated.

Still rock-hard inside of me, he nudges me tenderly onto my back again, seeming to take pity on my completely boneless state. He's gentle now, moving inside of me, and I'm grateful for it as my body recovers.

"I totally won that round," I whisper as he slides in and out of me. My eyes are still shut, but I can feel his smile beam down on me.

"And *I* totally let you win."

"Did not."

"Did to," he counters as my eyes pop open, and I can feel my body start to ride each wave of pleasure he offers me.

His pace quickens as he sees the life return to me, the desire build in me again. Painfully hard, his cock is poised for release and I arch my hips to accommodate his large size.

I watch him thrust inside of me, his eyes shut now, lost in sensation like I was only moments ago. And I feel myself join him on that ride of ecstasy, spiraling upward. Higher and higher, I climb, my pulse thundering in my ears till I feel my soul free-falling as he shatters inside of me.

My body quakes as I cry out, till all that is left is a low shudder from deep inside me as every muscle goes slack in my body.

Still above me, braced by his forearms, he smiles into my half-cloaked eyes.

"For the record," he says with a hint of smugness, "I'd lose to you, any day."

CHAPTER 15

~ CASS ~

I touch the red button on my iPhone and end the call with my mom, my blood pressure still teetering on the brink of dangerous.

If I shut my eyes right now and listen to the sound of the waters of Newton's Creek flowing over rocks behind Kim's townhome, I can almost pretend that I'm back in Annapolis, enjoying the ambiance of Spa Creek in Lacey and Mick's backyard.

I wish I were there right now, seeming so distant from reality.

"Come here right now and look at this," Kim calls into me through the screen door.

I throw back the rest of my coffee and step inside.

Sitting at the counter alongside her, I stare at an enormous number on her computer.

"What am I looking at?" I ask.

"That, my dear, is the total amount of donations that have come in since that free commercial you kindly arranged for us on national TV."

"It wasn't a commercial. We just figured showing a few cute dogs might help."

She taps her screen where the number is, leaving a slight fingerprint. "Oh, baby, did it ever help. Do you know how many spay and neuter surgeries this is going to cover? Not to mention dog food. And vet care—God, that heartworm positive dog we just pulled in yesterday will be able to get the treatment he needs and we don't even have to stress over it."

She shuts her laptop. "Look, I know what you're going through has got to be the pits, but it's sure making an impact on our bottom line."

I step back from the counter and pour myself another cup of coffee, black, as usual. God forbid I have an ounce of that sweet creamer that Kim enjoys and have to see it appear on my ass in the form of an unwanted bulge. After indulging in Annapolis, it's time to pay the piper.

I pause before answering. I'm feeling conflicted since even though my life feels like it's in total chaos right now, I wouldn't exactly describe it as "the pits" either. After our brief getaway in Annapolis, there's a part of me that feels almost rejuvenated, as though those gentle breezes blowing over the Bay somehow refreshed my soul.

But she's right. The reality is, I'm wearing a ring I have to return, and pretending to be engaged to a man I can't resist liking... a lot.

"Yeah. This weekend, I got calls from eleven more local families who want to become foster parents," I tell her. "A few of them are stopping by the adoption event today so I can meet them, and I'll do house checks on them this week."

"That's fantastic." She cocks her head slightly, her smile diminishing. "So why do you look so down?"

Sinking into the seat beside her, I can't wipe the frown from my face. "I just got off the phone with my mom again. God, I think my parents are ready to have me committed. First a viral video, then a fake engagement. Now I let it slip to my mom that I'm going to his parents' house for dinner and she's starting to think the engagement is the real deal."

"Hmmm," Kim murmurs evasively.

"What do you mean, 'hmmmm'?"

"What do you mean, what do I mean?" she asks innocently.

"I mean that you sound like you're thinking it's the real deal, too."

Kim tilts her head thoughtfully. "You're getting a little paranoid, sweetie."

"Don't *sweetie* me. I saw that look in your eyes." I shake my head dismissively. "God, this was a mistake. I shouldn't go tonight. I've never let any relationship get to the point of having Sunday dinner at a guy's parents' house. Geez, I didn't even have Sunday dinner with *my* parents. Sunday dinner was usually three separate microwaveable meals and I'd take mine to my room to eat. This is ridiculous. Why am I going tonight? Why can't I seem to say no to this guy?"

The right side of her mouth curves upward, and she stares at me for a long moment.

"What?"

She shakes her head. "I just never thought I'd see this."

"See what?"

"You—freaking out over a man. You're not exactly the type."

"Well, I've never worn a ring on my finger from a guy who has no intention of marrying me. I mean, hell, I've always said I'd never even *get* married and now I'm pretending that it's what I *want*."

"So it's not what you want?" she clarifies.

"No!" I vehemently confirm. "God, no. You know that. Marriage is fine for you and Allie. But you know it's never been in my playbook. This whole thing is completely—" I pause, struggling for the right word. "—FUBAR," I finally finish.

"FUBAR?"

"Fucked Up Beyond All Recognition."

Kim cocks her head. "Is that a Logan term?"

"How'd you guess?"

"He loves his acronyms."

Silent, my lower lip forms a pout.

"Aw, hon. I hate seeing you this way. Look, forget the ring right now. Forget the engagement. Do you like Dylan?"

"Of course. What's not to like?"

"Do you have fun when you're with him?"

"Yeah, I do. I really do."

"Okay, so, someone once told me back when I was dating Ryan that I should just enjoy myself—not stress so much over the future. Just enjoy the day."

"Seize the day. Carpe diem," I mutter sarcastically, curling my lip. "Yeah, that sounds like the kind of bullshit Allie would say."

"Actually, it was you. Not Allie. You fed me that line of bullshit standing right here in this kitchen, and you were right. So just forget about everything else and enjoy the time you have with Dylan. Tonight's going to be a blast. Allie and I will be there. The kids will be there. Anna makes amazing twice-baked potatoes—seriously, you'll love them. And Lord knows you need a few carbs in your life, hon." She drapes her arm over my shoulders and squeezes. "Life is good. You've got a bunch of new foster parent applications in, you're making us a boatload of donations, and your best friend is walking down the aisle in less than a week."

Cringing, I sink my head into my hands. "Ugh, you're

right. You're getting married and I'm sitting here all focused on me. What kind of a friend am I?"

"The best kind. Don't worry about it. You're giving me something to focus on other than all the wedding plans." She gives me an air-kiss—a habit she picked up from yours truly. "Now go upstairs and get ready for the day because it's going to be a good one."

As I trudge upstairs to my room, I ponder how easy Kim makes it all sound. Just enjoy the day. Don't think about the future.

Had I really given her that advice? Stupid of me, if I had. It's impossible not to worry about the future when every cell in my body seems to cry out for his constant presence.

My phone rings beside my bed. I glance over to the display and see his name. Speak of the devil… or an absolute angel considering all he's done for me lately.

"Hey, Dylan," I answer.

"Morning, Cass," he answers—two simple words that somehow have me wishing I could hear them from him every morning for the rest of my life.

Holy crap. What's happening to me?

"I was headed down to Cincy to check on the gym," he says. "Construction is pretty much complete. I'd love to show it off, if you're up for it."

I bite my lip. "I can't. Allie and I decided last night to hold a last-minute adoption event today, since we're getting such great press right now. Someone emailed me about a couple litters of pups found up north, and I don't have enough foster families for them if I can't unload some of my current dogs."

There's a long pause. "Wow. You don't waste any time, do you?"

"I can't. Lives are on the line," I respond, and feel a tinge of pride as the words come out of my mouth. Today, as I look at the next twenty-four hours of my life, I feel like what I will be doing actually matters. That's not exactly something I felt as I cinched on my Buckeye Princess gown every morning, or even back in New York as I'd speed-walk my way down Madison Avenue for another go-see.

I like this feeling.

"Care for some company? I can handle the reporters while you handle the dogs," he offers.

"Oh, I don't think there will be any reporters there this morning. It's just an adoption event."

"They'll be there," he warns.

And it turns out, two hours later as I stand in the heat with two dogs wrapping their leashes around my legs, Dylan was right.

There are three reporters from newspapers in Cincinnati, Dayton, and even one from Columbus, asking Dylan questions and snapping our photos as I try to wrangle dogs and focus my attention on prospective adopters.

Allie is at my side, but Kim is with Ryan and their wedding planner today. We somehow managed to wrangle three more volunteers, though, and with their help, I think we've found possible homes for at least four of our dogs.

If just a handful of these new foster applications come through for me, I'll definitely be able to take in those two litters by mid-week. I savor the satisfaction of it, sweeter even than the smile Dylan sends me as I pack up my backpack with applications at the end of the event.

After dropping Pie off back home (I don't think Pie appreciated the ride in Dylan's tight McLaren as much as I always do), we have enough time to drive to Cincy to take a look at his gym.

It's huge, though he says the next one he's building near Washington, DC, will be even bigger. There are boxing rings and an MMA cage, and plenty of areas for individual workouts. Four large rooms are set to the side for classes. Two of them have mats for sparring.

"Wow," I say under my breath. "It's gorgeous, Dylan."

He smiles. "Gyms always look nice when they're shiny and new like this, don't they?"

"It's not at all like I pictured. When I hear about a gym where a person learns how to fight, I picture something grungy, like in *The Harder They Fall*. You know, Humphrey Bogart." I frown, remembering Dylan's antipathy for black-and-white films. "But I guess you didn't see that."

"No, I missed that one," he replies with a low chuckle. "That's not the kind of atmosphere we're going for. We're family-friendly. Haven't you seen our commercials?"

"Well, sure. But you can't believe what you see in commercials."

"I won't tell Halton's Used Cars that you said that."

I giggle, my breasts now pressed against his chest as he wraps his arms low on my waist. "Please don't. Their residuals are my sole income right now."

His lips meet mine, and a purr escapes me. With the gym completely empty, all I can hear is the whir of the loud air conditioning unit and my heartbeat thumping in my ears as my tongue teases his.

If we weren't headed straight to his parents from here, I swear I'd toss him down on one of these mats and have my way with him.

From the ridge of him pressing against my belly, I'm pretty sure he's feeling the same way. His hands trace up my back to the base of my neck, tunneling into my hair.

With a sharp inward breath, he pulls himself a couple inches from my mouth. "Unless you want to make headlines again, we better stop this."

"What do you mean?"

He nudges his chin to the left and I glance in that direction, seeing a security camera aimed right at us.

I burst out laughing. "No, I think we better let things die down a bit before we get ourselves into *that* kind of trouble again."

After we hit the road, he holds my hand for most of the drive to his parents' house.

"Stop looking so nervous," he scolds me as we approach Newton's Creek. "I told you they didn't watch the video. To them, you're still the girl who came to my dad's rescue the other night."

Funny, I'd almost forgotten about that night at Allie's opening. It seems like a lifetime has passed since then. Time certainly speeds up when a girl suddenly finds herself wearing an engagement ring, even if it all is a ruse.

"Oh, come on, Dylan. It doesn't even matter that they didn't see it. They know it's out there. It's embarrassing. Wouldn't you feel a little awkward if you had to meet my parents?"

"You bring up an excellent point. Shouldn't I meet them?"

I furrow my brow. "Who?"

"Your parents."

My back straightens. "Why?"

Glancing at my ring, he shoots me a smile. "Well, according to America, we're engaged."

"Lord, no. I told you—they know we're going to break it off soon."

I can't help noticing the crestfallen look on his face.

"I mean, we are, right?" I add. "And if they did meet you, they might… get attached. You know?" Attached. Like I am. I've caused my parents enough of a headache this past week. I don't want to add to it.

His brow creases. "How soon were you thinking we should break up?"

I shrug. "I dunno," I say, kind of the same way that Connor responds when Kim asks him who left the toilet seat up again.

"You're still having fun, right?"

"Of course."

"Well, then why break it off until it gets... tiresome, you know?" he asks, staring at the road in front of him, looking slightly agitated.

Tiresome. *Ouch*. That word somehow stings. Call me crazy, but I'd rather walk away with a pleasant memory, untarnished by words like "tiresome."

I feel my stubborn pride surge. "I've always been a 'stop while I'm ahead' kind of girl," I say, my voice more curt than it should be.

A trace of irritation flashes in his eyes as he exits the highway, and I immediately regret saying it. Even though it's the truth.

"So, you'd be fine with that. Just breaking it off?"

No. Hell no. But I feel my bottom lip quiver as I say, "I'm going to have to be, aren't I? I mean, we're faking it."

He pulls to the side of the country road and throws the car into park. Turning to me, his eyes blazing with something that looks dangerously close to fury, he stares at me.

"Think I'm faking *this*?" His hand reaches behind my neck and pulls me over without compunction, his kiss searing me to my core. I feel his teeth scrape against my own, as our mouths open completely to each other.

His taste enters me, firing me like the foundry he built with Connor last week, intense enough to melt metal. Goose bumps cascade over my skin as his hands scrape against me, moving from my breasts to my back to pull me closer despite the bucket-like seats of the car.

Devouring each other, we fuse every square inch of our bodies that we can in the confines of the sports car.

His touch is demanding, the harsh caress of his skin against mine making every nerve ending in my body spring to life. One hand kneads the pads of his fingers into my scalp and his other hand touches my cheek. I hear myself moan, a plea for more, as I angle my face to feel more pressure of him against my lips.

Brazenly, my hands explore him, dragging against the planes of muscles of his lower back, tugging at the bottom of his shirt till I feel his warm flesh underneath my fingertips.

I can feel the wellspring of desire building inside of him just as it is in me, and I'm cursing the sunlight that pours into his car, reminding me that I'll have to wait a lot longer before I feel him inside of me.

Heat pools at my center, aching for pressure, for release, but all I end up receiving is a rush of cool air as it strikes my lips when his mouth leaves mine.

I'm panting, bleary-eyed, slapped by the reality that I've become completely dependent on the feelings he brings me.

And that thought terrifies me.

His gaze slices through me. "I'm not faking my reaction to you, Cass. Are you?"

My breath quickens. "No."

Giving an abrupt nod, he says, "Good. Let's go to my parents."

I swallow. He wants to go to his parents *now*, with my body practically trembling from aftereffects of that kiss?

I nearly tell him to turn around. I can't exactly face his parents when I'm eyeball-deep in a flood of hormones. But then he flicks on his signal and we turn into the long driveway leading to the Sheridans' regal home.

The nerves that were sparking with desire only a moment ago suddenly have my palms sweating and my stomach sinking.

"We're here," he says with a smile.

CHAPTER 16

- DYLAN -

After she's handed a glass of one of those sweet Ohio River Valley wines my mom loves so much, I see the worry in Cass's eyes dissipate, and the next kiss I give her—a chaste one this time, considering the company—tastes of pear and apple blossom on her lips.

I don't know what she's worried about. My parents think the world of Cass. Nothing can undo that.

Not even a viral sex video.

As I steal a second helping of Mom's twice-baked potatoes and return to my seat next to Cass, I try to make sense of the upwelling of panic that shot through me when she started talking about breaking things off.

Outside of business, I've never been much of a planner. I tend to fly by the seat of my pants in relationships just because history shows that they are always destined to end, anyway. I suppose the fact that this never bothered me doesn't say much about me.

But the idea of ending things with Cass shakes me. I know we just got engaged to distract the public and hopefully restore her reputation. But I didn't count on ending it so quickly. I could see us prolonging this—me, flying her up to Chicago for a weekend or two, showing her the city. Her, with her feet firmly planted in Newton's Creek now that she's taken a bigger role at Allie's rescue, able to see me when I come to visit my family. And I can picture us meeting in New York City mid-week sometimes, when she's got a commercial or spread to shoot, because whether or not she realizes it, her phone is going to be ringing off the hook next week.

We should keep this going a while. It'll be good for her career, I remind myself. I'm almost able to convince myself that I'd be doing it for her rather than for me, even though I know I'm full of shit.

I glance her way. She, Kim, and Allie are absorbed in a conversation about wedding plans while my mom takes down copious notes about anything that needs her attention before the big day. I find it fascinating how, even with the best wedding planner that money can buy, they still have managed to find a million things that need their personal attention.

Without anything to add to their conversation, my eyes drift to my brothers and Dad.

"The numbers that Anderson sent were impressive," I hear my dad telling Ryan and Logan as my brothers sink their teeth into their racks of ribs. "I can see why you're considering it."

"Considering what?" I can't help asking. Even though my family keeps the inner workings of JLS far out of my reach, I know enough to recognize that Anderson is JLS's Chief Operating Officer.

"Going public," Ryan answers casually.

"*What?*"

"I've had Anderson talking to some financial institutions this past year," Ryan explains. "Not seriously at first, just because Logan came on board and lightened up my load. But with Kim and I getting married, we're talking about… you know, *expanding*."

"Expanding JLS?" I ask, thinking expansion is certainly more in line with Ryan's corporate mindset than the God-awful idea of going public.

What the hell is Anderson thinking?

"No, expanding our…" Ryan stops, darting a look at the kids who seem to be making some kind of igloo structure out of their combined rations of potatoes. He mouths the word "family" to me to complete his sentence.

"Okay, sure." I nod, having fully expected more Sheridans coming down the pike in the next couple years. "That's great. But what has that got to do with going public?"

"JLS is getting too big to continue being family-run."

"It's too much for the two of us. I mean the three of us," Logan quickly amends, darting a look at Dad.

Dad holds up his hands. "You two are running the show now. I'm just along for the ride."

I stare at my father, a man who, just a couple years ago would have had a stroke at the thought of letting JLS go public. "Dad, you've always said you'd keep JLS as a family-run operation. Not give shareholders control of where the company is headed."

"I did. And I spent my entire life in that office because of it. I should have been spending more time with my wife. With my sons. I didn't see it till I'd reached this…" he pauses, "point in my life," he finishes cautiously, glancing at the kids.

I dart a look at Ryan. "But you've been taking the company in a new direction this past year. What about all that talk about building smarter? Being more accountable for the impact we have on communities? Was that all bull—"

I cut myself off when I see Cass's eyes flash toward me from the conversation she's having with her friends and my mom, her look silencing me. She's right. This isn't a conversation to have in front of a couple of kids.

"Was it all for show?" I finish through my teeth.

"No. We'll still have a say in how things are run. We'll be the primary shareholders. But we just won't have all the power anymore. I'll pass off being CEO to someone else."

I swear someone might have to scrape my jaw off the paving stones of the patio right now. "I can't believe you're thinking about doing this." My eyes turn to my father. "Dad? You're seriously okay with this?"

"Son, I don't want any of my boys to make the mistake I did. I think of all the memories I could have made with my family, years after we were financially settled. Memories are precious things, Son. I'd gladly trade in a few zeros on my bank account for more good memories with my children. I have no call to stop them from going public."

"Why do you care, Dylan?" Logan's tone has some bite to it, and I watch Allie's hand move to his knee, reining him in.

"Because it's our name attached to it. Because it was founded by our grandfather." My fingers coil into a fist instinctively—and I swear it's not because I want to punch my brother. It's because I want to grab onto JLS and not let go. "Because for 28 years all I've heard from Dad is that he wanted it to stay in the family."

"Oh, is that why you've been working so hard at JLS all these years?" There's enough sarcasm in Ryan's tone to fill an aircraft hangar.

"Boys, *enough*." My mom's voice slices through this

conversation like a titanium alloy knife. "Anymore talk like this and poor Kim will have second thoughts about marrying into this clan in six days."

"Ooh, I'd rather hear them fight than hear any more talk about the wedding. I think the barbeque sauce isn't mixing well with my nerves," she mutters, holding her stomach.

It's more likely it's the heaps of sour cream and butter my mom puts in her twice-baked potato recipe. But I know enough about women not to tell Kim that when she has a white dress she'll need to fit into at the end of the week.

"You'll be fine," Mom says, patting her knee, "if my boys can focus on being a *help* this week rather than a *hindrance*."

I swear that last word was directed more at me than anyone.

My brothers and I call a truce for the rest of the evening, letting the hours pass in a blur of more wedding talk that has Kim turning a light shade of green, while the kids burn off a sugar high from roasted marshmallows by having a swim in the pool.

Hours later, though, I'm still on edge when I climb into my car, stealing a quick glance at Cass before I turn on the ignition.

"Why didn't you say anything?" she asks immediately.

I *knew* she was going to say something.

"About what?" I ask innocently.

"You told me that you wanted to work at JLS. You've always wanted it. So why don't you step up to the plate now? With you on board, maybe they wouldn't be interested in going public."

I press my lips together silently for at least a minute. My answer will seem childish; I know that already. So I'd rather wait for the subject to change. But I can still feel her eyes on me, awaiting my answer.

"I've worked hard to get where I am, you know? Sheridan

Gyms has pulled a hell of a profit these past few years. I've proved I could be an asset at JLS. But obviously, they'd prefer I keep my nose out of it."

"Maybe they just don't think you *want* to take on any of the work there. You have your own franchise to manage."

I shrug. "I play a role in every new gym that opens, yes. But past that, I bring in some good managers who make sure the gyms are being maintained the way I envisioned. I'm busy, but it's not like I couldn't take on my fair load at JLS."

"So, talk to them."

"I'm not approaching them, hat in hand, Cass. My brothers have always gone after what they wanted. If they wanted me there, I'd hear about it. But they don't. So... fine. End of story."

"But—"

"End of story," I say again, my tenor more definitive. "So did you enjoy yourself this evening?"

She smiles. "I had a great time. You were right about your parents. It never even came up—our little *incident*."

That's a nice way of putting it, I think with a smirk.

"Besides, they're so focused on making sure Kim's wedding goes perfectly," she continues. "They've really turned it into quite a production."

"Well, I feel like Ryan is going a little overboard—turning his wedding into some kind of publicity stunt for JLS."

"Ha! You wouldn't know anything about publicity stunts, would you?" she accuses with a knowing grin.

"True," I admit.

"The pony rides and bouncers are just to make it fun for the kids and all their friends. Not for publicity. And you know how much Connor and Hannah like fireworks. Ryan does nothing halfway when it comes to pleasing them."

"Yeah, but this display will rival the one in New York City

on the Fourth of July." I flick on my turn signal to head toward Cass's, and she darts a look toward me.

"Dylan, why are you turning?"

"Because this is the way to your place."

She grins. "Turn around. Kim said she'd let Pie out for me tonight. I thought we'd go back to your hotel."

A smile sweeps across my face. "Oh, really?"

"Yeah. I'm like Connor and Hannah. I like fireworks, too."

CHAPTER 17

~ CASS ~

I'm feeling indulgent as the scent of champagne and berries lingers in the air of Dylan's hotel suite with a dramatic score playing from his TV as Errol Flynn and his band of merry men storm the castle.

Still naked after lovemaking, I roll my head onto Dylan's chest and watch the expression on his face instantly transform from bored out of his mind, to one of mild amusement.

He hates it.

How can anyone hate *The Adventures of Robin Hood*?

"You hate it," I say in sullen disbelief.

His head sunken into a pile of down pillows, he laughs. "I don't hate it. It's a cute show."

"No. I saw the expression on your face before you knew I was looking at you. You hate it."

"I don't. It's just—a chick flick."

"It's a classic."

"A classic chick flick," he amends. "It's a nice story. It's just that—"

I lift my head from his body. "What?"

"Him and his guys in the woods… they're all just a little too…"

"Too what?"

"*Happy*."

"They're merry men."

"Yeah, exactly. Merry men. They're laughing, like, constantly. I mean, are they all on Prozac or something? Because they laugh at everything. And it just doesn't cut it. Especially when they're doing it in tights. They need to be tougher to be taken seriously. All this—merriment, you know—would never fly in movies these days."

"Which might be what's wrong with films today," I defend.

"Okay, so you have a point." He pauses, watching Errol Flynn burst through the prison doors to rescue Maid Marian. "And I dig the whole rescuing the damsel in distress thing. I can see why you'd like that. It's very—"

"Chivalrous."

"—well, dated, is what I was going to say. These days they've always got the women rescuing themselves. And I mean, that's good, too. I like Hannah having role models of girls rescuing themselves, you know? But at the same time, I feel like men are starting to get a little lazy. What's wrong with a guy coming to a woman's rescue once in a while?" He glances down at the smile on my face. "Do I sound like a sexist for saying that?"

I lose myself in his blue eyes momentarily, realizing something I hadn't before.

He rescued me.

He didn't have to do what he did—he could have moved on with his life after our little scandal without the slightest impact. No—actually he probably would have done all the better for it. Publicity can only help him, and "doing the Buckeye Princess" probably would have only added another tantalizing layer to the Bad Boy persona that defines Dylan Sheridan.

But I would have been fired, and probably only offered the lead in a few cheap porn movies had he not stepped in and turned things around.

He saved my honor, just like in the movies.

He rescued me.

"No," I finally say. "You're not sexist at all. You're one of the good guys."

"Good." He scoots down a little off the pillows and wraps a lock of my hair around his fingertip. His other hand slides down to a breast and I feel my nipple pucker under his touch.

"So, now that I've watched the movie *you* wanted to watch, I'm wondering what I get in return?"

I grin as his hand moves down my belly sending shivers up my spine. His fingers channel into my curls, finding me oh-so-ready for this. I savor his exploration of me, and angle my body to tell him just where I need his touch the most.

"What is it you want in return?" I ask, unable to mask the hope in my words. It's only been an hour since we last made love—sometime around the point when Maid Marian was eating a leg of mutton with Robin Hood. And I'm already starved for him again.

"*Rocky,*" he answers.

Confused, I angle my head toward his, just as he takes a nipple in his mouth, momentarily stealing my words from me. His tongue laves the tender skin, just as his finger slides into my body.

"Rocky?" The word is shaky as it escapes me.

He lifts his mouth from me.

No, no, don't stop doing that, I want to scream.

"I want you to watch *Rocky* with me. Now there's a classic."

I feel my face pinch, wanting to frown at his words. But I can't—not when his mouth has moved to my navel and my legs instinctively open to him.

"I take it from your silence that you agree," he says, just as his tongue moves to the sensitive bud, shooting off fireworks throughout my body.

It's not a classic, I want to say, but I'm struck mute as his mouth investigates every moist fold that seems to quiver beneath his touch.

"Ohhh…" I murmur. Then I activate the last of my brain cells that aren't thoroughly drenched in hormones to force out the words, "That's not a cl—ooh…"

What was I saying just now? I can't remember—can't even remember my name as Dylan's tongue flicks against me, making every muscle in my body coil up, taut as Robin Hood's bow. I sense movement and I force my eyes open to see Dylan's hand reaching for the pile of clothes at the side of the bed. His hand emerges with a condom, and every nerve in my body wants to give him a round of applause for getting it without even lifting his talented tongue from me.

Two fingers slide inside of me and his mouth works me, making my breath come in tiny gasps, and the world seems to disappear from my sight as I slam my eyes shut, savoring the sensation.

He knows just where to caress me and when, as though our minds are one when we are like this. I don't even have to guide him to where I need his touch the most.

His rhythm is gentle, slow and deliberate as his fingers

invade me. And my body responds with thick moisture he takes in his mouth.

Higher and higher, I seem to fly till I become rigid under his touch, and then feel the apex of my satisfaction, coming hard against his mouth. I can't hold back the scream, and to hell with the people in the next room over. I can't be bothered with propriety or decency right now while I'm on fire, writhing beneath him, feeling his teeth and tongue on me, milking the last of my orgasm from me.

I sink into the sheets again.

Barely conscious, I see him slip the condom over himself. "Rocky," he begins again, "was a classic."

"Define classic," I challenge him.

"Something that transcends time," he says, sliding into me.

My body rejoices from the invasion, and again I'm struck speechless.

"Something that is as effective today as it was years ago," he continues, and I can't help considering how what he's doing to me right now would definitely fall into the realm of "classic," by his definition.

"Unlike your merry men," he adds, and then smiles when my eyes flash in response. "Shh…" he says, kissing my mouth before I can argue. "I just wanted to see if you were still listening…"

My ears shut down sometime around then, only allowing the sensation of touch to send signals to my brain.

He teases my depths, letting another climax slowly build inside of me. I watch him thrust into me, and while I used to relish the sight of his tight abs and hard length bringing me to new heights, this time it's the feeling of it that seems to arouse me the most. The feeling of being completely joined with this man.

This man I love.

Oh, damn… How did I let that happen? I don't fall in love. Love brings nothing but disappointment and a broken heart.

I know the reality of love, and should feel panic gripping me right now. Yet as he moves inside of me, all I can feel is satisfaction from it, as though this elusive emotion adds more to this experience of being joined with him than I ever thought possible.

I feel myself sinking further into it, savoring this feeling for what it is right now, without worrying about what will happen in the future. It's a revelation of body and mind. And if there is any fear inside of me at this moment, it's only at the knowledge that sex without love will forever pale in comparison to this.

His thrusts become faster, more urgent, the friction of his body against my center each time he's fully immersed in me making my body climb up to the heights again.

Love has ruined me, I think as my hips move in unison with the rhythm he's set for us, till finally I shatter beneath him again, feeling his last surge of control leave him before he sinks onto me.

But what a wonderful way to be ruined, I realize with a heavy sigh as his body moves to my side.

My eyelids dropping in exhaustion, I see darkness, listening to the steady breathing of both of us as we regain our strength.

Minutes later, fully satiated, I manage to open my eyes and see that the credits of *Robin Hood* have long ended and another classic has started up on the cable network I turn to on sleepless nights like this.

"Sorry you hated the movie." I offer him a smile.

"Stop putting words in my mouth. I didn't hate it," he says, tucking a tendril of my hair behind my ear and then resting his hand at the back of my neck.

"Okay. Dislike it, then. I should have started you off with

something else. Maybe something with John Wayne—like *Fort Apache* or *The Longest Day*."

"Make me watch *Robin Hood* again and I'll be *living* the longest day," he says, then smothering my ensuing laugh with his kiss.

CHAPTER 18

~ CASS ~

There are always more dogs to save.

Isn't that what Dylan had told me way back when we'd had dinner at Francesca's? At the time, his words were a source of inspiration for me. Now, they overwhelm me.

I've been holed up in my room for the past hour, my shades pulled shut because we've called the police twice already for photographers camped out in our bushes. Apparently, Dylan's proposal is still trending on the web, which tells me that it must be a pretty slow week in the news.

But I can't even let that bother me because I'm staring at the photos of some more unwanted dogs who are on the kill list—seven more dogs than I have fosters for right now.

Letting my eyes drift away from my screen for a moment, I soak in the sight of the sun pouring in through the narrow slit in my blinds. It's late afternoon in the middle of summer and I'd be sweating in my forty-pound dress right now.

I hated my job. But there is something to be said for having a job that requires zero emotional investment. At the end of the day, I'd peel off that dress and head home, never thinking twice about the hours I spent as the reigning Princess Buckeye.

But this? I'm not even getting paid to place these dogs in foster homes, yet their lives weigh so heavily on me. Even as photographers follow me around all day and people stop me on the street to offer their congratulations for my so-called engagement, my mind is still on these precious animals, their sad eyes haunting me every hour of the day.

I reach for my phone and tap on Allie's number in my contacts list. "How did you do this?" I ask her when I hear her voice.

"Do what?"

"Choose who lives and who dies. I—" My voice cracks as I click shut the photo of a dog needing my help that someone sent me—a dog that I don't have a home for just yet. "I have a newfound admiration for you. You did this for years. I've been doing it barely a week and I'm about ready for a strait-jacket and a padded cell."

"Oh, hon. I know it's hard. But you just have to focus on the ones that you can save. That's the only way you can do it. And for every one that you have to say no to, just hope that there's another group who will step up and take them in. We're not the only rescue."

"It feels like it, though."

"Just take it one dog at a time, you know? You're getting that program going so well. It's a lot to take on, and you should be really proud of yourself. I think I'll even be able to find someone to take it over when you leave."

When you leave. Her three little words seem to haunt my thoughts just as much as the sight of all the abandoned dogs.

When I leave.

I remember around this time last summer, I was counting down the days till I could get back to my life in New York. Yet now I seem to be dreading it. And when I hear my phone ring a moment after I hang up with Allie and the name of my agent pops up on my display, I'm surprised that I don't feel the excitement that I used to.

"Cassidy Parker," I answer.

"Cassidy, hi. It's Jenna Pietro. Did you get my message Friday about Halton's running your car ads again?"

"I did. That's great news, Jenna. I'm sorry. I should have called you back this morning. It's been a little crazy here." And my priorities seem to have changed, I don't dare to add.

"I can imagine. But it's about to get even crazier. I've got an ad agency wanting to meet with you about a shampoo ad campaign. At least three national commercials, and they really want you. So you can be sure I'm going to make them pay handsomely."

My breath catches slightly. Did she really say *national*? Did she really say *three*? Did she really say *they want me*, rather than the usual, "Show up at an audition with about 500 other blondes and hope for the best?"

Dylan was right. An engagement did more than distract people from our little sexcapade, it put me square in the spotlight as someone who actually might be worth hiring.

"That's great," I finally sputter.

"They want to see you this Friday."

I bite my lip. "There's no way. Kim is getting married the next day. We've got the rehearsal dinner at four. Even if I stayed the night before in a hotel or someplace, I still wouldn't be able to drive back here in time."

"Oh, we don't want you to miss out on that. Everyone's got their eyes on the Sheridans these days. They'll fly you up Friday morning and you'll be back in time for the dinner."

I feel my eyes protrude. "Wait. They'll fly me up?"

"Yes. I'll email you your flight itinerary."

"Uh, you mean, they're paying for my ticket?"

She laughs, and I know I might sound backwoods to her right now. But she's got to remember that last time I was in New York, I was forking over my own subway fare to make it across town for an audition or go-see.

"Yes. They're flying you up. First class, Cass. They want you. It's pretty close to a done deal. Just show up, smile pretty, and I'll reel them in."

"Okay," I say, staring across my room in a daze. A smile perks up my face as I consciously decide that if I'm dreaming right now, I might as well enjoy it.

As I set the phone down, I hear some momentary barking from Pie, and then voices downstairs, telling me that Kim has brought the kids back from picking up their outfits for the wedding.

Shutting my laptop, I allow myself a distraction.

"Hey, guys!" I greet them as I bound down the stairs. I shoot Kim a questioning look at the sight of the kids' tired faces. "Everything go okay?"

"Fine. Did you know there was another photographer parked outside?" she asks, trying to conceal the irritation in her voice, but not doing a good job of it.

"I was afraid of that. I called the police and Harvey asked the guy to leave a couple hours ago, but I just knew he'd be coming back. I'll call the police again."

"No need. I chased him away."

"How'd you manage that?"

She raises an eyebrow. "Hell hath no fury like a protective mom."

I grin, wishing I could have seen *that*. "I'll stay the night at Dylan's again, okay?"

Kim bites her lip. "Would you mind? I don't mind myself, but it's the kids. I don't like them getting photos of them."

"It's no trouble. I'll be out of here tonight." I give her a reassuring squeeze. "Guess what?" I say, my eyes darting from Kim to the kids.

"What?" the kids pipe in before Kim can even open her mouth.

"My agent called and an ad agency is flying me up to New York Friday morning to meet with them about a set of shampoo commercials. National, Kim," I add, taking her hand in my tight grasp.

"Oh my God," she says, breathless.

"Yeah. Who would have thought?"

The kids clap furiously.

I hold up my hands. "But let's not talk anymore about it. I don't want to jinx it." My eyes track among the three of them. "So how did it go today? Did everything fit?"

I can't mistake the cringe I see hidden behind Kim's eyes. "Well, Hannah's dress is beautiful. She looks like a princess. But I think she's a little burned out on the wedding prep, though. I can't say I blame her there." She gives the little girl's shoulder a reassuring squeeze.

"Oh, I don't blame you either, little princess. It's pretty overwhelming. Does your dress look nice, though?" I ask, glancing at the hanging bag that Kim put in the open closet.

She lifts her little shoulders a couple inches and drops them. "It's okay."

I raise an eyebrow. This is odd. That's just not a normal Hannah reaction to anything with frills, bows, lace, and sparkles, all of which are abundant in her flower girl dress.

My eyes drift to Connor. "How about your tux? Do you like it?"

"Uh, we actually didn't get to it yet," Kim answers for him. "Hannah looked like she needed a break. So I figured I'll just take Connor tomorrow."

I bite the inside of my cheek, thinking of Kim's already

intense wedding schedule this week. "Why don't you hang out with me, Hannah, and Kim can knock that out today? I'll do your makeup and curl your hair," I offer, and watch a spark of life come back to Hannah's eyes. Every girl loves a makeover.

"Really?" she asks.

"Really. How's that work for you, Kim?"

Kim sends me a grateful look. "Sounds great," she answers, mouthing *I owe you* when Hannah isn't looking.

"Knock, knock," Dylan says, as he ducks his head in our already open door. "Did you just get back from somewhere, or are you headed out?"

"Both," Kim says, quickly ushering Connor right back out the door. "Thanks again, Cass. I'll be back in about an hour or so."

"Take your time."

"Hi, Uncle Dylan," Hannah greets him, her eyes still hauntingly sad.

"You're looking a little tired, Peanut."

Hannah's mouth forms a straight line before she answers, "It was a little too much stimuli for me."

I nearly laugh at her reply. The kid sounds like she's been hearing too much stuff from those doctors she sees for her ADHD.

"Yeah, stimuli stinks," Dylan says sympathetically. "Can I hang out with you girls?"

Frowning slightly, Hannah narrows her gaze on him. "Cass is doing my hair and makeup. No boys allowed."

"What if the boy ordered Chinese delivery?"

Cocking her head, she stares at him thoughtfully for a moment. "Egg rolls, too?"

"Anything you want."

His offer is enough to win her heart, and after he places his order, he joins us in the upstairs bathroom as I carefully put mascara on Hannah's sinfully long lashes. She's surprisingly quiet, and I'm worried that she might be coming down with something. I touch my palm against her forehead as I blend in a smattering of powder, surreptitiously checking for a fever. But she feels normal.

She might just be overwhelmed. Lord knows I can relate to that these days.

"She looks too grown up," Dylan comments, sitting on the rim of the bathtub. "Your dad would throw a fit if he saw you this way."

"Silly, I won't wear it outside. But it's fun." Her eyes glint with a trace of humor. But still, just a trace.

"Yeah, it's fun," I mirror her, angling a look at Dylan. "*Silly.*"

He musses her hair. "So if it's so fun, why do you still look blue, Peanut?"

The corners of her mouth crease. "I'm okay."

"No, you're not. Did something happen when you were getting your flower girl dress? Did you not like it?"

"It's okay."

I frown. That's two "okays" in the span of ten seconds. That's never good. "Are you getting nervous about the wedding?"

"No. I've been a flower girl before at Aunt Allie and Uncle Logan's wedding, remember?"

"You're right," I reply. "I've never seen a cuter one either."

"I just—" She stops, and those creases in her mouth return.

"Just what, Peanut? You tell me, and Uncle Dylan will make it better."

She opens her mouth, then hesitating, snaps it shut again. Then she blurts, "I—I want to sing at their wedding."

"You want to sing?"

"Yeah. I had a solo in the school concert last year. And I'm really good. They even said so."

"What did you sing?"

"'Pure Imagination' from *Willy Wonka and the Chocolate Factory.*"

I hadn't been in town then, and I glance at Dylan to see if he'd seen the concert.

"I wish I could have seen that," he says in answer.

Before I can even agree with him, Hannah starts to sing, making my jaw drop three inches by the time she hits the fifth perfectly clear, perfectly flawless note.

I only saw that movie once as a kid, and up until about two seconds ago, I'd have told anyone that the only thing I remember is when that girl who chewed bubble gum all the time turned into a giant blueberry. It scared the hell out of me.

Yet ten words into the song, I can remember Gene Wilder singing it like I watched it yesterday.

She's pitch-perfect, each word sounding as though the song had been written with her sweet voice in mind, and I'm awestruck watching her, listening to the tones flow from her like a gentle ride into the land of—well—pure imagination.

Dylan and I sit, slack-jawed, completely entranced by her till the final note brings a bashful look to her face.

I'm clapping so hard I'm going to make my hands numb. "My God, Hannah. I never knew you could sing like that."

"Me neither." Dylan rakes his hand through his hair. "I mean, your dad has told me that you're a good singer, but I figured he was just being... well, a dad."

"You think? You really think I'm good?"

"Yeah. I mean, you know that, right?" I take her hand. "You could be on Broadway with a voice like that, sweetie. And *I know,*" I tell her with some authority. "One of my roommates a couple years ago in New York was trying to make it on Broadway. She was incredibly talented."

"She's on Broadway?"

I grimace. "Um, well, no. Actually she's waiting tables just *off* Broadway, last I heard. But anyway, you really have talent."

Hannah sits on the shut toilet. "I just kind of thought it would be so nice to sing that at the wedding. Maybe at the beginning, like that woman who sang before Aunt Allie came down the aisle last spring."

Dylan swats his hand through the air. "Kid, that soprano doesn't hold a candle to you. And she was a professional. If you sang that song you just did, there wouldn't be a dry eye in the house."

Hannah looks crestfallen.

Dylan's eyes widen and he scoops Hannah onto his lap. "No—that's a good thing, kiddo. A good thing. People cry at weddings because they're happy."

She shrugs in that *grown-ups are weird* kind of way. "It doesn't matter. Dad doesn't think I can handle it."

Dylan suddenly looks like he could tear the head off of a dragon. "He *told* you that?"

"No." Her voice is small, oozing with disappointment. "He hasn't asked me to do it. I keep waiting. You know, I've dropped some hints. Like, I asked if they were going to hire a singer, and they just said no. They could have asked me then. And Dad let me go to the auditions for the string quartet, and I even asked them if they knew 'Pure Imagination.' When they said they did, I was sure Dad would say something then. But he didn't say a word. He just doesn't think I can handle it."

"Oh, honey, maybe they just didn't want to pressure you. It's going to be a big crowd, you know."

"I know. But I can handle it. I love singing."

He smooths out her hair. "Then you just go right up to them tonight and say, 'I want to sing at your wedding.' I guarantee they'll be thrilled. If you want something, then you have to speak up for yourself. Don't assume they'll figure it out."

I stare at Dylan, again seeing that softer side of him that I find dangerously intoxicating.

"Really? You think?" The sparkle has returned to Hannah's eyes.

"I know," he says with a nod.

At the sound of the doorbell, she jumps up and heads for the stairs. "Chinese!" she cries, already distracted by the promise of egg rolls and fortune cookies.

"I'll answer it, Hannah. You just grab us some plates," Dylan calls after her over the ruckus of the dog barking downstairs.

He regards me cautiously as I stand, fists planted on my waist, staring at him.

"What?" he asks defensively, stalking out of the bathroom.

"What you said. About not assuming someone else is going to figure out what you want. Might want to take your own advice," I flash him a knowing look when he glances over his shoulder at me as he bounds down the stairs.

"What are you talking about?"

"JLS," I look into the kitchen as we head toward the door to confirm that Hannah is out of earshot. "You—waiting for your brothers to figure out what you want and ask you to join them at JLS. 'If you want something, then you have to speak up for yourself. Don't assume they'll figure it out.'" I do my best Dylan imitation and he glares at me as he rests his hand on the doorknob.

"I do *not* sound like that."

"Do too."

He opens his mouth to rebuke, but I lift a finger. "And they're your words, Dylan. Not mine."

He snatches my finger in his grip and tugs me toward him. "You're being a pain."

I giggle. "I know. And aren't you lucky you only have to put up with me for a few more days before you go home to Chicago?"

The words slipped from my mouth easily enough. But now, with them hanging between us, I feel somehow on edge, waiting for his reply.

"I'm lucky for every day I have with you before I go."

CHAPTER 19

- DYLAN -

I watch Dad lower himself into the passenger seat of my McLaren. He seems to be struggling. "Need help, Dad?"

"Son, these cars weren't designed for a man with back problems."

My brow furrows slightly as I shut the door for him and move to my side of the car. "You have back problems?" I ask when I climb in next to him.

"Have for years. Comes from spending too much time behind a desk. I worry about Logan doing the same. He's already got those shoulder problems from his time in the SEALs. He doesn't need to add to it going down the same road I did."

"What about Ryan? He's been locked behind a desk for longer than Logan has."

"Ryan's cutting back. He's being smarter than I ever was. Focusing on his daughter and the new son he'll have after this Saturday. That's what's important. So, where are you boys taking him tomorrow night? You're not planning on raising hell in Cincinnati or something, I hope. It might be a bachelor party you're throwing for him, but he's still a father. I don't want Hannah hearing tales when she starts school in September."

I scoff. "This is Ryan, Dad. There will be no strippers, inebriation, or dancing on the tabletops. We're just going to a whiskey and cigar bar south of here. You're welcome to come, you know."

"With all the meds the doctor has me on, I'd be smart to avoid whiskey. And from what I recall of Logan's wedding, you'd be smart to do the same."

I laugh. "I'm the designated driver, Dad. I'm well aware of my limitations."

My dad's eyebrows lift as I rev the engine, and then pull out of the parking lot.

"I'll say, this car is definitely worth it once I'm in it," he admits. "Maybe I should take it out for a spin or two rather than letting it collect dust in the garage after you go."

"I've always said you're welcome to. Just take Mom or that nurse with you, okay?"

I hear him grumble at the mention of *that nurse*. "Where did you even come up with the idea to buy something like this?"

I laugh. "There's a fighter I know—a belt winner, much bigger than I ever was in MMA—and he drove a McLaren. I had a little car-envy going on."

"Just don't let yourself turn into one of those men who collects cars. Or women. Nothing I find more distasteful than that."

I fight back a laugh.

"Glad to see you're settling down with a woman like Cass now. You made a good move, getting engaged to her."

There's an awkward silence between us. I know I told him that the engagement is a fake. The memory of sitting on my parent's couch and having to admit that I'd been caught by a security camera having sex with her—and the lecture I received from them afterward—has likely scarred me for life. So it's moments like these that I feel a pinch of fear that my dad's memory has slipped away again.

"Uh, Dad, you know it's all for show, right? You remember?"

In my peripheral vision, I see the frown emerge on his face. "I'm well aware of that, Dylan. Believe me, if I wanted to forget *anything*, it would be our little discussion a few days ago. But unfortunately, it seems to be the only thing I don't forget these days."

A sigh of relief escapes me.

"All I'm saying, Son, is that I like Cass. She's a good woman. And you'd be smart to do whatever it takes to hold onto her."

I shrug. "Well, the engagement seems to have done the trick in making that other scandal disappear."

He raises a hand to silence me. "I'm not talking about that bacterial video."

At a stoplight, I glance at him. "Uh, *viral* video, Dad. Not bacterial."

He cocks his head and gives me a look of diminishing patience. "I know. That was a joke, Son. Aren't senior citizens allowed to take a few cheap shots at this social media thing your generation has created? I'm just saying that Cass and you make a good team. I like her. A lot. I'm looking forward to seeing it—you getting married to her."

My fingers drum on the steering wheel impatiently. "Yeah, but, Dad, I told you that's just to distract the media for a while."

"I know. I'm not off in dementia-land, dammit. I'm saying

that I still want to see it. The days are getting shorter for me, Dylan. The memories I make are becoming more precious. Christ, I found myself sitting in front of a bowl of corned beef hash yesterday morning and I have no idea how I got there."

"You hate corned beef hash."

"Exactly. No idea how *it* got there either." He chuckles.

"That's not something to laugh about, Dad."

"Hell, if I don't laugh, I'll cry. Do you really want to see that?"

I shake my head. "Laugh, Dad. Laugh."

"You see my point." He attempts to stretch his legs in the footwell in front of him as best he can. "Dylan, I want to be able to see all my sons walk down the aisle. I'd like to enjoy the memory of seeing it for a while, before it gets stolen from me. You love her. You should marry her."

"I never said I loved her."

"Oh, for God's sake, Son. My memory isn't up to par, but my eyes are in working order. There's no mistaking the way you two look at each other. You get older, and you realize what a fool you've been for squandering away your days thinking they'll be in endless supply. But they're not, Dylan. I don't want any of my boys to rush into something they aren't ready for, but I don't want you to be a fool either. Don't be like me—struggling now to squeeze every last ounce of joy out of my days, always knowing that I wasted too many of them doing things I didn't want to do."

I feel almost offended by what he's saying. "Dad, you built an empire. You turned Grandpa's little company into something that will outlast you, and me, and probably even my kids, if I ever have any. And now JLS is saving our town. Look at Anders Street, Dad," I point out as we come to a stop in front of the light near Pop's. "The place was ready to blow away a couple years ago. Then JLS builds a community by the river and suddenly people are clamoring to live here. Ask Pops if your time at JLS was well-spent and he'll tell you that without our family's company, he'd be working for someone else right now, rather than working for himself."

"He wouldn't say that. He'd probably be happily retired now, enjoying his golden years with Louanne and their kids."

"He *did* say that. Just last week when I picked up donuts for Hannah and Connor. Dammit, Dad. Be proud of all you did."

He fills his chest slowly, artfully, with a sigh that is expelled over the next several seconds. "I am. But I'm prouder of my sons. It's not like the memories of the years behind that damn desk are the ones I'm fighting so hard to keep right now. It's the Christmases when you boys would barrel down the staircase to see whether Santa came. That fishing trip in Canada before my father died. The wrestling matches I'd get to see so damn rarely because I traveled so much—and that look on your face when you'd see me in the bleachers. It made me feel like I'd just been handed the world, seeing you look at me like that. Yet I missed nine out of ten of them—always in the office on the weekends. What the hell was the matter with me?" His voice cracks slightly.

"JLS is just a company, Dylan. After it goes public, it will probably end up with a name change down the road, anyway."

I open my mouth to argue, but his words silence me.

"And that's the way it should be, Dylan. I won't ask Logan and Ryan to miss out on the life that I should have allowed for myself, any more than I've ever asked you to give up your dreams to work at JLS."

I think about what Cass told me and take in a breath for encouragement. "But working at JLS *was* my dream, Dad."

I feel his eyes on me, but I don't dare glance his way, using the excuse of an approaching stop sign to keep me from looking at him.

"What?" His voice is soft, and if I didn't know for certain that it was my dad sitting next to me right now, I'd bet my life the voice came from some other man.

"I always wanted it. I'd see you go to work in the morning —I'd see the places you and Grandpa would build with such pride." I shrug. "I wanted to be a part of that."

"Well, why the hell didn't you say anything?"

"Oh, come on, Dad. You made it pretty clear that you wanted Logan heading JLS. And then when he got accepted to the Academy, you went straight to Ryan."

"You were—what?—maybe fourteen at the time, Dylan. What the hell kind of a father would I have been if I put that kind of pressure on you at that age? I wanted you to have time to be a kid like Logan and Ryan did. Give you a chance to explore your talents. And Lord, look at you. You found your own path. Just like I knew you would. You've built from scratch what Logan and Ryan had handed to them. I couldn't be prouder of you, Son."

I feel a pinch in my gut at his words. My dad was never one to lay it on thick, or to lay it on at all, for that matter. Praise fell into my mother's job description, not my dad's.

"Are you really going to let Ryan step down as CEO and take the company public?"

He stares at me a moment, his eyes resting heavy on me. "I think the real question is, are you?"

CHAPTER 20

~ CASS ~

With my two best friends climbing in next to me, I sink into a molded seat of Allie's hot tub and relax as the jets pummel my body. Settled, I glance at her new home, lit up like a dollhouse tonight, with the stars sparkling above it. It's a lot bigger than either of the townhomes she and Logan sold a few months ago. But probably smaller than what anyone might expect from someone with the Sheridan name.

It suits them well though, with a huge backyard for their dog, Kosmo, as well as the litter they agreed to foster after my trip north this week.

My eyes veer in their direction to the opposite side of Allie's yard, where the pups are jubilantly dive-bombing Kosmo. "How are the pups doing on their housetraining, Allie?"

She holds up a hand. "Don't ask. But we've only been at it for twenty-four hours, so I can't expect miracles."

Glancing at each other, Kim and I cringe in response. She's probably picturing the same thing I am—the demise of Allie's pristine hardwood floors.

"I shouldn't have let you take the pups. I had another option for them," I tell her. And I did—actually several options, thanks to the handful of new foster families that I approved this morning.

"Floors are meant to be stained," she replies with a grin. "The house looked too damn immaculate for my taste, anyway. Besides, they'll probably all get snatched up next week at your adoption event. It's going to be huge."

I smile in agreement. After the success of our impromptu event at Sally Sweet's last Sunday, I've decided to "go big or go home," as Dylan likes to say. So I contacted two smaller rescue groups from different counties to see if they wanted to piggyback with our event, hoping that all the press we've received might help them out, too. Among the three groups, we'll have about fifty foster dogs available, making this our biggest event for our fosters ever.

With the huge size, we're having it on the grounds of Allie's new shelter. That way, people can meet the dogs in the shelter, too.

JLS Heartland's foundation donated the funds for ads in local newspapers and Pop's is even going to have a booth there to sell coffee and donuts.

Kim frowns. "I'm so sorry that I won't be there to help you guys."

I glare at her with mock annoyance. "Yeah, really, Kim. If you were a real friend, you'd shorten your honeymoon so you can be there. *Really*." I roll my eyes lavishly, my mind picturing Kim and Ryan on the beaches of Bora Bora. I can't even imagine the concept of flying all the way to the South Pacific for a honeymoon.

Of course, I never imagined getting married, either. So that might be why.

"Good Lord, this is heaven," I mutter quietly, and I'm not even sure if my friends can hear me above the motor till I hear Kim's reply.

"Agreed. This is the best bachelorette party a girl could ask for." She reaches for the homemade milkshake we concocted with the Vitamix someone sent her as a wedding gift. She takes a long sip, leaving a mustache of chocolate on her upper lip. "I'm a mom. I'm not up for taking a limo down to Cincy and getting raging drunk. I've got a kid I have to face in the morning, you know?"

"Hey, I never said we'd get raging drunk," I defend. "I just suggested the limo part."

"Okay, okay. I guess I inferred it. But sushi, milkshakes, and a hot tub trumps a limo any day, in my book."

I nod my agreement, even though hearing the three listed together like that somehow sounds extremely unappetizing. "Of course, *you'll* get plenty of opportunities to jump in a limo, marrying Ryan. Not all of us have that in our future," I say, feigning a pout.

Allie and Kim share a look.

"You can't quite pull off that statement while you've got a diamond from Dylan, dear-heart."

Unconsciously, I find myself toying with my naked ring finger. I'd taken off the ring to go in the hot tub. But without it, I find I've grown accustomed to the weight of it on my finger. "Come on, guys. You know I have no intention of ever getting married. And this engagement is all a fake."

"There's nothing fake about that ring."

I shrug. "So, he'll just return it after we call the whole thing off."

Allie scrunches up her face. "Hon, you don't return a pink

diamond that you had to special order from an estate in the U.K."

Reaching for my milkshake, my hand stills. *"What?"*

She tilts her head. "Naturally pink diamonds are rare, especially in that size. I have no idea how he managed to find one, have it put in a new setting, and get it shipped to you overnight in time for your morning flight to DC."

"He hired a courier," Kim states bluntly.

I stare at her through the mist.

"Ryan told me," she answers my questioning eyes. "It's the only way he could have pulled it off. There's no returning a ring like that."

My mouth hangs open. I don't know much about diamonds, actually. I mean, seriously, why would I? So all this comes as a shock to me. When Dylan said causally that he bought it online, I was picturing him punching in a credit card number on the website of one of those jewelry store chains that advertise on the radio all the time. "Why did he get me a pink diamond then? Anything would have been fine."

"He told me that you said your favorite color is pink."

I remember the moment, standing in his hotel room, poised to launch myself at him.

My favorite color is pink, I had said. Talk about a guy who actually listens.

I shrink two inches deeper in the steaming water. "Oh my God. Why would he do that?"

"Well, duh. He loves you, you dolt," Kim answers.

"He doesn't love me. God, guys, he just did this to save my reputation as best as he could. You know. A distraction. That's what he called it."

"An *engagement* is a distraction. A pink diamond for a girl just because she loves pink? That's love."

It isn't. I can't let myself dare to think that it is. "We barely knew each other at that point. Hell, we barely do now. People don't fall in love that quickly."

"Ha. I totally disagree with you on that one. Allie?"

"I'm with you, Kim," she concurs, then angles a look at me. "What? Are you saying that you're *not* in love with him?"

"I—" I gaze at their knowing faces and realize I can't pull off a lie to my best friends.

At my silence, Kim's smile broadens like a Cheshire cat. "You are. Have you told him?"

My eyes widen. "No. Absolutely not. You know how I feel about that. Telling a man that you love him before he says it first is a huge rule breaker, in my book."

"Why? I mean, after the wedding, he's headed back to Chicago, right? So, give him a reason to stay a little longer. Explore this thing that you guys have together."

"I—can't tell him." I feel a lump in my throat, remembering, and give my head a shake. Tonight is about fun for Kim. Not about dumping my emotional baggage on my friends. "It's just one of my rules," I finish off-handedly.

"Well, it's a stupid rule. Toss it in the trash along with my 'don't date the boss' rule that I obviously broke since I'm marrying him," Kim says.

"And Logan's 'don't date a younger woman' rule that he broke to be with me." Allie sips her shake. "This is decadent. One more of these shakes and I won't fit into my bridesmaid dress."

I'm glad to see that Allie seems willing to let the topic drop. But I'm not lucky enough to get the same treatment from Kim. Her eyes are still on me. "So, why the rule, Cass? I've always wondered. Did a guy you were dating not tell you he loved you back when you told him?"

"No," I deny, thinking how much less it would have hurt if I had been deprived of the words from a mere guy I had dated. Feeling awkward, I glance out at the pups running circles around Kosmo. I bite my lip, seeing an opportunity to move the conversation along. "Those pups must be driving Kosmo nuts."

But now, Allie won't let it drop. "Who was it then, Cass?"

My shoulders sag, feeling like there's no way of escaping this question other than bolting out of this hot tub. But the hot bubbles on my skin feel too damn good.

I frown, the memory creeping out of the confines of my brain, and I swear I'm there again, eighteen years old, sitting on the top step of my carpeted staircase back home, listening to my dad finally tell my mother he wants a divorce.

"My father," I say, bitterness edging into my tone.

"Your father?"

I sigh. "Yeah. Pathetic, isn't it? They argued away the years, my mom and dad. I'd sit there and listen to every word of it just because I thought there would be that moment when one of them finally would say the all-powerful L word and everything would change. They'd realize how much they wanted to stay together. Then they'd hug and kiss and cry. The music would set in and the ending credits would roll." I glance at their perplexed expressions. "What? I'd see it in the movies all the time—all those sappy endings. So finally, when I heard my dad tell my mom that he wanted a divorce, stupid me bolts down the stairs and I tell him that I love him and I want him to stay with us and we can try to find a way to make our family work... together, you know? "

"And what happened?"

I shrug, trying to look like the memory no longer affects me. "Nothing. Absolutely nothing. He just looked at me, shook his head, and walked up to his room to pack a bag."

"Son of a bitch."

"It's not his fault, really," I can't help defending. "Looking back, I know he loves me. The word just isn't in his vocabulary."

Ignoring the lump in my throat, I struggle to down some of my milkshake. I hate that a memory that should be inconsequential can still have such control over me. It wasn't nearly the kind of experience that Kim needed to overcome these past years, or even the pain that Allie felt when her dad died suddenly. I'm so lucky, I tell myself.

I'm so lucky.

"But it hurt so bad that you don't want to subject yourself to that kind of pain again."

"Thank you, Dr. Phil," I respond to Allie with a smile. "I know it's stupid. But you're right. It hurts like hell—throwing your heart out there like that and then just letting it get trampled on. I just always hoped that if—God forbid—I ever *did* fall in love, the guy would be the one to say it first."

"I don't blame you," Allie says softly.

"Besides, Dylan and I have barely started dating," I continue. "Are you going to tell me that your guys spit out the L word two weeks into the relationship?"

My comment earns two frowns from my friends, and I know the answer. I should feel victorious, having made my point. But I don't. I feel empty inside.

I fight the feeling, trying to wipe my mind clear of our conversation.

I should be thinking about tomorrow—of my all-expenses-paid trip to New York for a few hours and the contract that might actually come from it. I should focus on the adoption event next week that brings me the sense of purpose that I've always longed for.

Life is turning around for me. I won't let myself ruin it by longing for love from Dylan or any man.

I reach for my milkshake again, thanking God for the satisfying taste of chocolate on my tongue, even though it's just not enough to fill the void in the pit of my stomach.

CHAPTER 21

~ CASS ~

New York City looks different from the inside of a limo.

My hand is still shaking from the events of the last hour as I reach for one of the water bottles the driver pointed out in the tiny refrigerator in front of me.

Turning the top, I hear the crack of plastic from the safety seal. I shouldn't even be able to hear such a slight sound amid the noise of midday traffic on 36th Street between Third and Lex. But this sleek car seems to shut a little tighter than the old Mazda that awaits me back in Newton's Creek.

I hadn't known that the ad agency would be sending a car to pick me up at the airport till the text I got this morning. And when I walked into baggage claim and saw the uniformed driver holding my name up on a small sign, I certainly hadn't expected the car to be a limo.

Part of me clung to the thought that he had the wrong Cassidy Parker for the entire drive into Manhattan. And the other part of me was thoroughly convinced I was still lying in my bed, sound asleep in Kim's townhome.

I'm still uncertain this isn't a dream.

Glancing at the sight of the gridlock surrounding me, I toss back a few thirsty gulps. My mouth is dry from talking so much. Usually at commercial auditions, there's not much talking and mostly just waiting—packed like a sardine in a room with a bunch of other blondes until my name is called. Then I'd have about thirty seconds to impress a bunch of people sitting behind a long table who look less than dazzled by my presence.

This meeting was entirely different. They actually smiled when they met me, shook my clammy hand, and showered me with praise about how I handled myself on television.

I shot a few smiles for their cameras and did a brief cold reading. They told me about the campaign—how they want it to feature me, showing off my freshly shampooed hair as I play with some shiny-coated puppies. They explained that my name's become synonymous with dogs and they'd like to exploit that angle.

As they walked me around the floor to introduce me to some people, they mostly just talked about my relationship with Dylan, and this morning's rumors of a reality show in our future. I laughed uproariously at that, telling them that the Sheridans are the furthest thing from the Kardashians that there ever could be.

"Even better," one of them said. "You look too much like Grace Kelly to star in a reality TV show."

And of course, after that statement, I was putty in their hands.

"Let this be just the beginning of our relationship," one of them said, hinting that there would be more commercials coming around the bend for me if these first three prove successful.

Still in dazed disbelief, I pull my phone out of my purse as we inch through the traffic toward the Queens-Midtown Tunnel.

Comforted by the photo I have of Dylan alongside his contact information in my iPhone, I tap on his number and wait, my heart in my throat, till I hear his greeting.

"Hi, baby! How'd it go?"

His voice somehow anchors me, as my soul still seems lost in the clouds.

"They want me." The three words flow from my mouth in a rush as though it wasn't reality until I told him. Funny— until I'd met him, I would have imagined myself calling my mom first, or maybe Allie or Kim.

But now, there's no question that it's Dylan's voice I need to hear right now. It's as though nothing can ever be real again, until I share it with him.

"Ha!" His shout of triumph comes from the other end of my call. "I told you they'd want you, Cass. They're smart. They know a good thing when they see it."

Me, too, I think, as I listen to him talk. I know a good thing when I see it. And there's nothing but good when it comes to Dylan Sheridan.

I babble as I tell him everything—about the commercials, the dog angle they want to use, the hints that there might be more work for me in the future. I'm not even sure if I'm making any sense because the words are flying out of my mouth as if I had a gallon of Starbucks this morning.

"I even had the nerve to ask if we could use rescue dogs in the commercials. And they didn't laugh at the idea. They actually liked it."

"Why would they laugh?"

"Because—I don't know—I'm just a high school graduate, you know? Not even halfway to getting my degree online. It's not like I went away to college and majored in advertising or marketing… or have any kind of business experience. What do I know?"

"You know plenty, Cass. You obviously know how to keep those rescue dogs in the spotlight. And *they* know that it will only make them look better by using a bunch of sweet, homeless dogs. The idea's genius."

With a sigh, I sink into the dark leather seat, my gaze tracking to the people bustling along the street outside my window. Not long ago, I was out there with them. And now, I'm sitting in a freaking limo with seats as smooth as butter.

"I'm still waiting to wake up, Dylan."

"You're awake, baby. And when I pick you up from the airport, I plan on showing you just how awake you are."

I giggle. "You'll have to be quick about it. We'll only have an hour before the dinner starts."

"I'm always up for a challenge."

I sigh—a sound I seem to be making a lot these days. "I still can't believe this. I'm just knocking wood till the contract is signed," I add warily. "But it really looks like I've got it. They're sending the contracts over to my agent this afternoon. I—I'm still in shock over here."

"I think champagne is in order."

I laugh. "That can be arranged, since I'm sure there will be plenty at the rehearsal dinner tonight."

He chuckles warmly. "I might just raise an extra toast to your success."

"Don't you dare. I don't want to steal Kim and Ryan's thunder."

"You're right. But aren't you going to tell them?"

"Oh, sure. I'll call Kim and Allie next. And my mom. But I don't want word spreading too much till the contract's signed. It still seems a little too good to be true."

"You deserve a little too-good-to-be-true after all you've

been through this last week. You held up like a champ, though. I'm proud of you, Cass."

I'm proud of you. His words somehow warm me from the inside out, long after I've ended our conversation.

The weight of that simple sentence feels so much more substantial just because it was said by him.

CHAPTER 22

- DYLAN -

"Mother of God, I thought those toasts would never end," Ryan mutters softly as I pull up a seat next to him and Logan at the outdoor bar overlooking the rolling hills of a vineyard.

The rehearsal dinner is approaching its third hour and Ryan's looking like he wishes he'd eloped.

"It was the same at my wedding," Logan reminds him.

"No kidding. I keep thinking I'll be able to use the excuse of getting the kids home, but they're having more fun than I am." He watches them running in and out of the rows of grapes with their cousins and second cousins.

The Sheridan clan has definitely accepted Connor into the fold, and while I'm relieved to see it, I'm not surprised. "Yeah, you don't want to be the bad guy and break up the party."

Logan tilts his head. "Well, Hannah really should get some

sleep tonight. You don't need her overly tired for her big performance."

Ryan's face beams. "No kidding. I never would have guessed she'd want to sing in front of a crowd that big. I mean, the school concert was pretty small compared to this. But she's not even nervous about it."

"Why should she be? She's incredible," I remind him.

He nods, watching her with pride. "But you're right. I better get her home."

He starts to rise, but I stop him, resting my arm on his shoulder for a split second. "Wait, Ryan," I tell him. "Listen, there's something I wanted to talk to you both about. I'm emailing you a few spreadsheets tonight."

Logan's eyebrows hike two inches up his brow. "You want Ryan to look at a spreadsheet the night before he gets married?"

"It doesn't have to be tonight. It doesn't even have to be this week, because I know you're headed out on your honeymoon. Just sometime before Anderson talks anymore to you about going public."

Ryan cocks his head. "What's this about, Dylan?"

"Nothing we need to discuss tonight. I just wanted you to have some numbers in your hands before you made any moves with JLS. I'd like the three of us to talk sometime."

He eases back into his seat, sharing a look with Logan. "So I'm here. Logan's here. Talk."

I frown, knowing that I'd rather they look at what I have to send them first before having this discussion. But it's not like either of my older brothers to put off what can get done today, so I should have foreseen this happening.

"All right. So, I know you're both thinking about going public with JLS to lighten your load. I get that. Running Sheridan Gyms kept me pretty bogged down the first years. But it's profitable now. Very profitable—and those are the numbers I want you to look at before you make any moves." I pause momentarily. "Because I'd like to propose that JLS Heartland acquires Sheridan Gyms."

Ryan's eyes widen. "Pardon me?"

"Our missions aren't too dissimilar. You build housing developments. I build gyms. And if JLS acquires the gyms, then I'll have the leverage to be able to modify my present gyms to have more adaptive equipment like I'm doing at the one near Walter Reed." I glance to Logan for some kind of feedback. I know he's more interested in rolling out with those plans than Ryan is.

"Look, I told you, if you need money from JLS's foundation for that, then we're all in," Logan assures me. "We don't have to acquire your gyms to get the job done."

"I don't need the money," I say, figuring it's got to be the twelfth time I've told him that since I showed him the plans. "And I'm not just thinking about how *I'd* benefit. Diversification can make JLS stronger, especially if housing goes south again."

Ryan lowers his chin. "So when Logan and I say that we want to cut back on our workload, you're proposing that we start *diversifying*? Acquire a new business?"

"It's not that different from when you started up the JLS Foundation last year."

"Yeah, but you're not hearing us, Dylan. We want to slow down. Have more time with our families. So far, you've only proposed something that will lighten your load, not ours."

I square my shoulders toward him. "Not if I come on board at JLS."

Dead silence hangs among the three of us for a moment.

"You want to work at JLS?" Ryan looks stunned.

"Yes," I say firmly. "That way I can still manage Sheridan Gyms, and I can take some of the leadership load off your plates."

"How much can you handle?" Logan eyes me warily.

"A third easily."

Ryan scoffs, "You'll take a third of the load, *and* manage the new acquisition?"

"Hell, Ryan, I can do that in my sleep."

Logan's laugh is a low rumble. "You think?"

"I *know*. Look, I know you guys all think of my gyms as being some kind of a damn hobby."

"That's not what we think, bro."

I stand. "Just take a look at the financials and tell me you've ever seen a hobby build that much capital. We're sound, and we're only poised to grow. Just like JLS. Now's not the time to be going public. I want in. I've wanted in all my life, but you all seemed pretty content with me on the outside."

Logan glances at Ryan, and then back to me. "We never knew you wanted in."

"Well, now you do. I have something to offer you guys. I'm not coming to you with my hat in hand. It will only help JLS's bottom line in the long run. And it will keep it in the family, the way Dad always hoped it would stay. The way it would need to be if any of our kids wanted to take it over when we retire."

Logan opens his mouth, but I raise my hand to cut him off. "Don't say anything more about it till you look at the financials, okay? If you're not okay with it, then fine. I tried. But at least take a look at what I send you. See what I've built on my own and imagine what I can do for JLS."

With a sharp nod, I walk away. My heart is racing because I hadn't known how much I wanted to be a part of JLS till I opened my mouth just now.

In fact, there's only one thing I want more right now.

Cass.

My eyes dart around the hall to find my fiancée. I don't

care why she's wearing my ring right now. I need to see her. I need... her, and the realization shakes me to my core.

I feel the buzz of my phone in my pocket and pull it out. My features harden defensively at a quick glance at the words of the incoming text. It's the fifth one I've received from our lawyers tonight, by the look of it. But I hadn't felt right checking my phone during the toasts, even as dull as they were.

With a tap, I open and skim over the attachment they sent. A smile eases up my face.

The tides have turned for Cassidy Parker. And I'm the lucky guy who gets to share the news with her first.

CHAPTER 23

~ CASS ~

My hand trembles, holding my glass as I'm introduced as Dylan's fiancée to another family member of the Sheridan clan.

Glancing at the watch on the man's wrist—I don't want to look at my own because that would seem too obvious—I see that I'm entering the third hour of this rehearsal dinner.

Allie and Logan's rehearsal dinner was so much easier, without the pressure of wearing a ring and pretending to be engaged to Dylan. I was able to fall into the woodwork back then, sipping my expensive champagne and flirting with the abundance of Navy SEALs that were in attendance.

But this is different. All these people are hugging me and acting like I'm next to be accepted into the fold. I feel like a fraud.

Dylan's dad eases up next to me, and his eyes meet mine

as I'm trapped in a conversation with some great aunt, and a third or maybe fourth cousin of Dylan's.

When there's a break in conversation, he asks, "Cass, care to take a walk around those vines with an old man? I could use a little break and you know how Anna gets when I wander off," he adds with a chuckle.

"Love to," I say, accepting the offer of his arm, and grateful that this man seems to have been reading my mind.

We escape the crowd to the vineyard where the kids are darting in and out of the neat rows of vines. I'm calmed by their laughter; it somehow anchors me. My heels sink into the dirt as we walk, and the sweet scent of the grapes tickles my nose.

"How did you know I needed to break free from all that?" I ask.

"I recognized that look on your face—the same look you had when you showed up for our family barbecue on Sunday. But tonight, it hasn't disappeared."

"This is a little more overwhelming than a barbeque."

"I'd have to agree with you there. But at least you don't have a damn nurse tailing you all the time."

He glances over his shoulder and I see her, holding her champagne glass, pretending she's a guest, but staying exactly fifty paces behind us.

"See?" He grunts. "Anna doesn't want me disappearing again. And I guess I don't blame her. But there's no dignity in growing old, just as I told you the other night." A smile flashes across his face. "See? I do remember some things."

"You remember plenty."

"I also *notice* plenty. You don't look like you're having a good time tonight. I'd have thought you'd be beaming right now."

"Why?"

He grins. "Well, my boy kind of let it slip about that ad

agency wanting to sign you for those shampoo commercials. That's a big deal."

"That scamp. He wasn't supposed to tell anyone. I haven't signed the contract with them yet. I don't want to jinx it."

He chuckles. "Don't be mad at him. He only told Anna and me. He's just proud of you."

I glow inwardly. I can't help it. The idea of Dylan being proud of me somehow makes me even happier than the fact that my whirlwind trip this morning seems to be resulting in a complete 180 of my once lackluster career. I'm determined not to celebrate until my agent says it's a done deal; God knows I've discovered how life can turn on a dime these days. But I still feel a glimmer of hope.

No. It's more than a glimmer; it's a shining ray of light bright enough to blind me.

And it's all because of Dylan Sheridan.

"I don't think I could ever be mad at Dylan."

He laughs. "Apparently, you haven't been around him enough, then."

"True."

"So, why did you look so uncomfortable in that crowd, Cass?" He nudges his chin in the direction of the reception area.

"Oh—I don't know. It's just overwhelming. All the congratulations I keep getting. I'm never sure what to say since I know it won't last forever."

"Your engagement with Dylan will only end if you and he want it to end." Pulling a grape off a vine, he pops it into his mouth. His lips suddenly pinch together as though it was a bit tarter than expected. "That's not really what's upsetting you tonight, is it?"

I look at him for a moment, curious how he can be so intuitive, and wondering if that is why he succeeded in business. "No, you're right. It's not. Family gatherings like this sometimes make me... I don't know." My voice trails and I let the silence speak volumes.

"Miserable, if you're at all like me," he pipes in. "If I really wanted to see my distant cousins and all their descendants, don't you think I'd invite them over for a Sunday dinner?" He laughs warmly. "No, I'm kidding, of course. How do they make you feel?"

I sigh, wondering how to answer. I'd usually come up with something vague, yet there's something about Mr. Sheridan that seems to pull the truth out of me. Maybe it's because I saw him once so vulnerable, that I feel I can let my own guard down.

"I feel like I'm always on the outside, looking in," I finally admit.

In my peripheral vision, I see him nodding, slowly.

"You come from a small family, I take it?"

"Only child," I answer.

"Parents are divorced?"

"Good guess. And I just didn't experience this whole extended family thing that you Sheridans have. I had my grandma till I was ten, and she was... incredible." I feel the warmth of a smile touch my lips at the memory of her, snuggled together on the checkered couch, watching old movies. I miss my grandma. "That's it, though. I have cousins, but just never kept in touch with them. So this big-family-thing kind of gets me... nervous, I guess."

"If you don't mind me saying, you didn't look nervous. You looked downright sad."

I bite my lip. "Oh, God, was it that obvious?"

"Only to Anna and me."

We walk a few more steps, letting the buzz of the bees in the grapes somehow have their own say in our conversation, till I finally stop and look back at the crowd on the terrace. "It's nice. What you have, I mean. All this family. All this support. All this… love." The last word almost gets stuck in my windpipe.

"Cass, I don't know what's going to unfold in this engagement you and Dylan have brewing. But I do know this. You are a part of our family—" He points to the crowd. "—of *that* family no matter what happens between you two. So just remember that."

I feel a knot in my throat and the sting of tears forming behind my eyes. "Thanks." My voice is small, and I feel like that girl at the top of the stairs again, aching for love.

"Speaking of Dylan, I think someone's looking for you," he adds, glancing over my shoulder.

I turn, and see Dylan walking across the vineyard toward me.

"Trying to steal my girl, Dad?" he chides.

"I'm too old and too married. But you'd be smart to make sure no one else does," he adds.

"Point taken," Dylan answers with a grin. "I bet you're about ready to call it a night."

"Yes," his dad and I reply in unison, and then our eyes meet and we share a laugh.

"I'm with you both on that." The sharp angle of Dylan's chin and cheekbones catch the light of the setting sun, making him look even more handsome. "Ryan's packing up the kids now," he continues. "They've got a long day ahead of them tomorrow. So I thought it might be a good time for us to slip away."

I turn to Dylan's dad. "Thanks for the walk. And the rescue," I tell him, unable to resist a hug.

"Anytime, Cass."

We walk him back to his wife and say our good-byes for the night. Once alone, as we trek across a field toward his car, I press my fingers against my temples.

"Headache?"

"Just a little one," I answer.

"Well, I know one thing that might make that headache go away."

"Oh, you do, do you?" I say coyly.

He chuckles. "Not that. Though I'm completely up for that, as well. But I got a text from our lawyers saying that Buckeye Land has a settlement they'd like to offer you."

"*What*? What are you talking about?"

He glances at me, seeming genuinely surprised by my reaction. "A settlement. A cash settlement. They let that video get leaked, Cass."

"Well, yeah. But I didn't think they'd offer me some kind of settlement for it."

His eyebrows rise an inch. "I should say they better—the way it turned your world upside down."

I shrug, considering where my life was two weeks ago. Now my agent is negotiating with an ad agency about putting me in three commercials. I've somehow had the good fortune to become closer to a family I absolutely adore. And I get to wear a gorgeous ring, even though I know both Dylan and the ring are just mine on loan. It's hard to feel spiteful. "I —I don't feel right about taking money from them. I mean, I did have sex in the break room."

"And they *did* leak the footage."

"Yeah, but Buckeye Land isn't exactly flourishing as it is. It's like taking money from a dying company."

Dylan laughs. "Oh, they're not dying anymore, Cass. Ticket sales are up drastically. Think about it. Two weeks ago, no one had even heard of them. Suddenly, they're a household name. In fact, our lawyers are arguing that they may have leaked that footage intentionally. And from how quickly they're offering a settlement, I'm betting that's just what happened."

"Sons of bitches," I mutter suddenly.

"Look. It's a hell of a settlement. You can buy yourself a nice condo in Manhattan or something."

A condo in Manhattan? Does he have any idea what real estate goes for in New York City? I glance at him. Of course he does. "How much are you talking about?"

He reaches into his pocket to retrieve his iPhone, and opens an attachment from his lawyers. "Take a look."

My eyes skim the document on the tiny display, the wording completely flying over my head and below my knees. Lawyers talk in a different language from the rest of the world. Then my gaze settles on a seven-digit sum that has me staggering.

I grasp Dylan's arm, stopping. "I need to sit down."

"Are you okay?"

"I'm serious. I need to sit down." My head spinning, I stumble to the split rail fence alongside the parking area.

Dylan sits beside me. "You okay?"

I stare at the number. "This isn't some kind of joke, is it?"

"No. No joke about it. You'll definitely have enough for a one or two-bedroom condo in New York."

"Or a house," I say quietly.

Dylan cringes. "I wouldn't get your heart set on a house in Manhattan for that kind of money."

"No. Not in Manhattan. Here in Newton's Creek."

"Hell, you could buy a fifty-acre farm for that kind of money around here. But is that what you want? To stay here?"

Yes. Not until this moment did I realize just how much I want to stay right here where I'm surrounded by people I love and a mission that holds my heart in its grasp.

"Yes," I say, jumping up from the fence and walking toward Dylan's car again, propelled by a new surge of energy. "Yes, that's exactly what I want to do. I can buy a big place and take in more dogs."

He matches my pace. "But what about your career in New York?"

"What about it? I mean, if my agent actually manages to snag these commercials or a few others, then I just fly up there and do it. But even if nothing comes of their talk, then I can live really well off of that settlement. Maybe get a job again at Pop's donuts to cover some of my expenses, or start selling sex toys again with the multi-level marketing company Allie used to work for."

Stopping cold, his eyes whip to mine. "*Sex toys?* I'm sorry, but *what?*"

I bat my hands through the air, still walking. "Long story. The point is, it doesn't cost that much to live here in Newton's Creek. And think of all the dogs I can save if I stick around."

He smiles at me. "I won't argue that point, George."

My eyes dart to his. "Huh?"

"George. I think I should start calling you George Bailey for all the difference you're making in the world, Cass Parker." He takes my hand, stopping me, and wraps his arms around my waist. "But I'll have a hard time explaining to people why my pet name for you is George."

His lips brush against mine, the slow, seductive movement lulling my racing heartbeat back into submission. My mouth opens to him, right along with my soul and I feel a sigh escape me.

He did this, I think again. This could have had a very different ending for me, but this man found a way to turn it around for me. No matter what happens between us in the days and weeks ahead, I resolve to always love Dylan Sheridan for that.

Even when he inevitably breaks my heart.

"How about staying the night with me at the hotel?" he says when his lips part with mine.

I think about the chaos awaiting me at the townhouse. Connor will be wired and Kim will probably be even worse off than her son. An escape to Dylan's suite sounds beyond tempting tonight.

But then I think of Pie, waiting to be let out into the backyard, and shake my head.

"No. The photographers aren't camping out in our bushes anymore. And there's no way I'm texting Kim to ask if she'll take care of my foster dog again the night before she gets married. She's been tolerant enough of me this week. I'm not pushing it."

"You're right." His lips caress mine again and I feel the warmth of his hands raking up the sides of my dress to my back. The pressure of his hard chest against me, such a minimal dose of contact, has me craving so much more.

As he kisses me, I feel my mouth quirk up into a wide smile before he pulls a half-inch away from me, watching me, letting his blue eyes latch onto mine.

"But the house will be pretty lonely tomorrow night, with Kim on her honeymoon and Connor and Hannah staying with your parents for the week," I say with a smile.

His eyes light. "Is that an invitation?"

Tilting my head, I murmur my acquiescence to him. I know Dylan will be leaving on Monday for Chicago. But that's two whole nights I'll have with him.

And I plan to enjoy every minute of it.

CHAPTER 24

~ CASS ~

A cascade of flowers in my hands, I walk down the aisle to the sweet voice of Hannah singing, and my entire heart is melting with each note.

I glance at Ryan, who is already standing at the end of the aisle with his brothers and I see the unshed tears in his eyes. He loves his little girl so much that it reminds me that not all dads are like my own. Some *can* express their feelings. Some can be hard-nosed corporate CEOs and still let a tear fall at the sound of his little girl's voice singing so proudly as her family joins with another.

My heart cracks. I'd trade my signed poster from *Vertigo* that I bought on eBay for a tissue right now.

As Hannah finishes her song, my eyes meet Dylan's who stands across the aisle from me. He looks so handsome in his light beige tux with a blue tie that seems to showcase those

Sheridan eyes. My heart fills completely, so enraptured by this man, so stunned by the effect that he has on me.

Correction: it's more that I'm stunned by the effect of *love* on me, this feeling of complete helplessness. Kim and Allie speak of love in a way that makes it sound as though the emotion somehow empowers them. But I can't feel that way, not knowing that every moment I spend with him brings me closer to the end.

Geographic differences have broken stronger relationships than ours. With only two weeks under our belts, the ties between us aren't that resilient. I can't imagine it will be long before this dies off. He'll be back in Chicago, catching the paparazzi's eyes with some new bombshell on his arm, and I'll be back here, in Newton's Creek, the place where I'm determined to make a permanent home for myself and as many dogs as I can squeeze into a house.

Everyone stands at the sound of the Wedding March, and goose bumps blanket every inch of my skin as I see Kim walk down the petal-covered aisle toward Ryan.

I reach for Allie to steady myself as we stand next to each other beside an arch of white roses. I feel her eyes on me, warm and comforting. And confident—so confident in this thing called love that she and Kim have welcomed into their lives. All the while, my eyes are probably filled with questions right now.

How? How can something last forever?

Why does it stick for some and not for others?

Will I ever see it in the eyes of a man as he looks at me? And would I recognize it if I saw it?

It wasn't long ago that it was Allie walking down an aisle toward the love of her life, facing a new beginning with him without the slightest fear or apprehension.

I glance at Jake and Anna Sheridan as they stand, hand in hand, watching Kim approach. What difficult years they must have had together, both being apart so often as he focused on building the family business into something that can last for generations.

It couldn't have been easy on either of them. Yet their relationship survived—somehow they made it—as though they had made some silent arrangement that they would never give up on each other like my parents did.

Glancing back at Kim as she takes her final steps down the aisle, her eyes are locked on Ryan's. I turn slightly so that I can see him—looking nothing like the cold, calculating CEO that he likes to portray. He looks utterly, completely defenseless to her, as though the slightest wave of her finger could slice him in two.

That's what love is—I know that now—that complete vulnerability to someone.

A small hand reaches for mine and my eyes track down to Hannah, who is nervously biting her lip. She'll have a new mom today, a step up from the one who barely ever takes the time to even call her. Her biological mom tossed her away last summer like unwanted baggage when Hannah didn't meet with her absurd expectations.

I feel a kinship with Hannah. She knows what it feels like to be denied love by a parent. She knows what it's like to see the ties that should bind people together disintegrate. Kim is just the upgrade in the Mom Department that this little girl needs, and I couldn't be happier for either one of them right now.

Ryan takes his fiancée's hands at the end of the aisle and I gaze at the point where they are joined, and it's like I can't even tell where one of them ends and the other one begins. My breath catches at the realization of it.

Listening to the pastor's words, I feel the weight of them more deeply than I did when I stood at Allie's side at the altar only a few months ago. As he speaks of love and commitment, the words make me ache, and I feel a burn on my finger that wears a meaningless ring. It singes me, shames me somehow, how I've taken something that should be so deeply meaningful and made a mockery of it.

And now Fate has exacted some kind of revenge on me for it, making me fall for the man who gave me the ring—fall completely and totally in love with him.

I glance at Dylan again, panicked suddenly. Just last night I had relished the idea of spending our last days together, inseparably, till he leaves town. But now, witnessing all the love around me—the kind of love that lasts—I feel a pressure building in my heart. An urge to flee.

I can't let myself continue to be swept away in a lie that is so much sweeter than the truth.

A tear escapes me as I hear Kim speak the vows she painstakingly wrote and practiced for weeks. Her voice is quiet—she's not the type to like being the center of attention like this—but they are genuine, and they seem to strike Ryan right in the heart. And then he speaks to her, and it's as though they are the only two people in the park right now, standing at this point where Kim says they shared their first kiss.

My eyes again turn to Dylan's parents in the front row, the grasp of their hands together, united completely. Just like the hold that Ryan has on Kim right now, as they slip bands on each other's fingers.

I want that, I decide. Every second of every day since that night my dad left, I swore up and down that I'd never get married and take a risk on something so tenuous, so fragile. But now that I've seen how love can be when it does make it through the tunnels of turbulence that life can bring, I want it for myself. A love that lasts.

Subconsciously, I find myself toying with the ring. I'd take it off right now if it wouldn't raise some eyebrows. The lie of it scorches me, and the irony it symbolizes slices open my heart.

Dylan Sheridan is my greatest love. But he is not my fiancé.

Suddenly all the jealously I promised I wouldn't feel for my friends as they enjoy their happily-ever-afters bubbles up inside me, as I wear this ring and play out Dylan's and my little charade. And I hate myself for it.

I can't do it anymore. I just can't.

My smile broadens automatically as I see Kim and Ryan kiss for the first time as husband and wife—a sincere reaction because even though I desperately want the love they share for myself, I'm still so deeply grateful they found it for themselves. As cameras snap and tears fall, I clap right along with everyone else, and Ryan and Kim walk back down the aisle *together*—the same way they'll be doing everything for the rest of their days.

As rehearsed, I take Dylan's arm and let him escort me to the end of the aisle.

"They did it," he says, his smile stealing my breath.

"They did." My own joy mirrors his, even though I feel like my soul is weeping, knowing that I can't live in this farce anymore.

"You okay?"

He always does seem to know when my mind is elsewhere.

"Of course," I chirp back forcefully, before being swept into what seems like a hundred hugs from people I don't even know. Their words sting me—comments like "You'll be the next one walking down the aisle" shredding me inside.

When the photographer completes the usual rounds of posed photos, I make a break for it, walking briskly out of the tent where champagne glasses are clinking endlessly and a string quartet is playing while people enjoy their hors d'oeuvres.

Just near the river's bend, I see townspeople gathering, already marking their spots with picnic blankets for the fireworks that will light up Newton's Creek after sunset. I hear the peals of laughter from children and families nearby, no doubt enjoying the bouncers and pony rides that have made Ryan and Kim's union something of a local holiday.

I think I'm the only person in the entire town who is feeling anything but complete and utter happiness right now.

Needing someplace where I can catch my breath, I head toward a small enclave of trees that I hope will shield me, offer me some privacy for a while. But I hear Dylan's voice behind me. "Cass! Wait up!"

I glance backward. "No. Go back to the reception, Dylan. I just need a little air."

"So I'll get some air with you."

"Really, I'd rather you didn't," I say, my eyes turning away from his as I continue toward the trees. I pick up my pace, ducking into the greenery, and letting the sounds of the creek soothe me. Nature seems to welcome me into her embrace, tamping down the chaos rising in my soul.

At the water's edge, I feel his hand reach for mine. "Cass, what's wrong? You've been fine all day. Did something happen?"

"Don't ask," I warn him. "Just don't. Now's not the time to be having this conversation."

"What conversation?"

I shake my head. "Just forget it, Dylan. Please. Let me just catch my breath and I'll be back in a few minutes. Then we can go back to playing our little farce for the evening." The words were sincere, but I hadn't intended to say them with such bite.

"Farce?"

I wrench my fingers from him. "Yes. Farce." I can't take back the word. I won't. Because it's the truth.

"I'm not playing out some farce with you."

"Well, what is it then? What would you call it? Charade? Travesty? I mean, it's easy for you. You can stand there during that ceremony and listen to all those words like love and commitment and not crave them the way I do. You've seen it—had it—all your life. But for me, this *family* thing that you Sheridans have—it's not something I've ever experienced before. And to stand there wearing your ring, feeling the acceptance from everyone around me, knowing that it's all a lie—it's more than I can handle, Dylan."

His expression is guarded. "What do you mean?"

"I mean, it's over." A sigh escapes me and I'm almost stunned by the relief I feel amid the anguish. "There. I said it. We knew we'd break-up sometime, so let's just do it now."

"Why? I thought we were hitting it off."

I stare at him. *Hitting it off?* Really? If that doesn't make me want to toss this pink diamond into Newton's Creek, I don't know what will. "Yes. You're right. We hit it off fine."

"So why stop now?"

I stare into his eyes, and I can remember the first moment I saw him, so many years ago, on my parents' TV. I can recall the tingling I felt in every nerve, the feel of that brown shag rug beneath my bare thighs as I sat there in my shorts. I can feel the heat of the summer air spilling through our open windows. I can remember it like it was yesterday—no, like it was two minutes ago.

Yet never would I have imagined back then that I'd know the man on the TV screen so intimately. That I'd have the contours of his face, the texture of his skin, the timbre of his voice committed to my memory forever. That I would know the feel of his heartbeat against my chest, and the caress of his lips against me. That I would hand him my heart so reluctantly, so involuntarily, and so completely.

Even then, back in those days when I believed in happy endings, when I truly believed that love could prevail, I would never have fathomed that I could feel so deeply for one man.

"I bought a lottery ticket last week, Dylan," I hear myself say.

The questions in his eyes are unmistakable.

"I don't do it often," I continue. "Maybe once a year when the jackpot gets really high. But maybe that says I'm more of a gambler than I like to think I am."

My voice cracks and I look away from him, watching the water tumbling over the rocks in the creek as it flows downstream to where Ryan and Kim are starting their lives together right now. "Playing this role—your fiancée—made me realize something. I really do want love, Dylan. Love like Kim and Allie have from their husbands. I do. And I know it might end up like it was with my parents. But if I'm willing to bet a dollar on the freaking lottery, then why can't I gamble my heart on the 50-50 chance that I might end up in a relationship like my best friends have right now?"

I look at him, and search for some trace of love in his eyes for me. I want to see it there, so that I can tell him what I feel inside so deeply. But I can't trust myself to recognize love, even if it is there in his eyes. So I keep my feelings buried inside, where they are safe.

"You've done so much for me, Dylan. And this time with you has been—" *The best time in my life*, I want to say. *The kind of time that I could only have with a man I love more deeply than I ever thought possible.*

But I don't say that. I can't. I'm not up for getting my heart broken like that again. I know how painful it will be when he doesn't say the word back to me. And I'm in enough pain right now.

"—it's been wonderful and fun and given me a glimpse into the kind of life I really want with a man," I finish instead.

His eyes become distant as he watches me, waiting for my next words. But none come.

I start to pull the ring from my finger, but he clasps both my hands in his. I savor the feel of his skin touching mine and the sensation sends a thrill to my core.

Keep it, I want to hear him say. *Keep it because I love you.*

But instead, his eyes grow cold. "Don't do this now. I don't want to upstage Ryan and Kim. You've worn it this long, may as well wear it till they're on their honeymoon."

His voice is devoid of emotion, almost as though he's doing a business transaction.

I nod automatically, the chill of his tone making my back straighten. "You're right," I agree. "Of course."

"I'm flying to Chicago on Monday. We can just let things die out naturally then."

I stare at him. "Right. Monday. Okay." Just as I knew things would end between us. He starts to walk away. "Dylan—"

He stops in his tracks, but doesn't turn to look at me.

I love you.

I *love* you.

Just say it, dammit, Cassidy Parker.

But I'm suddenly seeing myself race down the staircase of my childhood home to my father. *"I love you, Dad. Don't leave us. We can make this work."* And in stony silence, he left anyway.

I won't do that again.

"You... came to my rescue," I say instead. "First with the Brenna Tucker thing. Then with the damn video. No one ever rescued me before." My voice cracks as the tears escape me.

He turns, and I see a glimmer of emotion in his eyes. "You're worth rescuing, Cassidy Parker. Don't you forget that."

And then he walks away.

CHAPTER 25

- DYLAN -

"Tell me that's your first shot."

I hear my brother's voice behind me as Logan joins me at the bar.

"It's my first shot," I tell him, and glance at my watch. "Since nine o'clock," I qualify.

"There were stories about you getting completely drunk at my wedding after Allie and I left."

"Hell, that's not my fault. You're the one who invited about forty SEALs. They drink like... well... sailors."

"Because they *are* sailors," Logan laughs. "Yeah, I won't deny that. But there aren't any SEALs here now."

"Just you. Drink with me," I tell him, flagging down the bartender.

"I'm not wearing the trident anymore. And I've got a wife I'm driving home at the end of the evening. Think I'll stick with a couple beers."

"Suit yourself."

"So, planning on telling me why you're sitting at the bar moping when you've got a hot blonde as your date?"

"What? We ate together. We talked. We danced. Just like everyone would expect us to," I add with disdain.

"I take it there's trouble in paradise?"

"Hell, there never was any paradise between Cass and me. You know that. It was all for show."

"Was?"

"Yeah. Was. She said she's done play-acting. Wants to find the real thing with someone else."

He settles into the chair next to me. "Funny. I thought she found the real thing with you."

"Yeah, I kind of thought so, too," I grumble, glancing over my shoulder and seeing Cass dancing with my great uncle. I almost crack a smile at the way my extended family has welcomed her. Damn, that makes things more complicated.

"Did you tell her that?"

"Tell who, what?" I hear Ryan's voice on the other side of me before I see him.

I narrow my gaze on Ryan, my eyes tracking down to the platinum band on his finger. Lucky son of a bitch. "Shouldn't you be dancing with your wife right now?"

"She's in the restroom with Allie doing—whatever it is women do in there." He signals the bartender who brings him a beer. "So, tell who, what?"

"I was just asking Dylan if he finally told Cass that he loves her," Logan's big mouth blabs.

"No. Why would I? It's not like she's said it to me," I inform him and almost cringe at how childish I sound right now.

Ryan signals the bartender to bring him a beer. "Oh, hell, she'll never say it first," he says.

I cock my head. "Why not?"

"Her dad. Kim told me something about her dad leaving them, you know, when her parents split. Before he left, Cass said she loved him. She hoped that would be enough to make him want to work things out with the family. He never said it back. He just walked out on her. On them. So she's made it some kind of rule to never say it first. She doesn't want to get hurt like that again."

I frown at the full shot glass in front of me. I picture Cass as a kid, perched at the top of the stairs like she had once described. And I can somehow picture her young face so well, filled with hope, trying to force the happy ending that she longed for, then shattering at her dad's silence.

Dammit, Cass. Why didn't you tell me? I would have said it right there in the woods a couple hours ago.

I stand immediately, knowing that I can fix this right now.

Logan shoots me a look as I stand and Ryan grasps my arm. "Not so fast," he says.

"What?" I ask, glancing at his grip on me.

Ryan tilts his head. "About that offer you made yesterday —about you coming aboard at JLS."

I roll my eyes. "Aw, hell, Ryan, you're not really going to talk business at your own wedding, are you?"

"Damn right I will, if it will take another chunk of the load off my shoulders so that I can enjoy my family when I get back from my honeymoon."

I look at him warily. "What do you mean?"

"I mean, Logan and I talked about it, and we're taking the idea of going public off the table."

"You are?"

"Yep. You made a good offer. I looked at the financials for Sheridan Gyms and—good Lord, Dylan—you built a hell of a company. If we acquire it, we'll be able to build more of those gyms like you're doing near Walter Reed. Logan showed me the plans. That would be a real feather in JLS's cap, and with our size and ability to roll out with those designs, we'd be able to make it more profitable than you could on your own."

I bristle slightly. "Don't be so sure."

"You know it's true. And I like the idea of expanding JLS into building something other than just housing. I like even *more* the idea of having you on board, taking a full third of the load, if you really think you're up for it."

"You know I am."

"Then it's a deal, Dylan." He extends his hand. "We grow the company, share the load and the profits, and keep it in the family."

A grin edging up my face, I shake his hand.

"Dad'll love this news," Logan comments, watching my dad who at some point rescued Cass from my great uncle's two left feet.

"No kidding," I say.

Logan glances over his shoulder to see Allie and Kim approaching. "Our wives have returned," he says, clinking his beer glass against Ryan's before swinging his long leg over the stool to stand. He gives me a swift thump on the back. "Now that you'll be spending more time in Newton's Creek, I know this single woman who runs a dog fostering program who might be looking to settle down."

"And there aren't many single women in this town. So better snatch her up fast," Ryan adds, tossing his chin in Cass's direction just as she retreats to a table by herself.

They leave me there as they join their wives, the way brothers do after they get married, I guess. They never would have left me at a bar drinking by myself when they were single. But that's what happens when you find someone who means more to you than even the blood you share with your brothers.

Someone like Cass.

She's not facing my direction as she reaches downward. One high heel is resting alongside her and she massages her bare foot. She was smiling the whole evening as she danced, never letting on that her feet might be killing her, or maybe, just maybe that her heart was breaking.

I see my father walk toward her, bringing her a glass of water. His eyes meet mine, his expression heavy with meaning, as he steps away from her after patting her on the shoulder.

I glance at my shot glass again, still filled to the rim, and then look back at her as she sits at the table alone.

A memory comes to me as I stare at her—hazy, as though something experienced in a dream—or more likely under the influence of whiskey.

I can see her sitting in a strapless gown that night, not too dissimilar in style to the one she has on now.

I'm the irresponsible one, I had said to her. God, I remember it so well now as I look at her. How could I have forgotten it till now?

The irresponsible one.

It was easier to go through life pretending I was irresponsible, not speaking up about what I really desired for fear of finding out I might not be wanted. For years, I did it with my father and my brothers, waiting for them to ask me to take my place at the company that my family built—all while I acted like I didn't care one way or the other.

I'll be damned if I'm going to make the same mistake now with Cass.

I push my shot glass away from me without taking a sip, and ask the bartender for a Chardonnay. After sweeping the glass up into my grip, I walk over to Cass. She looks gorgeous, her skin luminescent against the purplish-blue hue of the taffeta draping her skin. She is every bit the princess she was once hired to be, and it has nothing to do with the way she looks, and everything to do with the way she cares for the people around her, the way she commits to a cause, the way she goes after her dreams with everything she is and everything she does. I don't deserve her.

But I intend to, one day.

When her eyes meet mine, I extend the glass to her. She cocks her head slightly before she accepts it, and I reach out my hand.

"I'm the responsible one," I tell her pointedly.

Her eyebrows rise, and recollection shows in her features as she shakes my hand. "The *responsible* one?"

"Yeah. My brother Logan? He's a former SEAL. A good guy, but a little unreliable at work now that he's married to some girl. And then there's Ryan. He was the rock our family's company pretty much relied on till he met a woman and discovered that there's more to life than building housing developments." I sit beside her. "Then there's me. I'm the responsible one. Picking up the pieces now that the two of them seem to be following their hearts more than their brains. They just asked me to come aboard at JLS Heartland. We'll be splitting the load three ways."

Her eyes brighten and a smile touches her lips. "Dylan, that's wonderful."

"It is, isn't it? That's what happens when a guy like me finally starts opening my mouth in this family rather than just mouthing off."

"I'm happy for you. And you're going to make your dad so happy."

I shrug, knowing there's one thing that would make Dad even happier than knowing his three sons will be working together now at JLS. I remember what he told me about wanting to see Cass and me take the next step together, make the commitment to building a life together. And I know I want it, too, more than I've wanted anything in my life. It should be too soon to feel this way. But truth is, I've felt it from the moment I opened my eyes and saw her that first morning I woke up with her in my bed.

She was mine then. She is mine now. I just have to convince her of that.

I glance Dad's way and see him, still watching me. He raises his glass to me and nods. Then he turns his back as though to say, "You're on your own now, Son."

I look back at Cass and it almost makes me shudder, locking eyes with this woman I want in my life for the rest of my days. "You did it, Cass. You're the one who convinced me to confront my dad and my brothers about my interest in working at JLS."

"I didn't do anything."

"You did. You taught me to speak up if I want something. Well, there's something else I want."

"What?"

I scoot my chair closer to hers and take both her hands. "You."

Her eyes meet mine and it steals the wind from my lungs. She is everything to me. I don't know how it's possible—to know something this deeply in my heart. But I'm not about to question it.

I somehow manage to catch my breath. "I want you, Cassidy Parker. I'm in love with you. I have fallen hard and fallen completely. And I know that you told me you never want to get married. But after what you just said to me in the woods, I'm wondering if there might be a chance I could convince you otherwise."

She stares at me, wide-eyed, and I see goose bumps cover her arms. Always a good sign.

I trace my finger around the pink diamond that looks so perfect on her delicate hand. "I love you," I say again, making sure she hears the words. "Keep my ring. Keep my ring on your finger for as long as you want, as long as you'll let me spend my days convincing you to take a gamble on me. Because I think our odds are pretty good that we'll end up like that," I say, nudging my chin in the direction of my parents, who are now joined together in a slow sway on the nearly empty dance floor. My throat tightens at the sight of them, still united after all these years, determined to savor their remaining time together no matter what life throws their way.

Just like my dad said.

Most of the guests have retreated to the river's edge to wait for the fireworks, and there's a stillness beneath the huge white tent right now that makes me feel like time is frozen, waiting to hear what Cass might say to me.

I blink twice, surprised to feel the moisture in my eyes. I'm not an overly sentimental guy, but I swear I can imagine it—Cass and me on a dance floor decades from now, just like my mom and dad are at this moment.

A tear drops from her eye. I catch it on the tip of my index finger. "Oh, God, baby. I didn't want to make you cry. Look, I don't want to pressure you. I just want you to be happy. Whatever it takes, Cass. Because I love you and that's the bottom line."

I steel myself momentarily, waiting for some kind of reply from her. She might not feel the same way I do, and I can't blame her. It's been a damn whirlwind these past couple weeks. And with her childhood, she might not be ready to jump feet first into a life with a guy who's really caused her nothing but trouble.

I'm ready for whatever she's going to say because I know I won't let it be the end. Even if I have to stand back a while and let her catch her breath, I'll still be here waiting for the day when she'll be mine.

"I love you, too," she says so quietly and meekly, I'd swear she sounded more like my little niece than the bold woman who once invited herself into my hotel room.

"You do?" I dare to ask, almost not believing what I hear.

"Yeah." Two more full, round tears track down her cheeks. "I do."

"You'll keep the ring, then?" I ask, almost in disbelief.

"For as long as you want me to."

My mouth meets hers, demanding, urgent, then moves to her cheeks where I kiss away the tears.

"Then keep it forever, Cass." I pull her close, my heart filling to capacity, and then stretching to fill a little bit more. Fireworks sound in the distance, and I have to laugh at their timing, the explosions somehow mirroring the emotions bursting inside of me. "Keep it forever."

EPILOGUE

YEARS LATER

~ CASS ~

Clasping Dylan's hand, I gaze out at the Chesapeake Bay that surrounds me at nearly every angle. The water laps up against our little private peninsula, the rhythm of it seeming to speak to me, bringing me a message from a loved one who's left us.

Anna Sheridan reclines in her Adirondack chair keeping a close watch on her grandchildren as they crab off the dock.

"Your mother loves it here," I say, giving my husband's hand a reassuring squeeze.

"She does," he affirms with a slow nod I catch in my peripheral vision.

"Your dad would have loved it, too."

He chuckles warmly. "No. He was a freshwater man. Would rather his sons get a vacation home together on a lake maybe in Canada or the Finger Lakes in New York."

"He would have loved it. And not because of the water." I glance over at Dylan and know I don't need to say more. By now, I can read my husband's expressions well enough to know that he understands what I'm saying.

Jake Sheridan would have loved this place because his boys bought it together.

In that final year, as he slipped away from us completely, the pride never left his eyes at any mention of the work that his sons were doing together at JLS Heartland, making the company grow, diversify, and touch people's lives in ways that I can hardly even believe sometimes.

Like JLS, Newton's Creek is thriving now, a bustling little downtown area that looks like something out of an old post-card, every piece of architecture preserved, and every business along Anders Street family-owned, rather than owned by some faraway conglomerate.

The picture is just as promising for Allie's shelter, where I started working as a full-time staff member not long after Dylan and I got engaged. The three dogs that sit on the dock with Hannah and Connor are among the hundred or so foster dogs I've welcomed into our home since then. And there have been hundreds more fosters I've been able to rescue, thanks to a lot of people who seem to love giving dogs a second chance at life as much as I do.

We usually hire a dogsitter to take care of our fosters when we make the trip to Annapolis, but I've grown so accustomed to squeezing them into my minivan as I scoot around town, I thought we'd try a longer road trip and see if they like the Bay as much as I do.

A smile touches my lips. I still think it's funny—the image

of me driving my behemoth minivan, packed with dogs, instead of having children in the back seat like all the other minivans I see driving down Anders Street.

A laugh escapes me. *Well, that won't be the case for much longer.*

Dylan's gaze meets mine, a question in his eyes until he sees the sparkle in my own, and he chuckles along with me, knowing the news we are planning to share today.

"Hey, guys! The package arrived!"

I hear Kim's voice and turn to see her and Ryan walking around the side of the house. A box is in her hands, and his are filled with a squirmy two-year-old who looks like she's ready for her afternoon nap.

Logan and Allie step out onto the back deck with us.

"Shh!" Allie scolds. "We finally got Annie down for a nap. If you wake her, there will be a price."

She's dead right about that. Baby Annie, named for her grandma, has a set of lungs on her that can let out a mighty wail. I'd bet money she'll end up like her cousin Hannah one day, always on stage, belting out tunes as the lead in the school musicals.

Kim touches her hand to her lips. "Oops. Sorry. Want us to hang it up now?"

"Not without us watching," Anna says as she strides up the lawn with Hannah and Connor. "It's about time this place became officially ours."

Dylan tried for years to convince his brothers to go in on a vacation home with him in Annapolis. But none of the properties Lacey—who is now not just my friend, but also our real estate agent—emailed me over the years really grabbed the attention of all three of them.

That is, until this house came on the market.

I'll never forget the day I got the email with the link to

this property, because it was the same day Jake Sheridan left this life. She'd sent it to me before we were even able to share the news with our friends and extended family that his difficult and painful struggle had come to an end.

Weeks passed before I even managed to click on the link that Lacey had sent. But when I saw it, with its sweeping views of the Bay and sunny rooms that seemed to be filled to capacity with a warmth I couldn't mistake, I knew this would be the place where the Sheridans could come together and remember the man whose memory continues to shape our lives.

It was just what we needed at the time.

And it's just what we need now, months later, as we are ready to stake our final claim on this little bit of heaven.

Logan takes the box from Kim's hands and slashes it open with the pocketknife he always has stashed in his pocket. "Okay. Let's see if this looks as good as it did in the catalog."

A grin touches his lips as he pulls it from the box and points it toward his mother first.

Dylan gives an approving nod as he sees it. "What do you think, Mom?"

Her eyes are warm. "I think your father would approve," she says, and I feel my throat catch, hearing her words as I look at the sign.

The Sheridans, it reads in platinum-colored lettering just underneath the street address, framed in wrought iron.

"Cool," Connor says, and shares a nod with his sister.

"About time we got rid of the old sign," Hannah adds.

"Special order, honey. It took a while for it to come in. But the best things are worth waiting for," I point out to her, giving a sideways glance to my husband, thinking of the new life inside of me right now.

Trailed by the dogs, Logan heads to the garage to get a

toolbox, and the rest of us march through the house to the front door.

"Wait. I feel like we need a picture," I say, pulling out my phone from my pocket as Logan unscrews the old sign which bears the name of the prior owners, the Bakers, whom Lacey told me built this house together many years ago.

For some reason, I feel a lump in my throat seeing their name removed, and make a mental note to return it to the widow whose name was on the closing papers Lacey faxed us a while back. Somehow I feel the urge to meet her, this woman who could fill this house with so much love that it still seemed to linger after she moved out, welcoming us when we first stepped through the doors. It was at a time when we all needed to feel something—*something good*—so desperately after the loss of the man whom I was proud to call "Dad" in the last years of his life.

I snap another photo as Logan hangs the new sign next to the door, and Ryan checks it with a level.

Shaking his head, Dylan snorts. "You're so OCD, bro."

"No teasing your brother," Anna scolds.

As usual, Ryan ignores Dylan as he pulls the level away. "Perfect," he says. "Just like this place is—perfect."

Dylan shares a look with me. "Well, if it were perfect, I think it would have at least one more bedroom."

"What are you talking about? With the kids sharing rooms, the place is big enough for the eleven of us."

I smile, and feel Dylan come up behind me, wrapping his warm arms around my waist and pressing his palms against my belly. I turn my head halfway, so that he can see me give him a nod.

"Make that the twelve of us," he tells them.

I hear their gasps, but choose to ignore them as my husband curls his finger beneath my chin and lifts my lips toward his.

I know it's too early, but I'd swear I can feel the movement of our child inside of me now, stirred by the love in my heart for this man and the family we have together. And I know, with every ounce of my soul, that it will last forever.

FROM THE AUTHOR

More Sheridans have arrived! Remember those cousins that Logan mentioned early in this series? They have their own stories which take place—quite literally—in paradise. In my new HOMEFRONT: ALOHA, SHERIDANS series, you'll be able to check in on many of the friends you've made in this book. So I hope you'll grab the first, *A is for Alpha,* right now.

It's always difficult for me to say good-bye to characters. With this book, it was even a little harder, because I, too, have a parent suffering from vascular dementia. I suppose that's why I needed to make sure this branch of the Sheridan family ended their story in a special place, the former house of Edith Baker—a bayside retreat some of you might recognize from the Special Ops: Homefront series. It's curious how deeply I wanted to assure my readers—and myself—that life will go on, and there will be days filled with sunshine and love no matter what we face, so long as we march forward and keep our hearts open. I want to thank all of you who allowed me to take this journey with you over this series. Somehow, you feel like family to me at these times when I tap in the final words of a story, because you keep these characters alive for me each time you read one of my books.

If you enjoyed this book, I hope you will do me the HUGE favor of writing a review. I'm an independent author, and with so many books available to readers, it's your reviews that set me apart from the rest, and assure potential readers that I might be worth a try. So I truly can't thank you enough for helping.

My immeasurable thanks to my incredible friends, Chuck and Danielle who, book after book, year after year, haven't yet put my phone number on their caller block list or started dodging my emails. To my husband, I'll paraphrase something that Cass said in this book because it's something I've said so many times to you before: Nothing is ever real until I share it with you. To my family, I can't express how grateful I am that you allow me the time and support to bring these characters to life.

I'd like to thank K-9 Lifesavers and the countless local rescue organizations who give their time, energy, and, very often, money out of their own pockets so that they can give precious animals a second chance at life. Like Allie, Kim, and Cass, I wish I could take home every rescue you have and still always have room for more.

I love to hear from readers! You can contact me through my website at www.KateAster.com and also sign up to find out when my next book is available.

Thanks again for your unwavering support! I am so very happy you found me!

BOOKS BY KATE ASTER

~ SPECIAL OPS: HOMEFRONT SERIES~

Romance awaits and life-long friendships blossom
on the shores of the Chesapeake Bay.

―――――――

SEAL the Deal

Special Ops: Homefront (Book One)

The SEAL's Best Man

Special Ops: Homefront (Book Two)

Contract with a SEAL

Special Ops: Homefront (Book Three)

Make Mine a Ranger

Special Ops: Homefront (Book Four)

BOOKS BY KATE ASTER

~ SPECIAL OPS: TRIBUTE SERIES~

Love gets a second chance when a very special ice cream shop
opens near the United States Naval Academy.

───────

No Reservations

Special Ops: Tribute (Book One)

Strong Enough

Special Ops: Tribute (Book Two)

Until Forever: A Wedding Novella

Special Ops: Tribute (Book Three)

Twice Tempted

Special Ops: Tribute (Book Four)

BOOKS BY KATE ASTER

~ HOMEFRONT: THE SHERIDANS SERIES ~

When one fledgling dog rescue comes along, three brothers find
romance as they emerge from the shadow of their billionaire name.

More, Please

Homefront: The Sheridans (Book One)

Full Disclosure

Homefront: The Sheridans (Book Two)

Faking It

Homefront: The Sheridans (Book Three)

BOOKS BY KATE ASTER

~ HOMEFRONT: ALOHA, SHERIDANS SERIES ~

Even on a remote island paradise, a handful of bachelor brothers
can't hide from love when they leave the Army.

A is for Alpha

Homefront: Aloha, Sheridans (Book One)

Hindsight

Homefront: Aloha, Sheridans (Book Two)

Island Fever

Homefront: Aloha, Sheridans (Book Three)

BOOKS BY KATE ASTER

~ BROTHERS IN ARMS SERIES ~

With two U.S. Naval Academy graduates and two from their arch
rival at West Point, there's ample discord among the Adler brothers
… until love tames them.

BFF'ed

Brothers in Arms (Book One) - available now!

Books Two, Three, and Four
are coming soon.

*Sign up at my website at **www.KateAster.com***
to be the first to hear the release dates.

BOOKS BY KATE ASTER

~ FIRECRACKERS: NO COMMITMENT
NOVELETTES ~

For when you don't have much free time… but want a quick, fun

race to a happily ever after.

————————

SEAL My Grout

Firecrackers: No Commitment Novelettes (Book One)

Available now!

Novelettes Two, Three, and Four

are coming soon.

*Sign up at my website at **www.KateAster.com***

to be the first to hear the release dates.

LET'S KEEP IN TOUCH!

Twitter: @KateAsterAuthor
Facebook: @KateAsterAuthor
Instagram: KateAsterAuthor

www.KateAster.com

Made in the USA
Columbia, SC
10 September 2021